PLAY...ON

Laur...
bad...
broth...
pay h...

It was even worse that Rory flaunted Lady Isabel Maxby as his openly adoring mistress.

But now he had the effrontery to turn the full force of his charm on Lauren. And even more infuriating, ignore her pretense of indifference.

Smiling, he put his hand on her cheek. The air seemed motionless around her, and all sound died away except for the pounding of her heart. A bewildering weakness spread through her, and her whole body ached with desire as he pulled her gently to him. Luxurious shackles bound her, and she was a willing prisoner as he kissed her on the lips.

This was folly, she knew—but oh so sweet. . . .

A Highland Conquest

A
Highland
Conquest

by
Sandra Heath

A SIGNET BOOK

SIGNET
Published by the Penguin Group
Penguin Books USA Inc., 375 Hudson Street,
New York, New York 10014, U.S.A.
Penguin Books Ltd, 27 Wrights Lane,
London W8 5TZ, England
Penguin Books Australia Ltd, Ringwood,
Victoria, Australia
Penguin Books Canada Ltd, 10 Alcorn Avenue,
Toronto, Ontario, Canada M4V 3B2
Penguin Books (N.Z.) Ltd, 182–190 Wairau Road,
Auckland 10, New Zealand

Penguin Books Ltd, Registered Offices:
Harmondsworth, Middlesex, England

First published by Signet, an imprint of Dutton Signet,
a division of Penguin Books USA Inc.

First Printing, February, 1994
10 9 8 7 6 5 4 3 2 1

1

IT was cool beneath the trees in the Mall, and many fashionable riders made full use of the leafy shade to escape from the relentless blaze of the July sun. The summer of 1819 had been almost unbearably hot so far, and London sweltered after a cold winter and an indifferent spring.

Lauren Maitland managed her difficult chestnut mount with consummate ease, her equestrian skill so natural and accomplished that she barely needed to give the task any thought at all. Slender and graceful, with large green eyes and tumbling ash-blond curls, she wore a primrose riding habit and veiled black silk top hat that became her very well. She was quite at ease in elegant society and blended very well with the *beau monde,* but at the same time there was something eye-catchingly different about her. Perhaps it was her confidence on such an awkward mount, or maybe it was simply the stylish cut of her clothes. Whatever it was, she turned heads as she rode with her cousin Hester, and Hester's husband, Alexander Kingston. But Lauren was so lost in thought that she remained unaware of the stir of admiration she caused, for although physically she was in St. James's Park in London, mentally she was thousands of miles away across the Atlantic in her home city of Boston, Massachusetts.

She felt guilty because she was enjoying herself here far more than she'd ever dreamed possible. Today was the fourth of July, and she wished she were at home instead of in the very land from which her countrymen were rightly celebrating their independence! There were times when she wondered why on earth she had allowed herself to be pressed into coming, for in her opinion there hadn't been any real need. It had been her father's doing. When she'd inherited a British fortune through her late mother's family, the Ashworths, he had insisted that it was a necessary courtesy for her to come to London to meet her cousins. She'd given in, but now she felt as if she were consorting with the enemy, even though it was six years since America and Britain had been at war.

She glanced unhappily around as the cream of London society enjoyed the hot summer afternoon, for there was another more personal and poignant reason why she felt it was wrong to be enjoying herself here. During that last brief war, the man she loved had forfeited his life. How many nights had she spent despising these people? How many times had she wished them in perdition for taking Jonathan from her? Her hands tightened on the reins, but that was the only outward sign she gave of the bitterness that still lingered deep within even though she had been made so welcome here.

Jonathan Ryder had been an officer on the USS *Chesapeake*, and one of the forty-eight hands lost off Boston in the unsuccessful confrontation with HMS *Shannon*. That had been in 1812, and she had never gotten over him. But here she was, having a very agreeable time in the heart of the enemy's capital, staying with her extremely amiable British cousins and indulging in the many fashionable diversions provided by one of the greatest cities in the world. She shouldn't be doing it, least of all on the fourth of July!

Beside her, unaware of her inner conflict, Hester was obliged to concentrate upon her riding, for she wasn't a particularly accomplished horsewoman. She rode a pretty dapple-gray mare, and was dressed in a sky-blue riding habit with a matching feathered hat. Suddenly she noticed her American cousin's downcast eyes and reined in.

"Is something wrong, Lauren? You seem somewhat preoccupied," she asked with concern.

Lauren halted as well, forcing a quick smile to her lips. "I was just thinking of home."

"But of course, for it's the Fourth of July, isn't it? They will all be having a fine time rejoicing in their escape from us wicked British." Hester smiled warmly. She was small and raven haired, but with the same green eyes that both of them had inherited from their shared Ashworth family connections. She was from the junior branch of the family, but due to two sudden deaths, Lauren was now the sole surviving member of the senior branch, and this was why she had become heiress to the considerable fortune.

Alex hadn't noticed that his companions had halted, and rode on as Hester looked anxiously at her cousin. "What's wrong, Lauren? You'd tell me if you were unhappy, wouldn't you? I mean, I know you're a long way from home, but you aren't alone, truly you aren't. Alex and I are delighted to have you with us, and if you fear that we secretly resent you for inheriting, you could not be more wrong. Alex is really quite disgustingly wealthy in his own right, and—"

Lauren leaned quickly across to put a reassuring hand over Hester's. "I know you don't resent me, and you mustn't fear that I think any such thing. You and Alex have made me very welcome, and I've enjoyed my stay here more than I ever expected."

"We've loved having you here, and we'll both be sad when you go home again."

Lauren returned the smile. "I'll miss you too, Hester. You and Alex must come to Boston to stay."

"I'll warrant you never dreamed you'd say that," Hester replied with an impish grin.

"That's very true."

Hester was silent for a moment. "What was he like?" she asked suddenly.

"Who?"

"Why, Jonathan Ryder, of course. You've hardly spoken of him, and I haven't really liked to ask."

In reply Lauren undid the golden chain around her neck and opened the little locket attached to it. Silently she held it out to her cousin.

Hester gazed at the tiny head-and-shoulder likeness it contained, and the curl of sandy hair which had been so cleverly arranged like a miniature plume. In his United States naval uniform, with his soft brown eyes and smiling lips, Jonathan Ryder had been very dashing indeed.

Lauren gazed at the locket for a moment, and then had to look away, for the pain was so keen that tears had sprung immediately to her eyes.

Hester glanced at her. "You still miss him very much, don't you?" she murmured, closing the locket and giving it back.

Lauren nodded. "Sometimes it seems so very fresh still, as if it happened last year instead of six years ago. And before you say it, yes, I do know that it's too long to still feel as I do."

"I wasn't going to say that," Hester said gently.

Lauren gave a self-conscious smile. "My father does, frequently. He says it's long since time I was a wife, and he's right. All my friends have been married for some time now, and yet here I am, twenty-seven and still not even vaguely attached."

"Not for lack of interest," Hester pointed out, thinking of the host of eager suitors who'd clustered around Lauren from the moment she'd arrived in London.

"The prospect of a fortune usually stirs the male heart," Lauren replied sagely.

"They didn't all know about your fortune. Sir Richard Finchley certainly didn't." Hester mentioned this gentleman in particular because he had been especially smitten and persistent. Her glance became a little curious then.

"Actually, there's something I've been longing to quiz you about."

"Oh?"

"Yes. Why did Sir Richard suddenly cry off where you were concerned? One day he was dancing ardent attendance upon you, and then he suddenly ceased to call. What happened?"

Lauren toyed a little uncomfortably with her reins. "What happened was that I was guilty of a rather large untruth. You see, I didn't care for him at all, but while we were riding in Hyde Park one afternoon he became particularly persistent. He simply wouldn't take a hint, and so I cast around for something which would put him off once and for all. It occurred to me that if Jonathan were still alive, I wouldn't be pursued in such a way, and so I invented another fiancé back home in Boston. I called him Captain George Hyde, because we were in Hyde Park and I happened to notice St. George's Hospital. I said that I was dizzily in love and would be marrying in the new year when I returned to Boston."

Hester stared at her and then laughed. "You actually said that?"

"Yes, although I'm not really proud of myself. You see, to convince him beyond all shadow of a doubt, I went so far as to show him my locket, and I pretended that Jonathan was this fictitious George Hyde. I wish I hadn't now." Lauren hesitated regretfully. "Anyway, it worked and I haven't been bothered by dear Sir Richard since."

"I wouldn't have been as considerate as you, Lauren. If he were to pester me, he'd get a very swift *dismissal*, not a gentle fobbing-off to spare his feelings."

"I just wish I hadn't used Jonathan."

"It wasn't a very horrendous sin."

"No?"

"No."

Lauren smiled a little ruefully. "I wish I could get over him."

"The pain *will* pass in the end, you know. You'll suddenly meet someone else, and then you'll begin your life again," Hester said gently. "But I *do* understand, for I know how I'd feel if I lost Alex." Her glance moved after her adored husband, who'd now reined in a little further along the Mall to wait for them.

He wore a brick-colored coat, fawn top hat, and beige breeches, and looked every inch the leading Corinthian he was. Tall and muscular, with startling golden hair and long-lashed blue eyes, he was very much a follower of the fancy. In a society where a gentleman was admired if he indulged in manly sports, from pugilism and fencing to hunting, shooting, fishing, and tooling the ribbons of a coach and four, he was one of the foremost players. But there was also a very romantic and gentle side of his nature—when he'd set out to woo the former Miss Hester Ashworth, he had done so as tenderly as any great lover. It was a love match of the highest order, and he and Hester worshipped each other.

Another gentleman rode up to Alex suddenly, and Hester's breath caught with quick delight. "Why, I do believe that that's Rory he's talking to!"

"Rory?" The name conveyed nothing to Lauren as she turned to look as well. The other gentleman was the same height as Alex and as elegantly dressed, but his face was in shadow because his top hat was tugged low over his forehead. He wore an indigo coat and cream kerseymere breeches, and the diamond pin in his unstarched neckcloth flashed now and then in the dappled light filtering through the lacework of branches overhead. He was mounted on a particularly large and rangy bay thoroughbred, which was in such a mettlesome mood that it danced around constantly, striving to be off rather than stand still while its rider indulged in polite conversation.

Hester smiled. "Yes, it *is* Rory! I had no idea he was in town!"

"Who is he?" Lauren asked.

"One of Alex's two oldest friends. The other is Fitz,

who I've told you about recently. Come on, for I long to speak to him again. It must be two years since last he deigned to leave his highland lair and honor London with his presence!" Hester kicked her heel and urged her horse toward the two gentlemen, and Lauren rode after her.

Alex turned with a broad smile as they approached. "Look who's here, Hester!"

Hester beamed and she reined in beside them. "I know, I espied him from afar. It's wonderful to see you again, Rory."

"The pleasure is mutual, Hester," the gentleman replied, removing his hat before taking her hand and raising it to his lips.

Her fingers closed warmly over his. "Why have you stayed away so long? What is it about Glenvane Castle that you needs must lurk constantly within its walls?"

"I fear it's a long and disagreeable story, Hester," Rory replied. His voice was soft, with the faintest trace of a Scottish accent, and as Lauren looked at him she saw that he was memorably handsome. He had fine-boned features that were coolly aristocratic, and yet at the same time darkly wild and exciting, as if he were a disconcerting blend of nobleman and pirate. The nobleman was there in his grace of manner, which told of centuries of privilege and blue blood; the corsair was evident in his rugged complexion, expressive gray eyes, rather unruly coal-black hair, and air of restless, pent-up energy. Rory Ardmore would probably be as much at home on board a privateer as in his Scottish castle.

Alex hastened to introduce Lauren to him. "Rory, this is Hester's cousin, Miss Maitland of Boston. Lauren, may I present Rory Ardmore, eleventh Earl of Glenvane?"

Rory smiled and drew her hands to his lips as well. "Miss Maitland."

"Lord Glenvane." She met his eyes, and found their directness exceedingly disturbing. This was a man no one would ever take for granted.

He looked at her for a long moment, and then returned his attention to Alex. "Are you still residing at the same Grosvenor Square address?"

"Naturally. Where are you staying?"

"The club. I'm not here for long, and will be returning to Glenvane again in a few days' time. I've been attending to certain legal matters which should have been dealt with over a year ago."

"Nothing awkward, I trust?" Alex said.

Rory gave a faint smile. "No, just the formal relinquishing of any claim to a share of the estates of my late wife's family."

Alex and Hester stared at him, for they had had no idea that he'd been married.

Their astonishment amused him. "It's a very long and disagreeable story."

Hester was quite flustered. "Why didn't you tell anyone you were married?"

"It's an episode I prefer to forget."

"Oh." Hester quite obviously longed to pry a little further, but Rory's manner precluded any questions. She glanced at Alex, who raised an eyebrow but said nothing.

Lauren was curious as well, and found herself wondering greatly about the late Lady Glenvane.

Alex cleared his throat and changed the subject. "How are Jamie and Mary?"

"Nothing has changed as far as my wastrel brother is concerned. He's still single and still as charmingly beyond redemption as ever. More often than not he's to be found in one gaming hell or another, and the duns are frequently a little too close for comfort."

Alex grinned. "As you say, nothing has changed."

"Acting responsibly was never Jamie's forte, I fear, and the day is fast approaching when for his own good I will be obliged to teach him a very salutary lesson. As for my sister, well, if your command of mathematics has endured, you will know that she's about to celebrate her eighteenth birthday. The little hoyden who liked to ride bareback over the moors has become very much the proper young lady."

"A pretty one too, I'll be bound," Alex said.

Rory smiled. "We Ardmores are all a very handsome lot," he murmured.

"And so modest," Hester observed dryly, having recovered from the shock of finding out about his marriage.

Rory turned his head as a church clock struck the hour, and it was clear he was about to bring the brief reunion to a close, but Alex was anxious not to leave it at that. "Look, we can't just meet and part like this. We must see each other again before you return to Glenvane," he said quickly.

Hester nodded. "I agree, and what's more I *insist* that you dine with us, sir. Please come tonight."

"I'm not good company at the moment, I fear."

Alex raised an eyebrow. "I can't believe that. Besides, we are old friends, and I can't think of anything more agreeable than a chin-wag about the past. And talking of the past, Hester and I met Fitz and his new wife recently."

The ghost of a smile played upon Rory's lips. "So, you've made the acquaintance of at least one of your old friends' wives?"

Alex colored a little. "That isn't what I meant."

"I know. Forgive me. Actually, I'm rather surprised to learn that the lady has been persuaded to cross the Irish Sea, for I was under the impression that nothing Fitz said or did could lure her from Dublin."

"She made it clear to us that London wasn't to her liking," Alex admitted.

"And your opinion of her?"

"Ah, well, that we will discuss over dinner," Alex replied, exchanging a glance with Hester.

Lauren observed the glance, and thought back to the day Hester and Alex had encountered Lord and Lady Fitzsimmons in Bond Street. Their delight on meeting

Fitz again had been tempered with an instinctive dislike
of his beautiful Irish wife.

Rory saw the exchange as well. "My curiosity is
greatly aroused," he murmured.

"Sufficiently to honor us with your presence tonight?"
Hester pressed.

"You're both quite set upon this invitation, aren't
you?"

"Yes."

"Then I accept, of course."

Alex was pleased. "Excellent."

"But for the moment I fear I must bring this agreeable
meeting to a close. *À bientôt, mes amis.* Miss Maitland."
Rory's glance encompassed Lauren for a moment, and
then he urged his horse away in the direction of Consti-
tution Hill.

Hester gazed after him. "I can't believe he's been
married and widowed in the past two years. Who was
she, I wonder? And what happened?"

Alex shrugged. "The Lord alone knows. One thing
seems clear, however—the marriage was a bitter experience."

"Yes. Oh, how I wanted to ask him more!" Hester
replied with a sigh.

"Your base curiosity will no doubt be fully satisfied
tonight," Alex replied. "Now then, let's continue with
this ride before our horses become thoroughly out of
sorts." Kicking his heel, he rode on along the crowded
Mall, and Hester followed.

Lauren remained where she was for a moment, turning in the saddle to gaze after the now-vanished Earl of
Glenvane. The memory of his eyes remained with her, as
did the soft Scottish inflection in his voice. In spite of
his quick smiles and lazily amused eyes, there was
something deeply unhappy about him, something in-
triguingly unhappy . . .

Without a doubt, Rory Ardmore was the most interesting man she had met in a long time. A very long time.

2

THE drawing room windows stood open to the sultry July evening, and the leaves in the central garden of Grosvenor Square were very still as Rory's town carriage drew up at the curb outside Alex and Hester's handsome red brick town house on the east side of the square. Lauren, Alex, and Hester were waiting on the second floor, overlooking the square.

Lauren wore a new shell-pink gown and there were diamonds in her ears and around her throat. She had taken particular care with her appearance tonight, wanting to look her very best in front of Lord Glenvane.

Alex rose as the butler announced Rory, who entered the room and bowed to them. From the moment she saw him again, Lauren was uncomfortably conscious of the effect he had upon her, and she employed her ivory fan as she studied him. He was dressed in the same formal black as Alex, but somehow achieved even more excellence. His black corded silk coat was superbly cut to show off his athletic but elegant figure, and his close-fitting white trousers outlined the shape and length of his legs. Lace spilled from his cuffs, there was subtle embroidery on his satin waistcoat, and an emerald pin in his starched neckcloth. But beneath his cool outer composure she could again sense the restless contradiction of his character, the brigand concealed within the cultured man of fashion. It was a stirring and heady blend that drew her like a pin to a magnet.

She was both startled and shocked by the unforeseen

force of the feeling. All this time after losing Jonathan, she was suddenly at sixes and sevens again, and the cause of her disarray was a Scottish nobleman! If the attraction had not been so very real and intense, the situation might almost have been amusing. She, Lauren Maitland, the fiercely patriotic citizen of Boston, Massachusetts, was vulnerable to the merest smile from a dashing highland aristocrat! And this on the Fourth of July, of *all* days! The thought brought a blush to her cheeks, and she employed her fan a little more busily.

Alex drew Rory to join them. "A glass of something?" he asked. "Sherry, maybe?"

"Yes. Thank you." Rory smiled and inclined his head to the two ladies. His glance lingered a little longer on Lauren, a fact of which she could not help but be aware, for it caused her heart to beat a little more swiftly.

Alex ushered him to a chair and went to pour four glasses from the decanter on the nearby table. He pressed one into Rory's hand, and then opened the conversation, but the seemingly innocent topic he chose proved to be far more thorny and contentious than he could ever have anticipated.

"Have you been anywhere interesting since last we met?"

"America. Briefly."

"Why, by happy coincidence—" Alex began, turning to Lauren. But Rory shook his head and interrupted.

"It wasn't at all happy, and I have no intention of ever setting foot there again."

There was an uncomfortable silence, and then Alex gave a weak smile. "Really?" he murmured.

"I find nothing to recommend either the land or its citizens," Rory went on, not detecting the awkwardness that had entered the proceedings.

Alex and Hester glanced at each other, and Lauren's fan became suddenly still.

Rory studied his untouched glass. "I am more than glad to toast the Fourth of July, since it is a date which celebrates a very fortuitous parting of the ways," he murmured, raising the glass to the room in general and then draining it.

Lauren flushed a little, indignant at the cavalier manner with which her entire nation had just been condemned out of hand. It would have been offensive to her even if she'd found him personally repellent, but the fact that she found him so infuriatingly attractive somehow gave the insult twice as much sting.

"Are you much given to such sweeping generalizations, Lord Glenvane?" she asked coolly.

It was the first time he'd heard her say more than one or two words, and his gray eyes swung swiftly toward her as suddenly he realized from her Boston accent that she hailed from the opposite side of the Atlantic. "I—er—appear to have spoken somewhat out of turn, Miss Maitland," he murmured.

"Yes, sir, you do."

"Forgive me, but when you were introduced as Miss Maitland of Boston, I thought only of Boston, Lincolnshire."

"And that excuses you?"

He gave her a faint smile. "No, of course not, but I assure you that if I'd known—"

"You wouldn't have spoken as you did? Maybe not, but you would still have held your derogatory views about my homeland."

Alex gazed fixedly at something he suddenly found immensely interesting on the ceiling, and Hester fiddled uneasily with her peacock fan, wishing the clock would be turned back and the whole conversation begun again.

Rory was silent for a moment and then gave Lauren the coolest of smiles. "Would it be accurate to guess that there was a Maitland involved in the Boston Tea Party?" he enquired a little drolly.

"It would." It was the truth.

"I thought so." He searched her face for a second or

so. "I seem to have made an exceedingly bad impression on you, Miss Maitland."

"You have, sir," she answered, this time not so truthfully.

"I apologize, for it was unforgivable of me to allow my personal bitterness to get the better of my manners. Miss Maitland, can you find it in your heart to accept my remorse?" He gave her a repentant smile.

She couldn't reply, for the smile devastated her defenses. He was all she should shun, but she found him almost unbearably desirable. Plague take her foolish emotions! And plague take him as well!

He smiled again. "*Pax*, Miss Maitland?"

To her further chagrin the second smile stabbed her to the heart as well, but somehow she managed a rueful smile of her own. "*Pax*, Lord Glenvane. Besides, I hold equally entrenched and possibly erroneous views about Scotland and the Scots," she murmured, unable to resist getting her own back just a little.

"I detect the whiff of gunpowder, Miss Maitland, but nevertheless I will venture to ask what these undoubtedly erroneous views might be."

"That Scotland is a miserable, wet place, and that Scotsmen are all skinflints who like to dance in skirts to the accompaniment of a shrieking sack of wind called a bagpipe."

Alex strove not to laugh and Hester had to look away to prevent a loud giggle. A glimmer of humor passed through Rory's eyes. "Madam, regrettably I have to concede that on most of those points you are only too accurate."

The conversation ended there, for the butler came to announce dinner, and they adjourned to the pleasant green silk dining room at the rear of the house.

The French windows opened on to a balcony above the garden, and the warm evening air was heady with the scent of roses. It was dusk now, and there were lighted candlesticks upon the gleaming mahogany table, where a particularly elegant crystal epergne had pride of place. Tumbling with fruit, flowers, nuts, leaves, and cool moss, it was a veritable work of art.

They ate a leisurely and very agreeable meal of asparagus soup, poached Scottish salmon, and roast sirloin of beef, and then a footman brought the ingredients for the peach dessert which was Alex's speciality and which he always insisted upon preparing personally at the sideboard. It consisted of a thick glass bowl rinsed with brandy and filled with freshly sliced peaches, chilled champagne, and crushed sugar. The moment it was made, it would be brought to the table and spooned into smaller dishes with whipped cream.

When the footman had withdrawn, Alex went to the sideboard to commence slicing the peaches.

Rory smiled at him. "Do you recall the day Isabel ate all those peaches and was so sick afterward?"

"I do indeed."

"I don't believe she's liked peaches ever since."

Alex glanced over his shoulder. "Do you see much of her now that she's married to old Lord Maxby?"

"The late Lord Maxby—he went to his Maker about eighteen months ago," Rory stated. "And yes, I do see her quite often, for she has returned to Granton Park."

Alex was surprised. "I had no idea she was now a widow."

"A very rich and eligible one," Hester murmured.

"Indeed so," Rory replied, smiling a little.

Lauren glanced at them all. "Who is Isabel?" she asked.

Alex answered. "She was Miss Isabel Granton, and her family own an estate adjoining Glenvane. When we were children she was always following Rory around like an adoring puppy. Fitz and I teased him mercilessly whenever we were there on vacation from Harrow." He glanced at Rory. "Actually, I have always suspected that her adoration has continued, and probably always will."

Hester was appalled at such an indiscreet observation. "Alex!"

"Well, it's true. Isn't it, Rory?"

"Modesty forbids me," Rory murmured.

Alex raised an eyebrow. "Since when? Come on now, admit that Isabel was always besotted with you."

"A gentleman doesn't discuss such things," Rory replied with a grin.

Hester had been studying him. "May I be permitted a rather impertinent question, Rory?" she asked suddenly.

"You may."

"Is Isabel a part of your life now?"

Lauren lowered her eyes, not wanting to hear an affirmative reply.

Rory paused. "At this precise moment, yes, she is," he said.

Lauren became cross with herself as disappointment washed through her. This was quite ridiculous! She hardly knew him, and yet the details of his private life were inexplicably important to her.

Alex deemed it time to change the subject. "You said you were soon returning to Glenvane. When exactly do you leave?"

"I'm posting there the day after tomorrow."

"So soon? I was hoping we'd have a chance to see each other a little more," Alex replied.

Lauren was dismayed. The day after tomorrow? It was hardly any time away at all . . .

Rory continued. "I mean to be back there well in time for Mary's birthday at the end of next month. A young lady's eighteenth birthday should be celebrated with as much junketing and diversion as a young gentleman's coming of age, don't you agree?"

Alex continued to slice the peaches. "I do indeed. Actually, I seem to vaguely recall attending your own coming of age. I believe I spent a blissful week in an alcoholic haze. How long ago was it now? Eight years? Nine?"

"Don't remind me of the passing years, my friend. It

was nine years ago, and I am now the ripe old age of thirty." Rory toyed with the slender stem of his wine-glass.

Hester eyed her husband and then looked at Rory. "What's all this about a week of alcoholic haze?" she demanded.

Rory feigned alarm. "Please don't ask me to tell you about it, Hester, for it's more than my life is worth to sneak upon a fellow to his wife. Just take my word for it that we were models of good conduct and excellence."

"Do you really expect me to credit your coming of age celebrations with pious evenings of text reading and hymn singing?" Hester raised a wry, disbelieving eyebrow.

He grinned. "Hester, to claim such holy goings-on wouldn't convince you in the slightest, but actually we were reasonably decorous. Mary will have a grand ball, a fireworks display on the bowling lawn, a midnight boating party on the loch, several grouse shoots on the moor, a picnic by the waterfall on Ben Vane, and a stag hunt. Oh, and I have even managed to secure a promise from Madame Santini that she will give a recital."

"Madame Santini? The famous soprano?"

He nodded. "Fresh from La Scala, Milan, and at her warbling, glass-shattering best, or so I'm told. She's due to tour Scotland, and has agreed to come to Glenvane during her stay in Glasgow."

Hester smiled. "It all sounds most agreeable, Rory."

"Would you like to join in?"

Hester stared at him. "What do you mean?"

"That I am inviting all of you to join my many other guests for Mary's birthday celebrations at Glenvane Castle at the end of next month."

Lauren's heart almost stopped.

Hester's eyes shone, and she turned excitedly to Alex. "Oh, Alex, can we?"

"Yes, of course, although . . ." Alex looked uncertainly at Lauren. "Would such a visit be agreeable to you, Lauren?"

"I . . .I'm sure Lord Glenvane would prefer—" she began, but Rory interrupted her.

"I assure you that Lord Glenvane is determined to get you to Scotland, Miss Maitland. How else is your rustic colonial mind to be properly educated?"

"I'm sure I am beyond teaching, sir," she murmured, for his words cast her thoughts back to the first few minutes after he'd arrived, and his strangely antagonistic remarks about America. He'd mentioned personal bitterness as his reason, and she wondered greatly what that bitterness was.

"Beyond teaching? I doubt that very much, indeed I'm certain you'll be overcome with admiration when you see me in my kilt, doing the sword dance to the skirl of the pipes." He smiled.

The smile again laid waste her defenses. "I . . . I will not be able to contain my impatience, sir," she replied, managing to sound light.

"Nor I, for I have to introduce you to the many customs and delights of my homeland. Such as the noble haggis, for example."

"I think not, sir," she said with a slight shudder, for she had heard numerous awful stories about the ingredients of haggis!

"I regard your conversion as a matter of honor," he replied, and then glanced at Alex. "Is it settled, then? You will all come to Glenvane next month?"

"We'll be delighted, Rory."

"Excellent. Actually, I'd like to invite Fitz and his wife as well, but I've no idea where to find them. I've tried his club, but it seems he hasn't bothered to keep up his subscription."

"My fellow Corinthian he may once have been, but is no more, not since the advent of Lady Fitz," Alex replied. "If you wish to reach him, I believe they've taken a house up at Hampstead, somewhere near the Spaniard's Inn."

"Good. I'll endeavor to include them among my

guests." Rory glanced at him. "Am I right in suspecting there is an undercurrent whenever Fitz's wife is mentioned?"

Alex shifted a little uncomfortably. "Well, to be truthful, neither Hester nor I took to her particularly. We felt she was secretive to a fault, and we wouldn't care to trust her about anything, no matter how small."

"How odd."

"Yes, and then there is her strange reluctance to leave Ireland and come here. Not only that—she wouldn't take a house in London itself, but insisted upon remaining up in Hampstead. I could tell that Fitz was kicking against it a little, for you know how much he likes London life."

Hester sniffed. "If you ask me, Fitz has made a grave mistake," she said, but then she gave a slight laugh. "Oh, we're probably entirely wrong, and we certainly shouldn't allow first impressions to cloud our judgment so completely. After all, we've only met her once, and then briefly."

Alex pursed his lips. "I have the strangest feeling that I've seen her somewhere before, several years ago, although for the life of me I cannot think where. She certainly seemed oddly familiar. It wasn't an entirely agreeable feeling, rather like waking up in the morning and trying to recall a rather disturbing dream. One *knows* one was dreaming, and one is aware of the atmosphere created by said dream, but as to the content of the dream, that is another matter."

Rory smiled. "Well, even if you don't remember, and Hester doesn't change her mind, there will be sufficient other guests to make your dealings with Lady Fitzsimmons a matter of complete inconsequence. If I have my way, and Jamie and Mary have theirs as well, the house will be filled to overflowing. I only trust that with so many, it will not prove a boring occasion."

Hester smiled at him. "I cannot imagine that you would ever be guilty of anything boring."

"I'm flattered, and therefore your slave forever,

madam," he replied, reaching over to take her hand and drawing it gallantly to his lips.

"Do you really promise all the amusements you mentioned earlier?" she asked hopefully.

"The very same."

"I wish we didn't have to wait. The end of next month seems an age away."

"You must allow me time to make all the arrangements. Lavish hospitality takes a great deal of organizing."

"I know. Very well, I will try to contain yourself."

Alex at last completed the dessert, and with a flourish he bore it triumphantly to the table. Conversation drifted to other topics as the dinner proceeded relaxedly toward its conclusion, at which point they adjourned to the drawing room to talk for a little longer.

It was midnight when Rory departed, and Lauren couldn't help but be aware that Hester's curiosity about his marriage had remained unsatisfied. Once or twice her cousin had attempted to steer the conversation in that direction, but each time he'd skillfully managed to deflect her. Hester was frustrated but knew when to call it a day. She would have to accept that the Earl of Glenvane had no intention at all of talking about his late countess.

As he took his leave of them, Rory turned to speak just to Lauren. "I trust you do not mean to cut and run from my invitation to Scotland, Miss Maitland?"

"Cut and run? Sir, Bostonians are simply not capable of such cowardly acts," she retorted.

"Good." He smiled into her eyes and then drew her hand to his lips. "Until we meet again."

"Sir."

As his carriage drove away, Hester tapped Lauren's arm with her fan. "La, Coz, I do believe you've made a conquest," she murmured conspiratorially.

Lauren wished it were so, but rather doubted it, for on Rory's own admission, Isabel, Lady Maxby, had a place in his life.

3

IT required two carriages for the expedition to Scotland at the end of August, one to convey Lauren and her cousins, the other to carry their luggage and servants, including Lauren's maid, Peggy Donovan, who'd accompanied her from Boston. The journey to Glenvane Castle would have been accomplished with only five unhurried halts at various towns along the route, and the stay at Glasgow should have been the fifth and final one, but the next morning they had taken a wrong turn in the town of Dumbarton, which had taken them far off course and resulted in a sixth overnight halt.

It was sunset as the two carriages drove wearily over a wild moorland road where sweet-scented heather stretched into the gathering dusk. As befitted a member of the Four-in-Hand Club, Alex had elected to sit on the box beside the leading coachman, from time to time relieving him of the reins, and as he saw a cluster of buildings around a crossroad ahead, he pulled the team to a standstill in order to speak to Hester and Lauren.

"We're approaching a hostelry of some sort—at least, I believe it's a hostelry, judging by the lion and punch bowl sign which appears to denote inns and alehouses up here. It seems quite a substantial place, probably because it's the only inn for miles, so I think we should resign ourselves to being benighted yet again. We can return to Dumbarton in the morning and see where it was we went wrong."

The two women were in no mood to argue. They had

hoped to reach journey's end that night, but there was obviously no hope of that now, least of all in such wild country as this. Lauren supposed they should be thankful there was any sign of habitation at all, for there hadn't been so much as a cottage for the past five miles or so. She gazed out of the window at the sea of purple heather and the gradually rising landscape which led the eye to the first of the highland peaks. This would be a bleak and terrible place in the depths of winter, but in the summer it was beautiful almost beyond belief.

Thankfully, the building on the crossroads proved not only to be an inn, but a very superior posting house offering every comfort. It was named the Crown & Thistle, and the monarch whose face was displayed over the door was Robert the Bruce, not any foreigner from London! There were turf seats outside, where several gentlemen were taking their drams while enjoying the summer evening, and as the carriage drove beneath the low archway into the galleried courtyard, they found a number of other vehicles, from private traveling carriages and stagecoaches to carriers' wagons and a mail coach which was just leaving with much clatter and horn blowing. The appetizing smell of food hung in the air, and music drifted from an open window as a fiddler was playing the song 'Laird o' Cockpen.'

Because the inn was a posting house, one of the vehicles in the yard was a post chaise which was only waiting for a team of four to be harnessed before undertaking the rather hazardous exercise of continuing its journey after nightfall. The two postboys—actually small, rather sinewy middle-aged men—were standing together by one of the flights of steps leading up to the gallery, and they looked disgruntled, if not to say openly mutinous, for no one thought it wise to go on the open road once the sun had gone down.

Alex alighted from the box and came to assist Lauren and his wife out of the carriage. Lauren climbed down first, and paused to shake out her rather crumpled peach lawn skirts and smooth the sleeves of her brown velvet spencer. Then she adjusted the ribbons of her straw bonnet as she waited for Alex to help Hester down as well. Her glance moved around the yard, and her attention was suddenly drawn to a carriage which was drawn up close against one of the inn walls. It was a particularly handsome vehicle, with gleaming navy blue panels and highly polished brasswork, and the horses had been removed to the stables. The owner was evidently staying at the inn, for there was no sign of the coachman, or even a groom. Although the same could be said of most of the other vehicles in the yard, there was something about this one which aroused her curiosity. A cloth had been draped very carefully over the door panel which wasn't against the wall, and at first sight she thought the cloth must be protecting a broken window glass, but then she instinctively knew that the purpose of the cloth was to conceal whatever coat of arms was emblazoned on the door panel. She smiled a little, for the usual reason for such a desire for anonymity was an illicit assignation. Was some gentleman dallying here with a lady other than his wife?

The landlord had hastened out into the yard on hearing two more vehicles arrive. He was a large, very burly Glaswegian with wiry hair and bead-bright eyes which swiftly calculated that these newcomers would pay well for good service. He bowed to them.

"Welcome tae the Crown & Thistle, sir, ladies." he said. "Will ye be requirin' rooms?"

"We will, and good rooms at that," Alex replied.

The man gave a toothy grin. "Ye'll no' find bad rooms here, sir, and I can promise you the finest table in this part of Scotland. The very best mutton and beefsteaks, as well as blackcock and red grouse. There's salmon and trout too, should ye desire it."

"I'm sure that whatever you serve will do excellently," Alex replied.

Hester anticipated her meal with relish. "Red grouse? Oh, how I love it!"

"Maybe so, but it doesn't usually love you. In fact, most gamebirds seem to find a quarrel with your digestion," Alex reminded her.

"Oh, don't be such a damper, Alex, for if there is one thing I mean to enjoy while we're in Scotland, it's red grouse, and the season is perfect right now!

"Well, if it has the same effect as last time, don't say that I didn't warn you," Alex replied.

The innkeeper had heard the exchange. "The grouse served here is finer than any served in England, of that ye may be sure," he declared, his tone dismissive of anything that appeared on tables south of the border.

Hester smiled. "I mean to discover the veracity of that claim, sir," she said.

He bowed again. "Please enter my house, sir, ladies," he said, and led them toward the low doorway into the tap room.

Lauren was about to follow when curiosity got the better of her. Gathering her skirts, she hurried across the yard to the mysterious carriage and drew the cloth slightly aside to peep underneath. Sure enough, there was a beautiful gilded heraldic shield painted there. Lauren dropped the cloth back into place, satisfied that her suspicion was correct. Whoever had arrived in the carriage, whether it was a lady or a gentleman, was there to secretly meet someone other than their spouse.

Hester had paused in the taproom doorway to shake her blue sprigged muslin skirts. "Do come on, Lauren, for I'm so hungry I vow I could eat one of the coach horses!"

"I'm coming." Lauren hastened toward her.

Hester gave her a puzzled look. "Whatever were you doing?"

"Oh, nothing really. I'm afraid I was just being nosy."

Hester linked arms with her and they entered the inn, where the landlord had already seen to it that two suitable rooms were put at their disposal. They went up to refresh themselves before dining, arranging to meet again in the taproom in half an hour.

Lauren's room boasted two doors, one from the inn itself and the other giving on to the gallery around the courtyard. It was a simply furnished chamber with a large tester bed and a small pallet for her maid, a wardrobe with doors that groaned on their hinges, and a dressing table with a cracked mirror. It was very tidy and clean, and she had only been there a moment or so when one of the inn's maids came with a jug of hot water, fresh towels, and even some soap. The sun had almost set now, and lanterns were being lit in the yard below, so the maid soon returned to put a lighted spill to the candles on the mantelpiece.

Lauren's own maid, Peggy, came in shortly after that with the overnight portmanteau. Peggy had the slender, dark-haired looks of her Irish ancestors, and she'd been in Lauren's service for ten years, ever since they'd both been seventeen. Like Lauren, she had also come unwillingly across the Atlantic, but she too had found Britain less disagreeable than expected, even to the extent of finding a sweetheart among Alex and Hester's footmen. The maid had grumbled a little about leaving Boston for London, but she had positively complained about quitting London for this brief visit to Scotland, for it meant leaving her new love behind.

"This is a very wild place, Miss Lauren," she observed, putting the portmanteau down on the bed and then glancing out of the window, past the rooftops of the inn toward the mountains, which were now dark shadows against the fading sky.

Lauren took off her bonnet and tossed it on to the bed. "Have no fear, Peggy, you'll be back in London before you know it, and I'm sure that—er—Thomas, will be as delighted to see you again as you will be to see him."

"I hope so, Miss Lauren."

Lauren studied her. "Does this mean you won't be returning to Boston with me?" she asked after a moment.

The maid turned swiftly. "I . . .I don't know, Miss Lauren," she replied honestly. "If he asks me—"

"Do you love him?" Lauren interposed quietly.

Peggy nodded. "Yes, Miss Lauren."

"Then if he asks you, you must stay."

"But I don't like to desert you, Miss Lauren."

"You must put your own happiness first, Peggy. I loved and lost through no fault of my own, and I wouldn't like to think that you'd loved and lost because of your misplaced loyalty to me. If you and your Thomas love each other, you belong together, not on opposite sides of the Atlantic."

Peggy smiled. "Yes, Miss Lauren. Thank you, Miss Lauren," she said, hurrying to assist her mistress out of her peach lawn traveling gown and brown velvet spencer. Shortly after that, feeling much refreshed and with her ash-blond hair combed and pinned anew, Lauren was ready to go down to dine. By now she felt as ravenous as Hester had been earlier, for it had been some time since they'd eaten luncheon.

Wearing a light shawl around the shoulders of the lilac sarcenet gown she'd changed into, she went down a little early to wait in the busy taproom for Hester and Alex to come down to dinner. The door into the adjoining dining room stood open and a babble of voices emerged as the guests enjoyed their repast. Lauren went to sit on a settle by the yawning fireplace, where a large bowl of heather had been placed to brighten the soot-blackened stones. There were two huge hounds sprawled near her feet, and they hardly stirred as she took her place on the settle.

She couldn't help glancing around at the other people in the room and those she could see in the dining room, and wondering who was the owner of the carriage with the concealed door panel. There were several couples who fitted the possible bill, one with a lady who was far younger than her elderly companion and the other who were so loving and flirtatious that Lauren began to wonder if they would bother to wait until they retired to their bedroom! Then her gaze moved to a lady who sat on her own at a small table in the corner of the dining room. She was sweetly pretty, with almond-shaped blue eyes, honey-colored hair, and the sort of dainty features that always look vulnerable and appealing. She wore a demure pink lace gown that appeared very costly, and her hair was pinned up into a knot on top of her head. There were large pink opals in her earrings, and she kept glancing at her jeweled fob watch before glancing anxiously out toward the courtyard. But it was the fourth finger of her left hand which told Lauren that she was the owner of the carriage, for there was a white mark left by a very recently removed wedding ring. Yes, the more Lauren studied her, the more certain she became that the lady was a wife waiting for her lover.

Hester and Alex came down at last, and at first Lauren didn't hear them enter the taproom behind her, for her attention was still upon the lady in pink. The lady saw Hester and Alex, however, and her face blanched with dismay. It was more than just dismay—it was unutterable horror—and with great presence of mind she got up from her table and hurried out of the other dining room door into the courtyard, leaving her meal unfinished upon the table.

Startled, Lauren watched her shadowy figure hasten past the taproom windows and then up the wooden staircase to the gallery on the other side of the courtyard. Her actions were impossible to mistake. She knew Hester and Alex and didn't want to be seen in this place. Lauren's curiosity increased but she decided not to say anything to her cousins. After all, the lady's affairs were none of her business, and some sleeping dogs were much better left lying, she thought, glancing down at the slumbering hounds at her feet.

The landlord's boast regarding the quality of his table was well founded, for nothing could have been tastier or more succulent than the roast mutton, which was served with potatoes, greens, and red currant sauce, and which Lauren and Alex decided to sample. Hester stood firm upon the red grouse, but both Lauren and Alex thought it looked overly rich and suspiciously buried beneath a spiced sauce. Hester brushed their doubts aside, however, and declared it to be absolutely delicious. Lauren was relieved not to be eating it, however, for although game was supposed to be hung for a long time, in her opinion this particular grouse had been shot on the glorious Twelfth itself, and had lain around on a larder shelf ever since.

There were no such doubts about the Corinth currant tartlets which followed, for they were light and delicate and met with universal approval. The meal was ended with a particularly tasty cheese, and each course was accompanied by a reasonably palatable wine, which the landlord swore was the very best Bordeaux.

In spite of their tiredness after the long day on the open road, they would have lingered a little after they'd dined, but among the rest of the company there was a large group of Glaswegian gentlemen on their way home after a climbing excursion to nearby Ben Vane. They became increasingly noisy as the whisky punch flowed and each member of the party was called upon in turn to deliver a toast, or "sentiment." These sentiments were expected to be a crisp sentence, a poetic phrase, a moral judgment, or a proverb of some sort, and each one was awaited with great interest. Lauren had listened with amusement to the somewhat slurred pronouncements. "May the hand of charity wipe the tears of sorrow." "May war never be among us." "May the wind of adversity never blow open our door." "May sincerity always dwell in the bottom of my heart." It was this last which met with howls of laughter, for the unfortunate gentleman who uttered it was a little fuddled, and declared that sincerity should always dwell in the heart of his bottom. At this point, with the prospect of a descent into vulgar-

ity suddenly entering the proceedings, Alex decided to
escort his two ladies from the room.

There was no real escape from the rowdy climbers,
however, for the night was very hot and Lauren was
obliged to leave her windows open. The sentiments continued, becoming more and more drunken and crude,
and accompanied by increasingly helpless laughter.
There was no harm in the gentlemen, however, and Lauren smiled a little as she lay in her bed listening to them.
It was some time before she fell asleep, and when she
did, she dreamed of Jonathan.

It was May, and USS *Chesapeake* was gliding down
the sparkling waters of Boston Roads to face the waiting
British frigate, HMS *Shannon*, a scene Lauren had actually watched from the shore, but which in her dreams
she saw from on aboard the *Chesapeake*. She and
Jonathan seemed to be alone on the deck, wrapped in
each other's arms, oblivious to all around them. The ves-
sel sailed relentlessly toward the enemy, and suddenly
all was confusion, with cannonballs thudding into the
timber, men shouting, and smoke darkening the air.
Jonathan was smiling into her eyes, as if still unaware of
anything but her, but then his smile faded, and his soft
brown eyes lost their shine. He grew pale, but when she
reached out, her hand passed right through him, for he
had become an illusion, there and yet not there . . . She
screamed his name, but then the scene was awash with
red. Again she screamed, but he had gone, and there was
the rattling of wooden pulleys as the sails were lowered.
The *Shannon* was victorious and the British sailors were
cheering, but she was alone with her grief. She stood
there on her own, the smoke drifting chokingly past her
as she gazed helplessly around, still whispering
Jonathan's name. The pulleys rattled again, much more
loudly and insistently, and suddenly she was wide
awake, staring confusedly up at the hangings of her bed
in a remote Scottish inn.

The tatters of the dreams still clung to her, trying to

drag her back to the past, but the present was all around her now. Slowly she sat up, pushing her hair back from her hot face. There were tears on her cheeks and her heart was pounding in her breast. The room felt claustrophobic and she flung the bedclothes aside and got up to go to the gallery door. She stepped out into the night air, lifting her face to the stars and closing her eyes as she inhaled the scent of heather from the surrounding moors.

It was then that she realized why she had dreamed so vividly of cheering voices and rattling pulleys, for not only were the gentlemen in the dining room still enjoying themselves noisily with the whisky punch, but a cabriolet had just driven into the yard below and the iron-rimmed wheels and the horse's hooves were still clattering on the cobbles. A drowsy stableboy emerged from the rear of the inn to attend to the newcomer, and the gentleman alighted. He removed his tall hat to run his hand briefly through his hair, and she saw that he was young and very personable, with dark hair and patrician if rather sensuous features that were momentarily caught in the light from a nearby lantern before he replaced his hat. He wore modish clothes, exceedingly well cut and bang up to the mark, and it seemed to Lauren that there was something oddly familiar about him. She watched as he asked the boy something and was directed up to the gallery opposite her room. The gentleman pressed a coin into the boy's hand and then proceeded up the wooden steps on the other side of the yard.

There was only one light burning as he walked softly along the gallery, and the door of the room concerned opened almost before he reached it. For a second or so Lauren saw who opened the door. It was the lady in pink, except that she now wore a flimsy nightrobe which was almost transparent in the candlelight from the room behind her, and her honey-colored hair was brushed in loose tumbling curls about her slender shoulders.

Lauren could almost sense her sigh of anticipation as

she flung her arms around her lover's neck and they pressed together in a passionate embrace before he almost carried her inside and the door closed softly behind them. Lauren gazed across at the lighted window, and after a moment the candles inside were extinguished. She wondered who the lovers were. It was very tempting to ask Hester about the lady, but perhaps a little cruel, for it was still no one's business but the two people concerned. She also wondered why the gentleman seemed vaguely familiar. She was sure she hadn't seen him before, and yet . . . Obviously he must be like someone she *did* know, although who it was she simply couldn't guess.

She lingered for a moment longer on the gallery, enjoying the coolness of the night, and then she turned back into her room, stepping carefully past Peggy, who was deeply asleep on her pallet at the foot of the bed.

She was awakened again at dawn when the gentleman left. The climbers had thankfully reached the end of the whisky punch, and the inn was quiet. Lauren heard the cabriolet being led into the courtyard and the gentleman's spurs jingling on the steps as he went down from the gallery. A moment later the cabriolet was driven away, and she listened to the dwindling sound as it came up to a smart pace over the moorland road. Then there was absolute silence, except for the first curlew among the heather.

4

LAUREN was dressed and ready to go down to breakfast. She wore the peach lawn gown and brown velvet spencer again, and her hair was combed and pinned in readiness for her straw bonnet, as they would be leaving the inn directly after they'd eaten.

She stood out on the gallery, looking down at the busy yard, where a private carriage was on the point of departure and a stagecoach from Glasgow had just drawn up. It was a scene of chaos and noise, with so much happening at once that it was hard to recall the furtive goings-on of the night. The carriage which had attracted her attention the previous evening was still in the same place and there was no sign of movement in the lady's room opposite. But as Lauren glanced across, the curtains twitched a little, and the lady peeped cautiously out. Her eyes met Lauren's, and with a visible gasp she drew swiftly back out of sight again.

Lauren smiled to herself, reading the lady's actions like a book. The unfaithful wife was very nervous indeed now that she knew there was someone at the inn who knew her, and by now she had somehow perceived that Lauren herself was with Hester and Alex. It was therefore very unlikely indeed that the occupant of the room opposite would stir outside until the Kingston carriages had departed.

She was proved right on this. After an excellent breakfast of ham and eggs, hot bread rolls, butter, and best black Bohea tea, they emerged into the morning sunshine of the crowded yard, and Lauren glanced up to see the lady's curtains still drawn. The navy blue carriage remained in its place against the wall, with the cloth over the door, and there was no hint of the sort of activity which suggested an imminent departure.

The landlord came out to bid them farewell. "I wish ye a fair journey," he said, and then added curiously, "May I ask where ye're bound?"

"Glenvane Castle," Alex replied. "We took the wrong road out of Dumbarton yesterday; otherwise we wouldn't have come this way."

"I fear it's easily done," the landlord observed sympathetically. "Ye're no the first of Lord Glenvane's guests tae have ended up here at the Crown & Thistle. I take it that ye're going there for Lady Mary's birthday?"

"You're remarkably well informed," Alex replied, wondering how the landlord knew such details when the inn was far away from Glenvane on the other side of Ben Vane mountain.

The man smiled. "Well, as I said, ye're no the first guest tae happen this way. Sir Sydney Dodd was here earlier this week, after taking the wrong road out of Dumbarton. And I can help ye as I helped him, for there's nay need tae go all the way back to Dumbarton."

"What do you mean?" Alex enquired.

"Why, ye can take the shortcut hard by Ben Vane." The landlord waved his arm in a generally northeasterly direction.

"Shortcut? In carriages?"

"Och, aye. 'Tis a fine enough road at this time of the year. Not in the winter, mind." The man chuckled.

"Which way do we go?"

"Just drive back the way ye came until ye reach the fork, then instead of going back tae Dumbarton ye take the other way up toward Ben Vane. The road passes in the lee of the mountain, and then down into Glenvane on the other side. The River Vane rises in a cave at the top, and spills out in a waterfall. There's shelter tae be had in the cave when the weather closes in, which it often does. Ye'll no need it, though, not with such fine carriages. Anyway, the road follows the river down tae Loch Vane, and ye'll see the castle soon enough, placed on a slip of land jutting out intae the water. It'll take ye about four hours, but about eight if ye go all the way back tae Dumbarton."

Alex nodded and smiled. "Thank you. We'll take your advice."

"Farewell, sir, ladies." The landlord bowed to them, and then watched the two carriages drive out beneath the arch to the road.

As they left the Crown & Thistle behind, Lauren's thoughts returned briefly to the secretive lady and her dashing lover, but then she put them both from her mind as she gazed out at the breathtaking highland scenery.

The carriages soon reached the fork in the road and left the Glasgow highway to begin the long climb over the moorland toward the hills that were topped by the soaring magnificence of Ben Vane. Curlews called, and a small herd of red deer fled toward the shelter of a copse of spindly oak trees. It was a beautiful late August morning, the sky was an almost transparent blue, and far away to the south was the shining mirror of the Firth of Clyde. The carriage windows were lowered and the heady moorland air was warm and almost intoxicating, as if it had passed over a hidden pool of the purest malt whisky. It was unlike any air Lauren had ever breathed before, and the scenery she gazed over was a perplexing blend of wild freedom and strangely gentle intimacy. The mountains and endless purple heather were wild and untamed, but the little burn that babbled beside the road, and the humpbacked stone bridge that eventually spanned it, were charming and almost familiar.

They saw hardly any people—just two barefooted women with shawls over their heads, carrying baskets of knitted stockings which they hoped to sell to the carriers who halted at the Crown & Thistle, and a shepherd wearing plaid which was kilted around his waist and then tossed over his shoulder. He sported a highland bonnet and tartan hose, and he strode over the heather with his dog at his heels. The carriages warranted only a brief glance, and then he continued on his way toward a small knot of wayward sheep by a stand of Scots pines.

The road climbed higher and higher, and they had to pause from time to time to rest the horses. Ben Vane loomed over them now, its craggy peak seeming to almost brush against the sky. From up here it was possible to see the grand sweep of almost the entire Clyde estuary, with its dotted white sails and matchless headlands. Civilization lay down there, but up here they were now quite alone, except for the mournful, haunting cries of the secretive curlews, heard clearly but seldom seen.

At last the road reached the crest of the pass and they saw the cave and waterfall of which the landlord had spoken. The mouth of the cave yawned in the side of the mountain, and a clear stream of water tumbled down into a pool where the blue of the sky was reflected as if in a mirror. The little River Vane, scarcely more than a burn, spilled out of the pool to pass over the road and then down the glen ahead toward Loch Vane. Beside the ford there was a cairn of stones, to mark the place where centuries of travelers had paused to rest after the long climb over the pass; the two carriages halted as well, for the horses were very tired.

The passengers alighted, and as Hester and Alex strolled by the waterfall and pool, Lauren found a place on a large flat rock beside the ford where she sat gazing at the wonderful panorama of Loch Vane in the valley far below. Surrounded by mountains, the loch shone like a vast sapphire, its surface dotted with a string of emerald islands which seemed to have been embroidered upon the water. It was at least ten miles away from them, but the air was so clear that it was as if she could reach down and dip her fingers in its coolness.

But it wasn't just the loch which took Lauren's breath

away. It was also Glenvane Castle, which seemed to almost rise out of the water on a slender tentacle of land reaching out from the superbly landscaped park on the far shore. Tall, gray, and clustered with Gothic towers and turrets, it clung to its foothold, as impregnable now as it had been in medieval times. Its reflection shone on the surface of water which was so still and clear that it might have been a looking glass, and altogether it was a scene so perfect in every way that it might be the setting of a fairy tale. Lauren stared. This was a magical place, the stuff of dreams . . .

At last the coachmen pronounced the teams sufficiently refreshed to continue and the passengers took their places again for the final stage of the long journey from London. After such a long and arduous climb, the horses picked up their heels to make the descent, and they set off through the little ford and then down the glen. The road meandered down the mountainside, and after a mile the way became narrower and choked with rowan and birch. The River Vane splashed at the roadside, the crystal water sweeping down between fern-draped banks, joined now and then by other burns until the splash of water had become a veritable roar amid the trees as the river cascaded eagerly toward the loch far below.

At last the road reached the floor of the valley and emerged from the screen of rowan and birch to cross a bridge spanning the now quite wide river, which was still a torrent of white water after its brief but hectic descent from the mountain. There was rich parkland all around now, with here and there a specimen tree to indicate the work of man enhancing that of nature. The road joined the one they should have taken from Dumbarton, and the carriages passed the fork, driving on toward the castle, which now seemed even more splendid and magical than it had from the top of the pass.

Lauren held her breath as she stared at Rory Ardmore's highland stronghold. Glenvane Castle seemed the very embodiment of Scotland's history, with successive centuries lying over it like veils. But the fortress had a softer side, for there was a terraced flower garden reaching down to the water's edge, with fountains, arbors, and lawns that swept toward a jetty where pleasure boats were moored.

Looking at the garden, Hester sat forward suddenly, pointing ahead. "There's Rory. He's walking with a lady by the shore," she said.

Alex looked as well, and then smiled. "If I'm not mistaken, that flame hair belongs to Isabel," he murmured.

Lauren looked at the couple walking by the shore. They'd paused by the jetty, and were standing very close as they spoke intimately together, unaware as yet of the carriages passing nearby.

Isabel, Lady Maxby, wore daffodil muslin which clung to her legs as she moved. Heavy ringlets of her memorable hair fell from beneath her wide-brimmed white gauze hat, and a cashmere shawl trailed idly along the ground behind her. She possessed a tiny-waisted, voluptuous figure, and was very elegant indeed—she might have been a living illustration from the pages of *La Belle Assemblée*.

Rory wore a fawn coat and cream breeches, and he carried his top hat under his arm as he smiled down into his companion's eyes. As Lauren watched, he took her hand and raised it tenderly to his lips. He lingered over the gesture in a way which could only be described as loving. Lauren had to look away, for nothing could have reminded her more sharply that the wisest thing would be to put all thought of Lord Glenvane from her foolish head.

Suddenly Rory realized the carriages were driving over the narrow neck of land toward the castle, and he turned to wave his hat aloft as they passed beneath the towergate into the dark courtyard within. The walls of the castle seemed to crowd over the narrow cobbled area, blotting out even the bright August sunshine, and the arrival of the two vehicles disturbed a flock of doves, which rose with fluttering excitement toward the openness of the sky beyond the turrets.

Alex alighted, and as he assisted Hester and Lauren down, they heard Rory hailing them. There was a deep archway leading from the courtyard to the gardens, and he and Isabel were coming through it, their figures mere shadows against the riot of sunshine and flowers behind them.

Lauren was glad to see Rory again after what seemed a very long time, but then her attention was drawn to Isabel, who was arrestingly lovely. The daffodil gown was made of layers of sheer muslin, with a dainty gold-buckled belt and a square neckline which plunged perilously low over her full breasts. There was a dainty sprig of heather pinned to her shoulder with a golden brooch, and another sprig fixed to the crown of her wide-brimmed gauze hat. The hat cast translucent shadows over her gloriously beautiful heart-shaped face. Her hair was that rich auburn which Titian delighted to paint, and her eyes were the color of a bluebell wood in April, but as Lauren looked she saw that the clarity of that blue was being spoiled by barely concealed anger. That same anger was also evident on Isabel's cheeks and in the whiteness of the fingertips resting on Rory's arm. Lady Maxby was clearly finding it a struggle to appear relaxed as she applied herself to the business of greeting the new arrivals.

Lauren wondered what had happened. Had she and Rory had an argument? That hardly seemed likely, not given the intimate way they'd been speaking together by the loch a few moments before.

Rory smiled warmly at them. "Welcome to Glenvane, my friends. We were beginning to wonder if you'd changed your minds about joining us."

"The journey wasn't all it might have been," Hester replied, returning the smile as he drew her hand to his lips.

Alex hastened to renew his acquaintance with Isabel. "You are as lovely as ever," he said, kissing her on the cheek.

"And you are as dashing, Alex," she replied. Her

voice was low and melodic. She smiled at Hester. "It's good to see you again, Hester."

"It's good to see you, too," Hester answered, the subtleties of her tone conveying to Lauren that there was nothing good about it at all. Lauren was a little surprised to realize this, for Hester hadn't given any intimation at all that Lady Maxby wasn't to her liking.

Isabel's bluebell gaze then swung to Lauren, and Rory effected the introduction. "Isabel, this is Hester's cousin, Miss Maitland. Miss Maitland, may I present Lady Maxby?"

It was the first time he'd looked directly at Lauren, and as he did so he seemed to gaze right into her soul. There was nothing brief about the look—it was intense and clear and it caused a frisson of emotion to shiver through her.

Isabel inclined her lovely head. "I'm pleased to make your acquaintance, Miss Maitland."

"And I yours, Lady Maxby," Lauren replied, tearing her eyes away from Rory.

"Miss Maitland is from Boston, Massachusetts," he explained to Isabel.

"She is?" Isabel seemed taken by surprise, and then her eyes swung accusingly toward him. "You neglected to mention that before," she said softly.

"Did I?"

"You know you did." Isabel gave a faint smile. "How neglectful of you to leave so much unsaid."

"You were ever inclined to dramatize," he replied shortly.

She raised an eyebrow and said nothing more.

Rory returned his attention to Alex. "I'm neglecting my duties as host. Come inside." He ushered them toward an ancient studded doorway. "We expected you yesterday! What happened to delay you?"

Alex gave a rueful grin. "A wrong turning in Dumbarton. We ended up at the—"

"The Crown & Thistle?" Rory finished for him. "Yes,

it happens from time to time, and indeed has already happened this week. Poor Sir Sydney Dodd managed to land there several nights ago."

Hester halted and looked curiously at him. "*Poor* Sir Sydney? Why do you say that? The Crown & Thistle may only be an inn, but it is a rather superior one."

"So it is, Hester, but I fear Sir Sydney has been laid up in bed for the past day or so, and he puts the blame fairly and squarely on the Crown & Thistle's red grouse dinner."

Hester was dismayed. "I do hope he's wrong, for I had the grouse last night."

"Well, you look as radiant as ever, so perhaps the red grouse is innocent," Rory murmured, taking her hand and drawing it gallantly to his lips.

They walked on across the courtyard, but as they reached the flight of three stone steps leading to the door, Isabel, unseen by anyone, tried to deliberately trip Lauren. A dainty foot in a yellow satin slipper darted out suddenly, and it was all Lauren could do not to take a very undignified, if not dangerous, tumble. Somehow she managed to retain her balance, and was saved from stumbling by Rory, who seized her arms to steady her.

"Are you all right?" he asked anxiously.

"Er—yes, I think so. I wasn't paying proper attention," she replied, meeting her assailant's glittering bluebell gaze.

"Are you sure? You could have hurt yourself quite considerably on these cursed steps. The stone is so worn away after centuries of use that—"

"I'm quite all right, truly," Lauren insisted, glancing at Isabel again.

The faintest of smiles curved the other's lovely lips as she walked on into the castle. Lauren gazed bemusedly after her. So that was how it was to be. Isabel, Lady Maxby, had for some reason appointed herself Lauren Maitland's enemy!

5

RECOVERING from the sharp brush with Isabel, Lauren followed the others through the doorway and found it gave directly into a vast baronial hall with an aged smoke-stained wooden roof. The uneven upper walls were whitewashed and hung with weapons and hunting trophies which were interspersed with heraldic shields, and the shields were draped with fringed lengths of the blue-and-green Ardmore tartan. More of the same tartan figured in the ancient banners suspended from the roof beams and in the painted carving on the paneled lower walls. There was an immense stone fireplace, on either side of which stood suits of armor, and, apart from various chairs placed around the walls, the only item of furniture was a huge sixteenth-century table which ranged down the center of the black-and-white tiled floor. Two more suits of armor guarded the foot of the grand wooden staircase which led up into the shadows of the next floor, where a half-gallery afforded a splendid view down into the hall. The scent of roses and honeysuckle filled the air from the three large bowls on the table, and the sound of piano music drifted from somewhere beyond the staircase as someone played a sweet, romantic lovesong.

Hester listened to the music for a moment. "Who is playing?" she asked.

"That will be Mary. Come, I'll introduce you. I fear that she and Fitz are the only others in the castle right now. Fitz expects his wife to arrive at any moment, and everyone else has gone for a picnic by the head of the loch."

A door opened at the far end of the hall and a steward entered. He rather reminded Lauren of the landlord at the Crown & Thistle, except that he wore a plaid kilt and black waist-length coat, with a lavish spill of lace at his throat.

Rory turned toward him. "Ah, Tam, would you see that some suitable refreshments are brought to the music room, and that these guests' rooms are ready and waiting as they should be?"

"My lord." Tam bowed and withdrew again.

With Isabel on his arm, Rory led his new guests toward the staircase, and the sound of the piano grew steadily louder as they ascended. They walked along a dark-paneled passage toward an arched door that stood slightly ajar. The room beyond was bright with sunlight, and its windows faced over the loch toward Ben Vane. True to most music rooms, it was sparsely furnished, with a few chairs and several cupboards for music sheets. There was a gilded harp in a corner, a violin propped up on the mantel shelf, and a collection of bagpipes of varying antiquity displayed upon the walls.

The piano stood in a shaft of sunlight at the end of the room. It was an elegant instrument, much decorated with mother-of-pearl, ebony, and ivory, and it had a particularly sweet tone. The lady playing it was charmingly dressed in a green seersucker gown, and there was a silk scarf of the blue-and-green Ardmore tartan pinned over her shoulder with a silver brooch. She had a peaches-and-cream complexion, dark eyes, and soft brown hair which was worn up on her head beneath a lacy day cap, with untied tippets which trailed prettily on either side of her face. She wasn't alone in the room, for a gentleman was leaning on the piano, watching her as she played.

Anthony, Lord Fitzsimmons—Fitz to his friends—was tall and fair, with pleasant features and hazel eyes, and he wore a sky-blue coat of such an excellent cut that it had to have originated in London's Bond Street. There was a discreet pearl pin on his crisply starched cravat, and he was smiling at Mary in a warm but rather fraternal way. She, on the other hand, was returning the smile in a way which Lauren thought was anything but sisterly. There was a telltale glow about Lady Mary Ardmore, but it was a lost cause, for Fitz was married to the mysterious Emma.

Mary's playing broke off as her brother and his guests entered the room, and quickly she rose to come toward them. She had an amiable and open smile, and was delighted to see Hester and Alex again. She also greeted Lauren warmly when they were introduced, and Lauren instinctively found herself liking Rory's sister as much as she'd disliked his mistress a few minutes earlier. Lauren also took to Fitz, who had the sort of easy charm and good-natured humor which made him comfortable to be with. It was easy to see why Mary was secretly in love with him.

Mary was disarmingly pleased they'd arrived at last. "Oh, I'm truly delighted you've come, for now you'll be here tomorrow night."

"Tomorrow night?" Alex repeated blankly, not thinking.

"It's my birthday ball," Mary explained smilingly.

"But of course! How dense of me." He grinned at her. "After all, that *is* the reason we're here, is it not?"

They all adjourned to the nearby solar, which was the name given to the chamber which served as the drawing room. Like the hall on the floor below, it was half paneled, half whitewashed, and this time the whitewashed portion of the walls was adorned with tapestries and highly polished gold and silver plates. The windows faced over the gardens and the loch, and were larger than those in the rest of the castle—hence the name solar.

They sat in amiable conversation for a while, but when Tam the steward ushered two maids in with tea trays, Lauren was conscious of Isabel's dark gaze upon her. The tripping-up in the courtyard had quite obviously been a mere beginning, for more was promised by those spiteful blue eyes.

But not long after that, something happened to temporarily banish all thought of Isabel, or even of Rory himself, from Lauren's mind. Footsteps that jingled with spurs echoed briskly along the passage, and then the door was flung open and a young gentleman burst unceremoniously into the room. Lauren's breath caught, for she'd seen him before. He was the lover of the mysterious lady at the Crown & Thistle!

He had obviously been out riding, for he wore a pine-green riding coat and light gray cord breeches. There was color on his cheeks and his dark hair was windswept, as if he'd been urging his horse at speed for some time. He hesitated for a moment as he saw Hester and Alex in the room, and Lauren knew that his ladylove at the inn had told him all about them being there as well.

Rory was irritated. "Is the castle on fire, Jamie?" he enquired a little coolly.

Jamie? It was Rory's younger brother? Lauren lowered her eyes quickly, her thoughts racing as she considered the implications.

Jamie shifted a little uncomfortably. "Forgive me, Rory, I didn't mean to . . ."

"I'm sure you didn't. Well? What's wrong now? I take it there's a reason for your lack of manners?"

Jamie's glance slid again to Hester and Alex, but as he saw no particular response on their faces, he relaxed visibly.

"I'm awaiting a reply," Rory prompted frostily.

Jamie looked swiftly at him. "I haven't any real excuse for my conduct, except that I've had words with Lord Findon, who appears to think he knows more about Glenvane than I do! And then when I got back here, I found my horse had gone lame. That's all."

Lauren studied at him. He was fibbing. Whatever his

reason for behaving as he had, it wasn't on account of Lord Findon or a lame horse.

Mary hastened to smooth the moment over. "Come and sit down, Jamie, and I'll pour you some tea," she said.

He gave the teapot a savage look. Tea was evidently the last thing he really wished to drink at the moment, but he obliged her and sat down to accept a dainty porcelain cup and saucer. Then he looked at Alex again.

"We thought you'd be here before this," he said, his tone now level and all that was courteous.

"Well, we *would* have been," Alex replied, and then went on to explain again about the Crown & Thistle.

Jamie remained commendably self-possessed. "That fork in Dumbarton has had much to answer for over the years. Er—were there many at the inn?"

Lauren watched him. She alone knew why he was asking such a question.

Alex pursed his lips. "There were quite a few guests, I suppose, but it wasn't exactly crowded."

Jamie glanced at him. "So it wasn't like a Mayfair reception, a crush to end all crushes, with every face familiar?" he ventured.

"Not a familiar face in sight," Alex replied.

Jamie smiled, for those few words were all the reassurance he required. "A few days ago you'd have met Sir Sydney Dodd."

"So I understand. Unfortunately, Hester would appear to have sampled the same red grouse dinner, but we trust she won't be laid up in bed as he apparently is."

Rory nodded. "He's far from well, and I wish he would let me send for the doctor from Dumbarton, but he insists that he's recovering without the attentions of any cursed quack."

Jamie turned suddenly to Fitz. "Oh, by the way, I forgot to mention earlier that Emma won't be here now until sometime this afternoon. A messenger arrived as I was leaving on my ride, and it quite slipped my mind."

Fitz sighed. "What on earth is keeping her? She should have been here this morning."

"I gather she has had trouble with her carriage. Repairs, or something." Jamie fidgeted with his cup and saucer.

Mary was concerned. "Oh, Alex, what a shame that you didn't encounter her on the way, for you could have brought her with you."

"Indeed so," Alex replied.

Jamie said nothing, but a nerve flickered at his temple as he kept his gaze lowered to the floor. In that moment Lauren knew that Emma, Lady Fitzsimmons, was the woman at the inn. Jamie Ardmore was embroiled in a liaison with the wife of one of his brother's oldest friends!

It was a shocking realization, and Lauren was hard put to remain outwardly composed and unruffled. She was beginning to feel like a secret agent, for ever since she'd come over the border into Scotland she'd been the unwilling witness of others' intrigues. First of all there had been the nighttime activities at the inn, then Isabel's as yet unexplained animosity. After that had come the realization that Mary was in love with Fitz, and now the fact that Jamie was conducting an affair with Fitz's wife. What else might there be? Nothing, she hoped, for it was very uncomfortable being party to so much that was meant to remain hidden.

Shortly after that, Rory sent for maids to conduct Alex, Hester, and Lauren to their rooms, for the other guests were soon due to return from the picnic and a boating party on the loch had been arranged for the afternoon.

Isabel suddenly got to her feet and volunteered to escort Lauren in person.

Lauren was both startled and dismayed. "It's very kind of you, Lady Maxby, but—"

"I don't mind at all, for I have to go to my own room for something, and it's on the way," Isabel insisted.

Lauren had no option but to accept the offer with

grace, but in truth she would have preferred to go with the maid. She felt that Isabel had an ulterior motive, and it wasn't long before the suspicion proved correct. Halfway along a paneled gallery that was hung with portraits of Rory's ancestors, Isabel paused suddenly.

"Miss Maitland, will you satisfy my base curiosity about your locket?"

"My locket?" Lauren was taken aback.

"Yes. I couldn't help catching a glimpse of it in the courtyard, and it really seemed so very like another one I know of that I must see if it is the same."

"I cannot imagine that it would be the same, Lady Maxby, for mine was made especially by a jeweler in Boston, but if you wish to see it . . ." Lauren allowed her to examine the locket.

Isabel turned it over in her hand. "Yes, it really is similar to the other one. May I see inside?"

"If you wish."

As she opened it and saw the portrait of Jonathan and lock of his hair, Isabel immediately raised her eyes to Lauren's. "Who is he?"

"He was my fiancé."

"Was?"

"He died at sea," Lauren replied briefly, not wanting to say anything more.

"Oh."

Lauren took the locket and replaced it inside her spencer. Enough of this beating about the bush—it was time to get to the point. "What do you really wish to know, Lady Maxby?" she asked bluntly.

The bluebell gaze was wide and innocent. "I don't understand, Miss Maitland."

"No?"

"No. Have I offended you in some way?"

"Yes, Lady Maxby, you have, for I do not care to be deliberately tripped up."

"Deliberately? Oh, my dear Miss Maitland, that was

an accident. Perhaps I should have apologized at the time—it was most remiss of me not to—"

"Remiss? Yes, it was." Lauren held her gaze. If Isabel intended to pretend it had been an accident, there was little more to be said, but an accident it had most definitely not been.

"I'm so sorry if I've upset you," Isabel murmured, beginning to walk on again.

Nothing more was said as they continued along the gallery, and shortly after that they reached the door of Lauren's room. Isabel was all cool politeness as she took her leave, but Lauren felt there was something almost menacing about the busy whispering of her daffodil muslin skirts as she hurried away.

Lauren entered the room. It was a handsome chamber in one of the turrets and enjoyed a grand view over the gardens and loch. The furnishings were very sumptuous, from the spacious four-poster bed to the elegant French armchairs by the fireplace. The bed was large enough to require a wooden step to climb into it, and there was an inviting windowseat upholstered in the same blue damask as the canopy and hangings. Behind a lacquer screen there was a dressing table, wardrobe, and wash-stand and elegant cheval glass. There were two gilt-framed paintings on the wall—a portrait of a lady in sixteenth-century dress and a landscape which included Loch Vane and the castle itself. Someone had put a bowl of honeysuckle in the hearth of the small fireplace and the air was scented and heady. Reflections from the loch far below shimmered on the ceiling in a soothing manner which made Lauren feel welcome the moment she entered.

Peggy had already attended to most of the unpacking, and was very carefully hanging her mistress's clothes in the capacious wardrobe. She hurried around the lacquer screen as Lauren came in.

"It's a lovely room, isn't it, Miss Lauren?" she said, bobbing a curtsey.

"Very lovely indeed, Peggy." Lauren took a deep breath of the honeysuckle and then teased off her little white gloves to hand to the maid. "I trust you've been shown your own accommodation?"

"I have, madam. I'm sharing with Mrs. Kingston's maid."

Lauren smiled. "Well, that will suit you both, will it not?"

"Oh, yes, madam."

Lauren went to the window to look out, and suddenly Rory addressed her from the doorway.

"I trust the room is to your liking, Miss Maitland?"

She turned swiftly. "Why, yes, Lord Glenvane, it's very fine indeed."

"It happens to be one of the most agreeable in the castle—at least, that's my opinion—so I wouldn't want you to think I'd banished you to a garret," he said, entering and coming to stand beside her at the window.

"A very luxurious garret," she replied, all too conscious of his closeness. Oh, plague take this man for unsettling her whenever she was with him. Why couldn't she remain cool, calm, collected, and above all, aloof! She must form a defense. Yes, that was definitely what she must do. If she simply reminded herself of how tender his manner had been toward Isabel by the lochside earlier, then surely common sense would soon return. But as he smiled into her eyes, she knew that it would be easier said than done.

He looked out of the window again. "Are you enjoying your stay in Britain, Miss Maitland?"

"Much more than I thought I would," she admitted.

"I wish I could say the same of my visit to America," he murmured, and then he looked at her. "I make no apology for bringing the subject up again, Miss Maitland, for there is something I wish to explain to you. You see, my attitude has nothing to do with your homeland in general, or indeed with your countrymen, just with my painful experience at the hands of one American lady in particular. I am referring to my late wife."

Lauren stared at him. "Your wife was American?" she repeated.

"Yes."

"Oh." It was all she could think of to say.

He smiled. "Yes. Oh."

"An inadequate response, I admit," she said, returning the smile.

"Were our positions to be reversed, I doubt if I could think of anything suitable," he replied. "My marriage was a disaster from the outset, and with hindsight I know I was aware of the problems before I uttered a single vow." He gazed out at the sparkling loch as memories washed painfully over him, then he drew himself together. "I really shouldn't be burdening you with any of this, but I want you to know, to understand . . ."

"If you wish to tell me, Lord Glenvane, then I am willing to listen." Oh, how willing, for she wished to know all there was to know about the master of Glenvane Castle. She could tell herself a thousand times over that it was foolish to be drawn to him, and she could remind herself that Isabel was probably his mistress, but nothing seemed to make any difference. She was a moth, helplessly attracted to his bright flame. She almost yearned to be burned, indeed she found herself contemplating that searing moment. What would it feel like to be taken in this dashing Scottish lord's arms? What would it feel like to be kissed and cherished, to be made endless love to by him . . .? Hot color flushed to her cheeks, and she moved quickly away from the window.

He misinterpreted her reaction. "Forgive me, for no doubt you wish to rest awhile after the journey. I trust we will meet again soon when everyone gathers for the boating party. Until then, Miss Maitland." He inclined his head.

"Until then, Lord Glenvane." Lauren gazed after him. His wife had been American? His marriage had been a disaster? She wanted to know more, to understand more . . . If only she hadn't turned from the window, then maybe he would have explained what had happened.

A few minutes later, when Lauren had changed out of her traveling clothes and was seated before the dressing table in her pink muslin wrap for Peggy to brush her hair, there was a knock at the door. It was Hester.

"Are you all right, Lauren? It's just that we've been put in rooms some way from here, and I feel a little as if we've deserted you."

"As you can see, I'm being very well cared for," Lauren replied, spreading her hands to indicate the room.

Hester glanced around. "You are indeed. I'm almost inclined to be miffed." She went to the window. "What a wonderful view! We have only the courtyard to look at."

"Our host has been here to personally explain that this is one of the best rooms."

"Rory came here?"

"Yes, a few minutes ago."

Hester raised an eyebrow. "As I said in London. La, Coz, I do believe you've made a conquest."

"I doubt that very much, for Lady Maxby is his love."

"Then he is a very poor judge of women."

Lauren smiled a little wryly. "I think he would probably agree with you."

"What do you mean?"

"Well, according to him he made a very unwise decision when he married his American wife."

Hester's eyes widened. "*American* wife?"

"Yes."

"So, that's why he spoke as he did in London."

"I believe so, but I really don't know any more than that."

Hester's glance encompassed her again. "I still believe you've made a conquest, Lauren. He seems to be going out of his way to be agreeable toward you."

"I'd like to think you were right, Hester," Lauren confessed a little unguardedly.

"You'd like to? Does that mean you——?"

Lauren wished she'd been more circumspect. "It means that I'm going to be all that's sensible, and leave well alone," she declared firmly. "The last thing I need is an unhappy entanglement, and that's what I'd get if I allowed myself to succumb in this particular instance."

"But——"

"No, Hester, just forget I admitted anything. Please."

Reluctantly Hester nodded. "Very well."

"Thank you."

Hester turned from the window. "I confess I'm all agog to see Fitz's wife again, and this extra delay, even if it's only a few more hours, has simply served to heighten my curiosity. I'm dying to know if my first impression of her was correct."

"It probably was," Lauren murmured.

"I beg your pardon?"

"Oh, nothing." Lauren decided not to say anything, after all she only had her intuition to go by, and it might be that she was wrong about the identity of the lady at the inn.

"Alex can't wait to see her again, either. He's still trying to remember where he saw her before."

"He's still convinced that he did?"

"Oh, yes. Absolutely." Hester sighed. "Well, I suppose I'd better go. I gather the boating party is set to commence at three, and Alex and I will go down to the garden just before then if you wish to join us."

"Thank you. I'll do that."

Hester gave her a quick kiss on the cheek and then hastened away.

Lauren went to the window and looked out once more. The loch glittered almost dazzlingly, and suddenly the waters of Loch Vane in August became the waters of Boston Roads in May. She thought of Jonathan again, and her fingers crept to the golden locket at her throat.

6

THE gardens at Glenvane Castle were very lovely indeed, and at this time of the year were at the height of their beauty. The beds were colorful with roses, pinks, and delphiniums, and fountains played in the sunshine as Rory's many guests gathered for the boating party. There were statues, raised lily pools, gazebos, and a shell-studded grotto which had been built over a disused well. The well was now sealed with an iron grille, and the grotto boasted elegant seats and some of the most heavily scented honeysuckle Lauren had ever known.

On seeing carriage after carriage of picnickers returning from the head of the loch a little earlier, she had wondered if the whole of Mayfair had upped and come to Scotland! When Rory had promised no lack of company he had not exaggerated, and the chatter and laughter in the garden was quite considerable. It was a very happy gathering, and there was no doubt that Lady Mary's birthday celebrations were a great success.

Lauren sat in the grotto with Hester, Alex, and Fitz, as well as a number of other people, some of whom she'd met in London. Fitz was in a withdrawn mood, as indeed he'd been since learning that his wife's arrival would be delayed until the afternoon. Lauren was still privately convinced that Emma and the lady at the Crown & Thistle would be one and the same, and if that were so, then the Fitzsimmons marriage couldn't be as secure as might be expected only a year after the wedding in Dublin. Fitz was most definitely preoccupied, and Lauren couldn't

help glancing frequently toward him. She wondered
what he was thinking, and, inevitably, she wondered if
Mary figured at all in those thoughts.

Aside from her secret musings about Fitz's private
life, Lauren was now feeling much refreshed and revital-
ized after washing and changing out of her traveling
clothes. Now she wore a pretty turquoise-and-white
striped lawn gown and her hair was pinned loosely on
top of her head and tied with a pink ribbon. She carried a
fringed pink parasol and there was a turquoise velvet
reticule looped over her wrist.

Beside her in the grotto, Hester was in vivacious
mood as she made little secret of her eager anticipation.
"Oh, I can hardly wait to be out on the loch. I *love* boating!" she said, smoothing the skirts of her cream silk
gown.

Alex poked her arm teasingly. "You don't always. I
seem to recall you were somewhat seasick when we last
went out on the Thames."

"That was at Greenwich, and there was a horrid wind,
to say nothing of a full tide and a luncheon of rather
doubtful salmon!" Hester protested.

"Yes, as doubtful as that red grouse you *would* have
last night," he observed.

"Oh, do stop going on about the grouse. I feel perfectly all right, and am sure there was nothing wrong
with it." Hester smiled at him. "In fact, please stop
grousing about the grouse!"

He grinned. "Very well, not another word will cross
my lips."

"Good." Hester looked past him toward the castle,
where Rory, Isabel, Jamie, and Mary had just emerged to
descend to join the gathering.

Mary was delightful in orange as she enjoyed pride of
place on Rory's arm, and Isabel, who wore forget-me-
not blue, was escorted by Jamie, a fact which she quite
obviously did not like, if her stormy face was anything
by which to judge.

Hester raised an eyebrow. "It would seem dear Isabel isn't amused about being eclipsed by Mary," she murmured.

Alex frowned at his wife. "Don't be so uncharitable. Isabel isn't at all as disagreeable as you think."

"No?"

"No."

Lauren glanced at Hester, and then leaned closer to whisper. "Do you think Lady Maxby is Lord Glenvane's mistress?"

"I don't only think it, I know it. Alex told me. He and Rory dined together at their club the evening before Rory left London, and it seems Rory admitted it then."

Fresh disappointment washed through Lauren, for there was a wealth of difference between wondering if that was how it was between Rory and Isabel and actually knowing it for a fact. Why she'd entertained hopes was a mystery to her. Rory had confessed in London that Isabel had a place in his life, and she should have had the common sense to accept the situation then. But whenever she thought of the handsome Earl of Glenvane, or worse, when she was actually in his presence, practical thought flew willy-nilly out of the window!

But events were in train which would cause Isabel even more displeasure than taking second place to Mary, for she was about to be relegated yet again, and this time by none other than Lauren. It happened as the whole party was adjourning to the jetty, where the pleasure boats, each large enough for a lady and a gentleman, had all been made ready with comfortable cushions and little hampers containing glasses and bottles of refreshing iced lemonade. Lauren was on Fitz's arm as their party proceeded after the rest when suddenly she noticed a brief but rather heated exchange taking place between Isabel and Rory. They'd drawn slightly to one side, and Isabel was very displeased about something. She even went so far as to stamp her foot, but Rory remained adamant. He shook his head and pointed to Jamie, who was waiting with Mary on the jetty.

Isabel's face was fiery as with an ill grace she stalked on to the jetty, and allowed Jamie to assist her into one of the boats. Lauren was so engrossed in watching Isabel's angry display that she didn't notice Rory pairing Fitz with Mary. It wasn't until he came over to her that she realized how he'd manipulated everything. "I trust you will not mind suffering my company, Miss Maitland?"

She looked hesitantly at him. "I'm very honored, Lord Glenvane," she said.

"The honor is entirely mine," he replied.

With a shy smile, she slipped her hand over his sleeve, and they proceeded on to the jetty, where the boats awaited. Hardly anyone else noticed what had taken place, except Jamie, Fitz and Mary, and Isabel, of course. The latter observed everything with stony-faced resentment as she was rowed away from the jetty. Only one other person glanced back with interest, and that was Hester. Lauren's cousin gave a very knowing smile. I told you so, the smile said, you *have* made a conquest! Lauren felt uncomfortable about the whole thing, for although she felt no sympathy at all for Isabel, whose conduct so far had been less than praiseworthy, the fact remained that she, not Lauren Maitland, had first claim upon the Earl of Glenvane.

Rory handed Lauren into the last remaining boat. He wore a dark gray coat with light gray trousers, and his unstarched neckcloth fluttered slightly in the soft breeze as he stepped down into the boat after her. She made herself comfortable on the cushions in the stern, and he discarded his top hat as he took up the oars. Soon the jetty and shore slipped away behind as the little boat cut through the dazzling water.

Lauren observed Mary and Fitz and wondered if he was quite as unaware of his companion's adoration as he made out. Maybe he was flattered to be the object of her

affections? He certainly paid her every attention and
found her agreeable to be with, for he was laughing at
something she said. It was a warm laugh, and he was
comfortable and at ease. As for Mary, well, the signs
were all there to be read, from the pretty flush on her
cheeks to the shyly lowered eyes.

With a sigh, Lauren lay back on the cushions, her
parasol twirling gently as she watched Rory rowing.
Why had he singled her out like this? It would be flatteringly agreeable to think that Hester was right, but somehow she didn't think that that was it. Perhaps it was the
unflatteringly simple fact that he and Isabel were temporarily at odds and he was endeavoring to make his
mistress jealous. If that were so, then he appeared to be
succeeding!

There was much laughter and good humor as the colorful flotilla glided on the loch. Some of the boaters
made for the nearest of the islands, which were dotted
everywhere, but others, like Rory and Lauren, simply remained out on the water. Lauren gazed toward the castle.
"You are a very fortunate man, Lord Glenvane," she said
after a moment.

"Fortunate?"

"To be master of all this." She looked around at the
magnificent scenery.

"Ah. Yes, I do not deny it, for I believe Glenvane to
be one of the most beautiful places on earth."

She nodded. "I think you may be right, sir."

"How long will you be here in Britain, Miss Maitland?"

"Oh, a few months more, I suppose. I mean to be
home in time for Christmas."

"Boston's gain will be Britain's loss."

"How gallant you are, sir."

"Meaning, how glib I am?" he murmured, smiling at
her as he rested the oars for a moment. "Yes, I suppose it
might have sounded like that, but in truth I was paying
you an honest compliment."

"Then I thank you, Lord Glenvane," she replied.

"You have a dry way with you, Miss Maitland."

"I didn't mean to sound dry, sir."

"You also have a way of confounding me. Here I am, practicing my devastating charm, and yet I have the uncomfortable feeling that you are laughing at me."

"That is not so, sir."

"I will take your word for it."

She studied him. "Actually, I've been wondering exactly why you've singled me out like this. Am I the stick with which to beat Lady Maxby?" She hardly knew the words were on her lips, and color immediately flooded her cheeks.

He met her gaze. "Is that how you see my conduct?"

"I . . . I cannot help but wonder."

"I fear you do not know me at all."

"That I cannot deny."

He smiled a little, and took up the oars once more. "You will know me better soon, I promise you," he murmured.

She felt quite dreadful as he rowed on across the loch. What on earth had possessed her to ask such an improper question? It was hardly surprising that he had responded in the way he had. She'd been put in her place, but in the nicest possible way! Embarrassed color lingered on her cheeks, and she did all she could to avoid catching his eyes. Of the many things of which she might from time to time have been guilty, forward and indiscreet enquiries did not figure on the list. She wished the boating party would end, and soon!

But it was far from over yet, and they were a long way across the loch, close to the choppier water at the mouth of the River Vane, when at last Rory shipped the oars. "A glass of lemonade would be very welcome after all that rowing, Miss Maitland," he said, nodding toward the hamper.

Quickly she put her parasol aside and leaned across, but as she did so her locket suddenly slipped from around her throat, and fell to the bottom of the boat. It lay open, its contents revealed.

Rory rescued it, and glanced at Jonathan's portrait before handing it back to her. "You are attached, Miss Maitland?"

"I was, Lord Glenvane, but Jonathan is dead."

"Forgive me, I didn't mean to—"

"You weren't to know, sir."

"When did he die?"

She took the locket as he handed it back. "You may wish you hadn't asked, sir."

"But I have asked, Miss Maitland."

"Jonathan was an officer on USS *Chesapeake*, and he was killed in the action against HMS *Shannon*."

He held her eyes for a long moment. "It would seem you have little reason to like the British, Miss Maitland."

"As little reason as you would seem to have to like the Americans, sir."

"The conflict between the *Chesapeake* and the *Shannon* was honorable. The same cannot be said where my wife is concerned." He paused, as if unsure of whether to continue or not.

Lauren saw his indecision. "Lord Glenvane, if you wish to tell me about it, then as I have already said, I am more than willing to listen."

"I thought earlier that maybe you were only being polite."

"I meant what I said. Please tell me about your wife."

"Very well. I met Fleur in New York, and fell hopelessly in love with her. At first she spurned my attentions, but then was suddenly all eagerness, which should have warned me. We married, and she accompanied me back here. I didn't realize it at the time, but she married me in order to support the worthless layabout she really loved, and she knew that he was following us here to Glenvane. She continued to see him, using the generous allowance I gave her to lavish attention upon him. But he became greedy, and she was rash. They stole my mother's jewels and fled to Glasgow, meaning to take passage back to New York, but I discovered the theft and followed them. I wasn't concerned about keeping Fleur, for her conduct had extinguished my love, but I was most definitely determined to get the jewels back. When I confronted them both, he soon proved to be a craven coward. Fearing a duel with me, he compelled her to return the jewels, and this she did. She brought them to my hotel, which was opposite their inn, but from the window she saw him leaving. He was going to desert her because she was no longer the fount of plenty as far as he was concerned. She hurried out of the hotel to try to halt him, but she ran front of a carriage and was trampled by the team."

Lauren stared at him.

He thought he'd offended her with such a tale. "Forgive me, I really shouldn't have—"

"There is nothing to forgive, Lord Glenvane. In my opinion, your wife behaved abominably, and I find it little wonder that your attitude toward things American has become somewhat jaundiced, but I trust that you will not continue to take her as the yardstick for all her countrywomen. I promise we aren't all like her," she said quietly.

He smiled. "Miss Maitland, you have more than redeemed your nation as far as I'm concerned, and I trust that you will soon be able to say the same of me." His glance moved fleetingly toward the locket.

"I do not think I will find it all that difficult, sir, because since I've been here in Britain I've been obliged to change my views."

"We aren't all black after all?"

"It would appear not." She smiled, and closed the locket before putting it and its chain back in her reticule. Then she attended to the business of pouring him some lemonade.

He accepted the glass. "Actually, your locket is very like one of my mother's."

"Oh?" Isabel had referred to another locket.

"They might be one and the same item, except that the engraving on yours is far more intricate."

He finished the lemonade and then took the oars again, but as the boat began to slide over the water once more, Lauren became conscious of a resentful gaze upon her. It was such a strong sensation that she glanced around to see who was looking. Almost immediately she saw Isabel and Jamie in their boat about fifty yards away. Jamie's attention was on the shore, where a carriage was crossing the bridge over the River Vane on its way to the castle, but Isabel was intent upon Rory and the long conversation he'd been having with his boating companion. Her expression was one of undiluted jealousy, and her lips were pressed together in a thin line.

Like Jamie, Rory was looking at the carriage. "Ah, it would seem that Fitz's mysterious wife has arrived at last. At least, I presume it's her, for the carriage looks like one of Fitz's."

Lauren watched the vehicle bowl toward the castle. It was the one from the Crown & Thistle. Her suspicions were right. Her glance moved to Jamie, who did not take his eyes off the carriage until it vanished into the castle courtyard. It was clear he longed to row back to the jetty immediately, but that would have been too obvious a thing to do, and so he was forced to dally out on the loch, knowing that when he did go ashore she would not come to him, but to the husband she was deceiving.

It was another hour before the boating party began to end, and the boats made their separate ways back to the jetty where Emma, Lady Fitzsimmons had come to wait. She was wearing a geranium gown and matching pelisse, and her honey-colored hair was hidden beneath an ivory jockey bonnet from the back of which a long geranium gauze scarf trailed to her hem. She looked dainty and defenseless, and not at all capable of a passionate illicit liaison with Rory's brother. But Lauren was soon to find out that appearances were most definitely deceptive where Fitz's wife was concerned, for defenseless the lady certainly was not.

Rory and Lauren were still on their way to the shore when both Jamie and Fitz made their boats fast and assisted their respective ladies on to the jetty. Lauren couldn't help watching closely as the two men in Emma Fitzsimmons's life approached her. Hester and Alex were among those returning to the jetty, and as Emma saw them, she looked to Jamie for reassurance that they were definitely unaware of anything that had taken place at the inn. His slight nod was all she needed, and a wide smile broke upon her face as she flung herself into Fitz's arms and kissed him on the lips. Jamie looked away.

Lauren drew a long disapproving breath. Hester and Alex's first impression in Bond Street had been right when they'd instinctively felt Emma Fitzsimmons wasn't to be trusted. But had Alex's feeling that he'd seen her before been founded on fact? Lauren looked at him and saw that he was studying Emma, evidently wondering the same thing.

The reunions continued on the jetty. Hester and Alex greeted the new arrival, and so did many others, including Isabel, with whom Emma was apparently very thick, or so it seemed from the effusive greeting.

"Bella! Oh, Bella, it's so good to see you again. You'll never know how much I've missed our little *têtes-à-têtes*!"

Emma then saw Rory assisting Lauren out of the boat, and again she turned swiftly to Jamie. Again he reassured her, and she put Lauren from her thoughts as she continued to speak to Isabel. But it was nevertheless of Lauren that she evidently spoke, for Isabel turned to glance at the boat and then nodded at Emma. The two women drew closer together, and Lauren felt uneasy about those two bent heads. They were unpleasantly conspiratorial and their manner didn't bode well for her.

She gave Rory a rather uneasy smile. "It would seem

that Lady Maxby and Lady Fitzsimmons are old friends," she said.

"Yes, they've been acquainted for several years, or so I've recently discovered," he replied. "Until my return here I had no idea they'd even met. Isabel has family in Dublin, and she met Emma when visiting them. They hit it off, as you can see."

"Yes. Can Lady Maxby shed any light upon Alex's conviction that he's seen Lady Fitzsimmons somewhere before?" Lauren asked, watching Emma walk arm in arm with Isabel, leaving a rather put-out Fitz to once again offer his services to Mary, who accepted gladly.

"None at all."

They began to move with everyone else toward the castle, but just before going inside, Rory hesitated for a moment and Lauren was obliged to linger as well. He faced her. "I fear my duties as host will claim my full attention for the moment, Miss Maitland, but I trust we will have opportunity to speak again properly after dinner this evening."

She gave him a hesitant smile. "Lord Glenvane, there really isn't any need to feel obliged to—"

"I'm not speaking out of a sense of obligation, Miss Maitland, but rather because I have enjoyed speaking to you today, and wish to do so again." He smiled.

It was if they were alone in the world. Everything else faded into infinity as Lauren was lost beyond all redemption. She could no longer protect her heart from this storming of its defenses. She was deeply and irrevocably in love with the Earl of Glenvane.

7

THERE was still another half an hour to go before it was time to go down to the hall, where everyone was to gather before dinner, but Lauren had been ready for some time and had become a little impatient. She stood by the window in a fuchsia taffeta gown, watching the evening sunlight dancing upon the loch and wishing she hadn't abandoned herself so completely to the intense attraction she felt toward Rory. But his parting words and warm glances that afternoon had left her trembling with anticipation about what the evening might bring.

She toyed with her little fan, hoping that she'd chosen the right gown to wear. Fuchsia suited her very well, for it seemed to bring out the silvery lights in her hair, and she knew that her diamond earrings were perfect with it. Peggy had pinned her long tresses up into an elaborate Grecian knot that was finished with a glittering diamond-studded comb. A white silk and lace shawl was draped lightly over her white-gloved arms, and there were fuchsia satin slippers on her feet. She was restless and the minutes seeming to be dragging by. Suddenly she could bear it no more, and decided to go down early. If there were no one else there, she could pass the time by examining the hall itself, for there was much to see.

But before she reached the door it opened, and Isabel came in unannounced. She wore a purple lace gown over a matching satin slip, and she brought with her the fragrance of violets. Her blue eyes shone as she closed the door behind her and leaned back against it.

"It is time to lay our cards upon the table, Miss Maitland," she said.

Lauren faced her. "Isn't it customary to knock before entering?" she enquired coldly.

"I don't require your permission for anything, my dear," Isabel murmured, straightening and coming a little closer. "I believe you may be laboring under a misapprehension where Lord Glenvane is concerned, and I wish to spare you any consequent humiliation. He's mine, and will remain so, no matter how much you may wish to the contrary."

"I don't have to listen to you, Lady Maxby, and I would prefer it if you left immediately!" Lauren replied sharply.

"I'm telling you this for your own good, Miss Maitland. You mean nothing to Rory, and you would do well to remember that. He was mine before you came on the scene, and he will still be mine long after you've gone. If you have any thought of maybe becoming the next Lady Glenvane, let me advise you that nothing could be less likely."

"Please leave."

"As you wish, but don't complain that you weren't warned. I fight for what is mine, my dear, and you will be severely bruised if you presume to encroach upon this particular preserve. Stay away from Rory, or you will rue it." Turning on her heel, Isabel opened the door and left. The door remained open behind her, so that the sound of her departing footsteps could be heard dying away into silence.

For a long moment Lauren remained where she was. Her pulse had begun to race from the moment of Isabel's arrival. Cards on the table? Oh, yes, they certainly were, but if Rory was so completely Isabel's property, why then did there appear to be friction between them? And why had he made such a point of declining her company for the boating party? It might have been, as Lauren had wondered, because he wished to make his mistress jealous. But on the other hand it could have been because Isabel's hold upon him wasn't as strong as she'd like. Whatever it was, no doubt more would become clear in the hours ahead.

Lauren looked cautiously out into the passage, fearing that Isabel might yet return, but there was no sign of anyone and so she left the room to go down to the hall. The castle was very quiet as she made her way in the direction of the grand staircase. She passed the music room and went along the picture gallery, but just as the gallery and staircase came into view ahead, she heard the voices of Rory and Jamie emanating from an open doorway on her left. She would have walked on, but then she heard her name mentioned, and instinctively she paused. The following few minutes were to prove unpleasantly enlightening.

It was Jamie who said her name. "I'm reliably informed that your Miss Maitland is a fortune—the Ashworth fortune, to be precise."

"You are informed correctly, but she isn't *my* Miss Maitland," Rory replied.

"Are you sure about that?"

"Quite sure. Why do you ask?"

"Because your attentions to her today were rather marked."

"I was merely being a good host."

"Indeed? Well, I'm afraid I thought you were smitten. In fact I've begun to wonder if Glenvane is about to acquire a second chatelaine from the other side of the Atlantic."

There was a long silence before Rory replied. "That is not so."

"She isn't of interest to you?"

"No."

The single word cut into Lauren, and she leaned back against the wall next to the door with her eyes closed.

What a fool she'd been to entertain any hope that he might return her feelings!

Jamie continued. "Then you will not object if I pursue her?"

Lauren's eyes flew open again.

"Pursue her?" Rory repeated.

"Well, pursue her fortune, actually, but since it and the lady are inextricably combined . . ." Jamie's voice ended on an almost visible shrug.

Rory drew a long breath. "I take it this is your response to my refusal to bail you out again?"

"The duns are at my door, Rory, and if you won't come across with the necessary funds, then I have to think of something else."

"I've supported you far too much in the past, Jamie, but still you've indulged your misguided passion for the green baize. How long is it going to be before you realize that the odds are seldom in your favor?"

"Those who don't gamble don't understand," Jamie replied.

"And those who do gamble are amazingly dense," Rory responded sharply. "Do you think yourself clever for plunging in over your fool head? If the duns are clamoring for your blood, you only have yourself to blame."

Jamie sighed. "That point has already been established. Oh, damn it all, Rory, all I'm asking is that you help me just this once more."

"That sounds all too familiar, Jamie, and I warned you last time that I wouldn't come across again. I meant it."

"Then I must needs find myself a wealthy wife."

"And you think the unfortunate Miss Maitland fits the bill?"

"She's most conveniently to hand. Look, Rory, of what consequence is it to you if I pursue her or not? You've already insisted that she isn't of interest to you, so I cannot see—"

"Then pursue her if you must," Rory interrupted, with an edge in his voice.

Lauren blinked back tears. How wrong she'd been where he was concerned! Far from regarding her with warmth, he appeared to hold her in virtual contempt. She should have trusted her head, not her heart. Isabel had warned her she would be humiliated; that humiliation had come with painful speed.

Jamie was speaking again. "You have no reservations at all?"

"Should I have?"

"I don't know. Look, Rory, you may not have intended to appear as interested in her as you did earlier today, but I wasn't the only one to misinterpret. Isabel wasn't exactly amused, as I think you already know."

Rory gave a slight laugh. "Isabel has, as usual, made her feelings forcibly known."

"Have you managed to reassure her?"

"Only one thing would really reassure Isabel, Jamie, and that is marriage, but I'm afraid it's as the old saying goes—I'm once bitten, twice shy. My experience with Fleur was sufficient for several lifetimes, and Isabel has always known exactly how I feel."

"Has she?"

"Yes, Jamie, she has. I've never deceived her on that score."

"So she remains the mistress, never to be the blushing bride?"

"At least she and I have been free to do as we please, which is more than can be said of you and *your* ladylove," Rory replied quietly.

Jamie was startled. "I beg your pardon?"

"Oh, come now, little brother, don't play the innocent with me. I know you are conducting a liaison with someone else's wife. I don't know who she is, nor do I wish to. I only know that it is so."

"How did you find out?"

"It didn't take a genius to recognize the signs."

"And you don't approve."

"Did you honestly imagine I would?" Rory's tone was acid. "Jamie, I have been obliged to play the part of the deceived husband, and I promise you it's a humiliating and painful experience, so you may be certain that I disapprove entirely of your liaison."

"Do you expect me to abandon it?"

"I would *like* you to, but I doubt if my wishes would make any difference in this instance."

"I love her," Jamie said simply.

"And she promised to love, honor, and obey her husband," Rory replied sharply.

"But I am free to marry, if I choose," Jamie pointed out, neatly returning the conversation to the matter of acquiring a wife with a fortune. "Look, Rory, I'm set upon pursuing Miss Maitland, but I've barely spoken two words to her since she arrived. You, on the other hand, appear to have a considerable rapport with her, and with your help I could—"

"I'm not a damned procurer!"

"No, you're my brother, and since you've declined to assist with the contents of your fat purse, the least you can do is assist me in the acquisition of Miss Maitland and her fortune."

"You seem to take it for granted that the lady is there for the winning."

"I have faith in my talents in the love stakes."

"Oh, vanity, thy name is James Ardmore," Rory murmured dryly.

"Will you help me?" Jamie asked again, a little impatiently this time. "You could start tonight, by seeing to it that I am the one who escorts her in to dinner, and maybe you can arrange it so that she and I sit next to each other at the table?"

"I'm not about to scurry around at the eleventh hour changing name cards. As to escorting her in to dinner— yes, I'll see to it if I can."

Jamie's satisfaction was qualified. "I trust you'll be all that's convincing?"

"I have as much faith in my thespian talents as you do in your amorous abilities. I promise you that the lady will not suspect anything untoward."

"Let's seal it with a dram of the mountain dew." Jamie crossed the room and there was the chink of a decanter against glasses. Then he returned to Rory. "Shall we drink to the Ashworth fortune?"

"As you wish."

"Very well. The Ashworth fortune."

"The Ashworth fortune."

The glasses chinked together, and with that Lauren gathered her skirts to hurry on toward the staircase. There she halted, so overcome with mortification that she had to try to recover her poise before going down to the hall, where some of her fellow guests had already begun to gather. She placed her shaking hands upon the gallery balustrade as she struggled to recover from the shock of what she'd overheard. Oh, how exultant Isabel would be if she knew! How smug and triumphant.

Wretchedness washed over Lauren and tears shone in her eyes, but then the wretchedness began to give way to seething rage. How dared Rory and his brother discuss her like that! How *dared* they presume to think they could lightly marry her off to settle gambling debts! The light of battle replaced the shimmer of tears in her eyes and she tossed a mutinous glance back along the gallery toward the open doorway.

So they intended to secure her, did they? And Rory was so confident in his thespian skills, and her gullibility, that he imagined his odious spendthrift brother would soon be her husband! Well, she would see about that! Lord Glenvane was about to find that the Ashworth fortune wasn't so easily brought into line—indeed, he was going to find it uncommonly difficult. She intended to thwart him at every turn and be ready for each move he made, commencing with the business of going in to dinner. Go with Jamie? She'd die first! As for cold-hearted Rory himself—well, she would make him wish he'd never been born. The lord of Glenvane Castle had bitten off more than he could chew in Miss Lauren Maitland, and if the War of Independence had to be fought over all over again, then so be it. The outcome was going to be the same as before as well, with victory going to America!

She took a deep breath. She must be cool, calm, and collected, for they mustn't guess that she'd discovered what was planned for her. She looked down into the great hall. From where she stood she could see into the adjoining dining chamber. Several footmen were putting the finishing touches to the magnificently decorated table. Silver cutlery shone, epergnes gleamed, and crystal glasses sparkled. There were crisp white napkins, little bowls of heather and white roses, and sumptuous porcelain, all laid out to perfection before the array of gilded red-velvet chairs. But her eyes went right to the little cards which denoted the guests' places. It had occurred to Jamie to alter those cards, but Rory had declined to take such action at what he called the eleventh hour. Well, *she* didn't think it was too late; indeed, she thought it was a capital and very timely notion! What would happen if he suddenly found "the Ashworth fortune", so sought after by his despicable sibling, seated at his own elbow throughout the meal? It might be amusing to find out! It might also be amusing to perplex dear Isabel by making her wonder if Rory was still intent upon showing favor to the American interloper. Yes, indeed. And serve them all right!

Gathering her skirts again, she began to descend the staircase. At the bottom she paused, but no one appeared to have particularly noticed her, not even Hester and Alex, who were on a sofa near the main entrance. She made her way carefully around the edge of the floor to the entrance of the dining chamber.

It was very like the great hall, with the same half-paneled walls and hammerbeam roof, but the upper walls were hung with tartan-patterned silk in the Ardmore colors, and were also adorned with several magnificent tapestries denoting Jacobite scenes involving Bonnie Prince Charlie. Evening sunlight streamed in through arched French windows facing over the terrace and gardens. It was all very lovely, but Lauren's mind was upon other things as she went in and began to walk down the table, inspecting all the cards as she did so.

She wasn't the only guest intent upon rearranging certain seating arrangements, for two other ladies were going surreptitiously about the same thing. The footmen paid them no heed, either because they weren't aware of what was going on, or because they chose not to see. Lauren took great care not to appear particularly secretive, and as luck would have it she'd chosen the side of the table where her own placecard lay about halfway along. Under the pretext of leaning across to examine a particularly pretty bowl of heather and rosebuds, she contrived to scoop the card into the palm of her hand, and then walked on.

Rory's place at the head of the table was flanked on either side by Isabel and his sister, and Jamie was to sit on Mary's other side. Lauren had no compunction whatsoever about exchanging her own card for Isabel's, and a smile played grimly upon her lips as she then retraced her steps down the table to her own place, where she carefully left Isabel's card, again without any of the footmen appearing to notice. Taking a deep, rather satisfied breath, she moved back to the entrance, where she surveyed the entrance hall again.

More and more guests were coming down now, and she was able to join them without anyone remarking. Hester and Alex were seated across the hall, close to the outer door, and so she made her way toward them. As she did so she passed Emma.

Isabel was with her, and she flicked her purple skirts disdainfully aside as Lauren passed, but Lauren merely smiled. Rory's mistress wasn't going to enjoy dinner tonight—indeed, Lauren hoped Isabel would be given indigestion when she found herself ignominiously demoted to the middle of the table!

Lauren walked on, threading her way around several other small groups until she reached Hester and Alex, who had now been joined by Mary and Fitz. They all greeted her warmly, and she thought how particularly pretty Hester was in silver muslin and pearls. Rory's sister wore aquamarine and opals, and by the shine in her dark eyes it was clear she hadn't expected to have Fitz's company now that Emma had arrived.

Lauren sat next to Hester and whispered so that no one else could hear. "Has Alex recalled yet where he saw Lady Fitzsimmons?" she asked.

"Not really, except that he feels it was three or four years ago, when he was either in Bath or Brighton. It was before I knew him, so I really have no idea. It's a mystery, is it not?"

"It is indeed."

Most of the guests had now gathered in the hall, and a babble of conversation echoed around the ancient rafters. Outside it was still a warm summer evening and sunlight filtered brilliantly in through the high windows. Jewels flashed, fans fluttered, and now and then there were bursts of laughter amid the general conversation. It was a very agreeable atmosphere and Lauren wished she could enjoy it properly, but that was out of the question now that she'd overheard so many unwelcome home truths about Rory. She wished she'd never come to Glenvane Castle or set eyes upon its handsome master.

There was a stir as Rory and Jamie appeared at the head of the staircase. Lauren surveyed them both, her green eyes bright with a warlike glint. Let battle commence!

8

LAUREN studied Rory and Jamie as they descended to join the guests. They both wore the close-fitting black silk evening coats and white trousers that were *de riqueur* for such occasions, but Jamie affected to be very much the tippy where fashion was concerned. His trousers were of the style known as cossacks, very full at the waist and gathered at the ankles, and his starched neckcloth was very voluminous indeed. On many a gentleman such modes might have appeared ridiculous, but the Honorable James Ardmore had the flair to carry them off.

Rory chose to be much more conventional than his younger brother. But being conventional did not make him dull—on the contrary, he showed a great deal more taste and sophistication. His corded silk coat needed no more than the excellence of its material and tailoring to make it perfect, his trousers were superbly cut, and his unstarched neckcloth was tied in a simple but effective knot which was the ideal setting for a solitaire diamond pin. He was coolly immaculate, but there was always a suggestion of fire just beneath the surface—ice with a flame within, the cool aristocrat versus the passionate buccaneer.

Lauren had to look away, angry with herself for still finding him so fascinating and irresistibly attractive. What was wrong with her? She now knew him to be totally uninterested in her, even to the point of aiding and abetting his dissolute brother in his aim to win her, and yet her senses were in turmoil just because he was near. This wouldn't do! Fiercely she reminded herself that to Rory Ardmore she was 'the Ashworth fortune', readily available to refill his brother's threadbare pockets. She felt her sense of outrage sweeping back, but at the same time she had the satisfaction of knowing she was one step ahead of their little plan. She was going to amuse herself at their expense!

The two men reached the foot of the staircase, where they paused to speak briefly to the first group of guests they encountered. Then they moved on to the next. Lauren knew that they would make their way toward her party; they had to if Rory was to see to it that Jamie escorted her in to dine. No doubt they were both confident that things would go as planned, but a rude awakening lay in store.

As expected, they did indeed wend their way over, and Rory greeted her as if nothing had changed since the afternoon. If it hadn't been for her providential eavesdropping, she would not have known he was anything but sincere. He had mentioned his thespian skills, and was indeed so convincing an actor that even Isabel, who had also joined the party with Emma, was also taken in. Isabel was far from pleased; after a while she could bear it no more and had to draw attention to herself. She gave Rory a brilliant smile.

"Rory, have you noticed Miss Maitland's lovely locket? I vow it is the very image of the one in your mother's jewel box."

"Yes, I've seen it. I agree, it's very similar."

"Such a pretty thing. It seems that Boston has a master jeweler to rival anything London has to offer. Miss Maitland, I really must compliment you upon your gown. It's such an exquisite color, and I'm all envy because you can wear it and I cannot. I've always yearned to wear that particular shade of pink, but when I've tried I fear it makes me look fit for interment."

"I'm flattered by your admiration, Lady Maxby," Lauren replied, her tone polite but her eyes cool. Did the woman really expect her to be all smiles after what had been said earlier?

"I trust you and I will soon become better acquainted, Miss Maitland, for I'm sure we have much in common."

I doubt that very much, thought Lauren. Then, from the corner of her eye, she saw a secretive smirk on Emma's face as she and Isabel exchanged knowing glances. So they thought they could toy with her, did they? Well, dear Isabel's feathers would be ruffled when she discovered the new seating arrangements at dinner, but Emma's could be satisfactorily ruffled before then!

She gave the latter an innocuous smile. "Lady Fitzsimmons, there is something I've been meaning to ask you," she said lightly.

"Ask me?"

"Yes. Tell me, haven't we met before somewhere?"

Hester and Alex looked swiftly at Lauren, but she wasn't intent upon Brighton or Bath a few years ago, but upon something that had happened much more recently. At the Crown & Thistle, to be precise.

This was the conclusion to which Emma immediately leapt, and her face became a little pale. "Met before?" No, I'm sure we haven't," she said, with swift recourse to her fan. Her almond-shaped eyes were wide as they swung anxiously toward Jamie.

Lauren savored being the cat to the other's mouse. "No? But I feel absolutely certain that—"

Emma interrupted her. "Miss Maitland, I can't imagine where we could possibly have met. I don't believe you were with Hester and Alex when I first met them in Bond Street a short while ago, were you?"

"No, I wasn't." Lauren smiled again. "Maybe I'm mistaken, or maybe I'll suddenly remember," she added wickedly.

Remember? That was the last thing Emma wanted! She said nothing more, and avoided any further discomfort by removing herself from the party altogether. Fitz glanced after her, but Lauren noted that he made no move at all to follow. On the contrary, he moved a little closer to Mary, who gave him a shy smile.

The dinner gong reverberated through the hall, and Lauren immediately forced her thoughts back to the matter in hand—that of confounding Rory and Jamie in their plan. She had a notion of her own, and the moment Rory turned toward her to suggest that Jamie escort her in to dine, she smiled and linked the elder brother's arm, as if innocently anticipating his own invitation! She did it so neatly that she was as convincing as he himself had been.

"I'm honored, Lord Glenvane," she murmured, turning her shoulder just sufficiently to exclude Jamie, who was ready and waiting at her other elbow.

Rory returned her smile without wavering, nor did he display any irritation he may have felt at this unexpected obstacle to his simple intention, but as they moved toward the dining hall and the other guests began to form a column behind them, she detected the brief glance he cast over his shoulder at his brother. Jamie had once again been obliged to accompany Isabel, whose bemused face was a picture to behold as she found herself supplanted yet again by the loathed visitor from across the Atlantic.

Lauren was delighted to have so neatly countered the opening skirmish in the war of the Ashworth fortune. The initial advantage was hers, she fancied, eagerly anticipating the next engagement.

The changed placecards caused discreet confusion— very discreet indeed, as far as Rory was concerned. If he was surprised to find Lauren next to him, he gave no outward sign, or none that any but the initiated would have noticed. His smile and grace of manner did not alter at all as he waited for the attendant footman to draw her chair out for her, but his eyes bore a rather quizzical expression.

Jamie was also puzzled as he took his place next to his

sister. His quandary was plain as he wondered how on earth he was going to commence his grand wooing across such a large table. Lauren felt no compassion for his difficulty. He had gotten himself into his financial scrape and he could get himself out again. Besides, she thoroughly disapproved of his liaison with Emma. He was willingly putting horns on poor Fitz, and Emma wasn't the hard-done-by wife who sought solace in the arms of a lover! No, Jamie and Emma were both despicably selfish, and Lauren had no time for either of them.

As Lauren took her seat, she stole a glance down the table at Isabel, who was speechless with disbelief on finding herself banished so far from Rory. Her cheeks were suffused with color, and became even more so when she perceived who now occupied her original place next to Rory. Isabel's bluebell eyes were positively poisonous as they rested momentarily upon her rival, for her humiliation was beginning to cause discreet comment around the table. Not only that, she also had to suffer the prospect of dinner with a fat viscount she disliked on her one side and an elderly clergyman who'd known her late husband on the other.

Lauren was satisfied that justice had been done, although she wished Hester wouldn't keep drawing the wrong conclusion. This latest business had merely served to convince Hester still further that Rory had formed a burning attachment for her American cousin. If only it were so, but the unpalatable truth was very different.

The dinner was excellent, and very traditionally Scottish. It commenced with the famous cock-a-leekie, a delicious chicken broth containing vegetables and prunes, and was followed by lavish fish courses of salmon, trout, and plump mackerel. The main courses consisted of buck venison, roast beef, and various gamebirds, all served with every vegetable and accompaniment imaginable, and for dessert there were jellies, fruit creams, and a veritable feast of pineapples from the estate's glasshouses.

Rory was attentive throughout, and in spite of everything, Lauren couldn't help finding the experience very enjoyable. He had many anecdotes to tell about the castle and its colorful history. She learned that it had briefly sheltered Mary, Queen of Scots, and her lover, the Earl of Bothwell, and that Bonnie Prince Charlie had hidden there as well. She also learned that there was a ghost—a gray lady who glided down the staircase at dawn and then went out into the gardens to the loch, where she walked into the water before vanishing. It seemed she was one of Rory's ancestors, an unfortunate Lady Margaret, who had anticipated her marriage vows and then lost her love when he'd drowned in the loch. Unable to contemplate life alone, she'd gone to join him in the same watery grave.

It was at the end of the meal, just before the ladies adjourned to the solar, that Rory's steward came apologetically to the table to speak quietly in his master's ear. From where she sat, Lauren heard what he said.

"Begging your pardon, my lord, but I think you should know that old Rab's wife has managed to get down here to tell you that he's changed his mind about leaving the croft after all. Now he says he won't go even if it falls down about his ears."

Rory sat back with a sigh." "Damn the old fool," he muttered.

"I suppose it was to be expected, my lord."

"Yes, for there never was a more stubborn old goat. Why can't he admit that he's too old to spend another winter out on the mountain? He and Aggie have earned a new home and a comfortable retirement, but he insists upon leading the life he's always led. It wouldn't matter if he were young and hale, but he isn't, and neither is poor Aggie."

"As you say, sir, he's a stubborn old goat."

"One who is about to discover that I am a stubborn young one."

The steward smiled. "What shall I tell her, my lord?"

Rory was silent for a moment. "Tell her I'll go there tomorrow and try again. I'll do all I can to see they're safely rehoused before winter. I'll ride out there first thing in the morning, and I mean first thing. Would you tell McGregor to have my horse ready at six?"

"Yes, my lord. Will you wish me to accompany you?" This was said with, as Lauren thought, a rather odd reluctance.

Rory gave him a rather wry smile. "No, Tam. Rab's mulishness will be sufficient on its own. You know what he's like about 1692 and all that."

"My lord." The steward bowed and withdrew again.

Lauren gazed thoughtfully at the table, for this was a side of Rory Ardmore that she could only admire. He was the concerned master, intent upon the welfare of those on his estate. She wished she couldn't find anything to commend him, for that would have made everything easier as far as she was concerned, but fate was determined to make difficulties. Her heart steadfastly refused to loathe him, and now there was something to admire as well!

Several minutes later it was time for the ladies to leave the gentlemen to their after-dinner port, except that in Scotland, due to historic connections with France, the men preferred claret. As Lauren went out with the ladies, she knew that she would be the target of attention from Isabel, and she simply wasn't in the mood. She wanted to be on her own, to have time to think clearly, and so she pleaded a headache and withdrew gracefully to her room. There she sat on the windowseat, watching the crimson spangles of the fading sunset flashing upon the surface of the loch.

She was still there when darkness descended over Glenvane, and Peggy had quite a shock when she came to light the room and turn the bed back.

"You startled me, Miss Lauren! I didn't realize you were here."

"I didn't feel like being closeted with a gaggle of women."

"Is there anything I can get you, miss?"

"No. Thank you."

At that moment there was a knock at the door, and Peggy went to answer it. It was Jamie.

"Lord Glenvane has sent me to enquire if Miss Maitland is well," he said.

Lauren's fury was suddenly rekindled, for it was quite patently another move in the Ardmore brothers' conspiracy to ensnare her.

Peggy turned inquiringly and saw her mistress shaking her head urgently. The maid had been in Lauren's service long enough to know what was expected, and she turned to Jamie again. "Miss Maitland is feeling a little indisposed, and has retired, sir."

"Would you please inform her that we trust she will soon be well again?"

"I will, sir."

Jamie walked away again, and Peggy closed the door.

Lauren immediately rose from the window seat. "Peggy, I've decided to go riding first thing in the morning."

"Yes, Miss Lauren." The maid did not see anything unusual in this, for at home in Boston Lauren had often gone out for a ride before breakfast.

"Would you see to it that someone is told I require a suitable horse at about half-past five?"

"Half past *five?*" Peggy stared.

"That's what I said."

"Isn't that a little early?" the maid ventured.

"Maybe, but I wish to be able to enjoy a long ride. When were you told the breakfast bell would ring?"

"Ten, Miss Lauren, but I gather no one really bothers to go down until about eleven, and then everything goes on until well after midday."

"So you'll attend to the matter of a suitable horse for half-past five?"

"Yes, Miss Lauren."

"And now I think I'll go to bed."

Lauren's green eyes were bright with determination as Peggy helped her undress. Lord Glenvane was going to encounter the Ashworth fortune out riding, for she intended to hide within view of the castle and then follow him when he went on the promised call to old Rab and his wife. On the way back, she would just happen to meet him. That would be something else for him to explain to Jamie, and something else for dear Isabel to swallow as well!

9

THE following day, Mary's eighteenth birthday, dawned as warm and sunny as nearly all its predecessors that summer, and Lauren was up well in time to go for the ride. She wore the primrose riding habit and veiled black top hat she'd had on the day she met Rory in the Mall, and her hair was loosely gathered into a net at the nape of her neck, leaving soft curls to frame her face.

The clock struck half-past five exactly as she went down the grand staircase to the hall, where there was already a great deal of bustle as preparations began for the ball that evening. Many huge bowls of flowers were being brought in for the decorations, the table had been removed so that the floor would be clear for the dancing, and servants were bringing sofas from the rest of the castle to place around the edges of the hall. A fashionable Glasgow orchestra had been engaged, and a dais had been erected overnight at the far end of the hall.

The steward, Tam, was overseeing everything, and he turned in some surprise as he saw Lauren.

"Good morning, madam," he said politely, executing a graceful bow.

"Good morning," she replied.

"I will conduct you to the stables, madam," he said then, bowing once more and preceding her to the outer door.

The morning air was fresh and the gentle breeze carried the scent of heather from the surrounding moun-

tains. She could hear curlews calling, and the more rau-
cous noise of waterfowl on the loch as a maid went
down through the gardens to feed them with scraps from
the servants' breakfast. The stables, which were approached through a narrow iron-studded door set in the
courtyard wall opposite the garden arch, proved to be
surprisingly spacious, with accommodation for a considerable number of horses, to say nothing of coach houses
containing the family's vehicles as well as those belong-
ing to the guests.

A bay thoroughbred mare had been saddled for her,
and as the steward helped her mount, she saw a large
dun stallion being led out as well. She guessed that it
was for Rory. The steward handed her the mare's reins.
"Will you be wanting a guide, madam? The land hereabouts can be very wild if you don't know it."

"I'll be all right, thank you, for I'm quite used to riding on my own. I won't stray."

"As you wish, madam."

He watched from the main stable archway as she rode
out and then around the perimeter of the castle wall toward the narrow neck of land leading to the main shore.
There she paused for a moment to look back. In the
early-morning sunshine Glenvane looked more perfect
than ever. Could there be anywhere more beautiful and
timeless than this? She felt as if she'd known it all her
life, and yet she'd only been here for one day. If there
were such a thing as having lived on this earth before,
then perhaps she had once lived here. Maybe this had
been her home hundreds of years ago . . .

It was a fanciful thought, and she smiled as she turned
the mare's head and kicked her heel to ride over the
bridge spanning the River Vane, and then across the park
toward an oak wood which spread a cool leafy shade
over a nearby slope. From there she would be able to observe Rory leaving on his mission to persuade 'old Rab'
to leave his croft.

She reined in out of sight, and then leaned forward to

pat the mare's neck as she waited. The woods echoed with birdsong, as if every feathered creature in Scotland had gathered in this one place, and out on the glittering loch the reflections of the islands shivered as the breeze swept low over the water. An osprey was diving for pike, and two men were rowing a small boat toward the far shore, where Ben Vane soared high toward the heavens.

The minutes passed and there was no sign of Rory. The mare became a little restless, but Lauren lingered, determined to give the master of Glenvane another unsettling time of it when once again he found himself in the company of "the Ashworth fortune."

At last he appeared. Mounted on the dun stallion, he rode from the castle at an easy canter. His top hat was pulled well forward over his forehead, casting a shadow over his face, but she knew every feature as if the sunlight fell full upon it. A yearning passed through her. Since Jonathan there hadn't been anyone to arouse her heart as this man did; perhaps not even Jonathan had stirred the deep emotions she'd known since meeting the lord of Glenvane. She wondered what Rory would have said if he knew how she really felt—that far from being an easy target for the younger brother, she yearned for the kisses of the elder.

As she watched, he suddenly turned his mount directly toward her. Filled with instant dismay, she maneuvered the mare further back into the woods and took refuge behind a thick screen of holly bushes. She heard the drumming of his horse's hooves and peeped out as he passed about twenty yards away from her. He rode with almost casual ease, as if his nervous mount's obedience were totally matter of fact. Lauren reflected that she would not have dared to take such a mettlesome horse for granted, even though she considered herself an accomplished rider. But the Earl of Glenvane was a masterly horseman, authoritative and yet sympathetic, in tune with his mount's every move.

"Why can't I despise you, Rory Ardmore?" she murmured, gathering the reins to follow him as he rode on up through the sloping woods.

After about half an hour the trees began to thin and the springy ground became rockier, but still Rory rode at a steady canter. Suddenly he emerged from the woods and rode over a heather-drenched moor, beyond which the lower slopes of a mountain rose majestically toward the endless arc of the heavens. Up here the calls of the curlews were clear and almost mournful, and the fragrance of the heather was almost intoxicating. The undulating sea of purple-pink stretched all around as Rory rode on over a ridge and vanished from sight.

Lauren reined in just before the ridge to glance back. The loch and castle lay in the valley far below, almost like miniatures which were oddly close at hand. It was as if she could reach down and take hold of them. Such a view commanded full attention, but she had to follow Rory, or run the risk of losing track of him. Gathering the reins once more, she maneuvered her horse toward the lip of the ridge, so that she could just see over without being seen herself.

She expected to see Rory riding on over the moor on the other side, but instead she found herself looking down a long slope toward another oak wood, on the edge of which there was a rambling croft set in a hollow, as if in readiness for the worst of the winter gales which must sweep over this remote and exposed mountainside. A wisp of smoke curled from one of the stubby chimneys, and chickens pecked in the little yard before the door. There was a fold beside the croft, as well as several outbuildings, and a black-and-white border collie barked as Rory rode toward the yard.

An elderly woman emerged. She was stooped and frail, with a plain red shawl wrapped over her head and around her shoulders. She paused as she saw who was coming, and then she went back into the croft, reemerging again a moment later with a man at her side. He was elderly too, but more sturdily built, and he wore a rough brown jacket, a kilt, and tartan stockings.

She vaguely heard Rab and his wife greeting Rory, but the breeze snatched their voices away. When Rory dismounted, Aggie led his horse into one of the out-buildings, and Rab accompanied him into the croft. The woman then joined them, and the collie sprawled before the threshold as if on guard.

There was nothing for it now but to wait for Rory to leave again. Lauren glanced around, wondering where best to position herself as if she'd just happened to be riding that way, but as she did so some red grouse burst noisily from the heather nearby, startling the mare so much that it was all Lauren could do to keep her seat. The mare reared and plunged, and Lauren couldn't hold her below the ridge out of sight of the croft. The moment the collie heard the commotion and caught sight of the terrified horse, it set up a clamor which seemed to echo all around the mountains.

Lauren was close to tears as she strove to keep a grip on the horse, but just as she began to regain full control, the creature's left forefoot struck a rock, and there was an ominous metallic clink as the shoe was cast. At last she managed to bring the mare back to the bit, and was able to dismount to inspect the leg. The creature was sweating and trembling, its nostrils and eyes wide, and its neck quivered as Lauren straightened once more to pat it. A cast shoe wasn't the only problem, for it seemed to her that the leg was now lame as well.

At the croft, the collie's noise had brought Rory, Rab, and Aggie to the door. Rory shaded his eyes against the sunshine and stared up toward Lauren. Then he left the croft to run up the slope toward her, and she could only wait, suddenly feeling very inept indeed. Far from engineering an idle encounter, she'd gotten herself into a fix! Here she was, miles away from the castle, with a horse she could no longer ride.

He reached her in a moment or so, his dark hair tousled and windswept because he had left his top hat in the croft. "Miss Maitland? I thought it was you, for I recognized your riding habit."

Lauren managed a rather embarrassed smile as she raised her little net veil. "What an excellent memory you have, Lord Glenvane."

"Are you all right?"

"Yes. Thank you." She couldn't meet his eyes, for she felt more than a little foolish.

"What on earth are you doing here at this hour?"

"I decided to go for a ride before breakfast, to sweep away the remnants of my headache. Some grouse frightened my horse and she cast her shoe when she struck that rock. I'm afraid she's lame." Truth and half-truth slipped from her lips with shameful ease as she bent to retrieve the horseshoe from among the heather.

He took it from her and examined it before following her example and checking that the mare wasn't harmed. "You have an adventurous spirit, Miss Maitland—too adventurous, perhaps, for this is a very remote place, and it's very fortunate that I happened to be here as well."

"Very fortunate indeed, sir," she murmured, suddenly beginning to realize that this was turning very much to her advantage. Now he would have to take her back to the castle, and how else could he do it but by taking her upon his own horse! What a stir *that* would cause if it were observed. Jamie would begin to wonder if his brother was hindering rather than helping him, and as for Isabel . . .Lauren couldn't help a flutter of satisfaction as she contemplated the anxiety which might be aroused in Lady Maxby's spiteful heart.

Rory finished examining the mare's leg. "You're right. She's lame," he said, straightening and then tossing the horseshoe away down the mountainside. "Well, shoe or no shoe, she can't be ridden back to the castle. I hope you are prepared to entrust yourself to my care, Miss Maitland, for it seems you must either wait at the croft until I can send someone with another mount, which may take some time, or you can ride double with me when I return after my business here."

"If you are prepared to endure my company, sir, I would prefer to return with you," she replied.

"Endure your company? Miss Maitland, I will consider it a pleasure to assist you," he replied, coming closer and taking her hand to draw it gallantly to his lips.

She smiled into his eyes, but inside she was resentful. How free and magnanimous he was with his compliments! She could almost believe what he said, except that she knew he only said it with Jamie's empty coffers in mind. He looked at her and saw her inheritance; she looked at him and saw . . .What did she see? Lord help her, she saw the man she loved! She was playing with fire by remaining here in Scotland. No matter how fiercely she waged her counter-campaign, no matter how justified she was in teaching the Ardmore brothers a lesson, in the end she would be the one to pay the real price.

She didn't realize she'd been silent for some time, or that nuances of her secret thoughts had flitted briefly across her face, but when he spoke again she knew she'd been less than completely guarded.

"Are you all right, Miss Maitland? You seem a little . . ."

"I'm quite all right, Lord Glenvane," she replied quickly. "I was just thinking about what you said. This *is* a very remote place, and I was indeed a little unwise to come all this way on my own."

He smiled. "Well, you didn't come to any harm, and I'm here to see you safely home again," he said, gathering the reins and then offering her his arm to escort her down to the croft.

Home? Oh, how she wished she'd never left! Boston was a safe and reassuring haven compared with this. But she returned the smile, and slipped her gloved hand over his sleeve.

They walked through the heather, and she smiled as the collie came bounding toward them. The dog capered all around, its feathery tail wagging, but at a single whistle from Rab it bounded away again, coming swiftly to the crofter's heel as he waited in the yard.

Lauren was led into the croft, where it was very dark and cool because the windows were very small in the thick walls. There was no ceiling, only bare rafters and the thatch, and a ladder led up to a sort of landing floor where Rab and his wife had their bed. The rafters were hung with strings of drying vegetables and fruit, from onions and mushrooms to apples and, surprisingly, apricots. There was an open stone fireplace and a well-scrubbed table where fresh-baked bread was cooling on a wooden rack. A kettle sang on the fire, and there were two settles on either side of the hearth.

Aggie smiled and nodded her head as she ushered Lauren to one of the settles. "Please to be seated," she murmured.

Lauren obeyed, arranging her rather cumbersome riding habit skirt and glancing around at the flagged floor and uneven stone walls.

"Some milk and bannocks?" Aggie enquired.

Lauren looked uncertainly at her. "Bannocks?" she repeated.

Rory sat down opposite. "A bannock is an oatmeal cake, Miss Maitland, and I can vouch for Aggie's as being the finest hereabouts."

The woman blushed with pleasure at such praise, and then hastened through a doorway into what appeared to be a small pantry. She returned in a moment with an earthenware jar containing the bannocks. Lauren took one, and on taking a bite she smiled at Aggie. "Lord Glenvane is quite right, for this is quite delicious," she replied honestly.

The woman went away again and returned with a little dish of sweetened milk which had been whisked so that it frothed like a syllabub. It was unexpectedly refreshing and went perfectly with the bannock.

Sweetened milk was hardly suitable for Rory, and he

and Rab were taking a glass of whiskey. They took up their conversation from the point where it had been abandoned because of Lauren.

"Now listen, Rab, you really must see the sense of leaving this place before winter. There's nothing to be gained by keeping this going, and it's pointless to remain here when there's a far more suitable croft further down the glen. If you won't do it for yourself, then think of Aggie. She's no longer in the best of health, and if you survive this coming winter, I fear you might face the one after that on your own. She was only able to come to the castle yesterday because Hamish McNeil was coming with his packhorses and could take her up on one of them. What if something happened to either of you? What then, mm?"

Rab didn't want to be persuaded. He had a weather-beaten face, and his bead-bright eyes were stubborn. "But this is ma home, your lordship," he replied, as if that were the cure-all answer. Then he drained his glass and then immediately refilled it from the jar in the hearth.

"And that is all that matters?" Rory remarked, not deflected from his purpose by the offer of another generous dram.

"Aye, my lord, it is."

"But, Rab, you must come around on this."

"Why, my lord? What harm does it do if we stay here? Or is it maybe that ye don't want us on your conscience?"

"That's most unfair, Rab," Rory replied, holding his gaze.

The crofter raised his chin mulishly, and Lauren was suddenly reminded of an old man who had been in the employ of her uncle in Philadelphia. The man had lived in the same isolated house all his life, and when he'd become too old to manage on his own, he too had refused to leave. At least, he had until her uncle had thought of the perfect solution.

Lauren lowered her dish of milk. "May I suggest something?" she asked suddenly.

The two men looked at her in surprise. Rory nodded. "By all means, Miss Maitland."

She smiled at Rab. "Forgive me for perhaps poking my nose in where it's not wanted, but is there any reason why you and Aggie can't move to the other croft and then come up here whenever you wish to see it?"

Rory smiled. "A reasonable enough suggestion, Miss Maitland, and one which has already been aired on more than one occasion, but unfortunately the other croft is a good five miles away, and although Rab may think he's still sturdy enough to walk here and back, his old legs know different."

Rab scowled. "There's naything wrong wi' my legs!"

Lauren nodded. "Nothing a good horse would not solve," she said.

Rab looked blankly at her, and then sniffed. "I've nay the money for a horse."

"No, but Lord Glenvane has," she replied, looking at Rory. "More than that, he has stables full of them."

Rory met her gaze a little quizzically, and she could see that he was amused at her munificence where his property was concerned.

Rab sniffed again, and Lauren felt rather than saw how his wife had come to stand anxiously by the settle.

Rory glanced up at Aggie and then fixed Rab with a very direct look. "What objection would you raise if I agree to Miss Maitland's suggestion?"

"A horse?"

"Yes, but only on condition you and Aggie leave here before winter. As to your freedom to come here whenever you choose, that goes without saying."

"Ye'll not move another man in here?"

"Is *that* what you fear?"

"Partly," Rab confessed reluctantly.

"Rab, I want you out of here because it's no longer fit,

and if that applies where you're concerned, it applies equally to anyone else."

"Even a young man?"

"Even a young man."

Aggie put a hand on her husband's shoulder. "Please, Rab, for it's far better than most would ever dream to get."

He hesitated, but then at last gave a nod. "I agree, your lordship," he said, holding a hand out to Rory, who took it gladly.

"The matter's settled, then. You and Aggie go to the lower croft, and I will provide you with a suitable horse."

Lauren spoke up quickly. "Two suitable horses, Lord Glenvane, and the wherewithal to keep and feed them. After all, if one should cast a shoe . . ."

"Your point is taken, Miss Maitland. Very well, two horses, their feed, and keep."

Rab sat back and gave Lauren a broad grin. "Oh, but ye're a bonnie lassie, and no mistake," he declared.

Aggie nodded as well, and gave Lauren a warm smile. "A true lady," she said quietly.

Rab refilled Rory's glass, and then looked a little curiously at Lauren. "Ye're not a Sassenach, are ye?" he observed.

"A Sassenach?" What was that? It sounded like an Indian tribe!

Rory grinned. "He's asking if you're English, Miss Maitland."

"Oh." She smiled quickly at Rab. "No, sir, I'm not, I'm American."

His jaw dropped. "American, is it? Was that not what—" He broke off sharply as Aggie jolted his shoulder sharply with her elbow.

Rory smiled a little. "Yes, Rab, just as my wife was," he said, draining his glass and then getting up. "I think we should be on our way, Miss Maitland, for I have much to do before tonight's ball." There was a subtle but tangible change in him, a withdrawal, and she could not help but be very conscious of it.

"Yes, of course," she replied, and hastily finished the bannock and milk before getting up as well. She accepted the arm he offered, and they went out of the darkness of the croft into the brilliance of the mountain sunshine.

10

RAB hastened to bring Rory's horse from the outbuilding, and before assisting Lauren up onto the saddle, Rory spoke to him again. "Remember now, you old scoundrel. I have your word upon this agreement, and Miss Maitland is my witness."

"My word is my bond, your lordship," Rab replied, stiffening as if a slur had been cast upon his honor.

"See that it is. I'll send someone up to attend to Miss Maitland's horse, and to make all the necessary arrangements regarding your move."

"Just don't let it be yon steward."

"I would hardly inflict him upon you, or you upon him for that matter," Rory replied.

"Thank ye, your lordship."

Rory turned to put his hands to Lauren's waist and lift her up sideways on to the horse, and then he mounted behind, with one arm firm around her for the ride back to the castle.

The horse was fresh and eager as it set off toward the ridge, where Rory reined in to wave to Rab and his wife. It wasn't the wave of a master to his servants, but of a friend, as Lauren could not help but observe.

He smiled at the comment. "Well, perhaps that's because they *are* my friends. I've been coming up here since I was a boy." Then he glanced down a little roguishly at her. "I'm relieved I only have the one stubborn tenant to call upon today, Miss Maitland, for I fear you might succeed in emptying my entire stables."

She colored a little. "Are you offended by my interference, Lord Glenvane?"

"Offended? No. A brace of horses is a small price to pay for the satisfaction of knowing Rab and Aggie will be comfortable this winter."

She looked back toward the croft. "I know it's none of my business, Lord Glenvane, but why doesn't Rab like your steward?"

He smiled. "Because Rab is a Macdonald."

"I still don't understand."

"Nearly a hundred and thirty years ago there was a massacre of the Macdonalds at a place in Argyllshire called Glencoe. The massacre was carried out at the instigation of King William III, and the people who obeyed his orders were the Campbells of Glen Lyon. My steward is a Campbell, and bitter old memories run very deep up here."

So that was it. Now she understood the odd reference to the year 1692 at the dinner table the previous evening. She smiled at him. "And where were the Ardmores of Glenvane when this happened?"

He laughed. "Minding their own business, for once. Oh, we have bloody fingers as well, Miss Maitland, but as far as Glencoe is concerned, we were as pure as the driven snow, which is why both the Macdonalds and the Campbells are happy to ally themselves with us, if not with each other. It's a difficult situation, however, and sometimes it requires the wisdom of Solomon."

She searched his face. "You are a good master, Lord Glenvane, and those on your estate are much more fortunate than most."

"I bask in your praise, Miss Maitland," he murmured, kicking his heel and moving the horse on over the ridge.

Now the vista of Glenvane was once again spread before Lauren, and she feasted her eyes upon the scene, for it was something she wished to keep in her memory forever. When she was home in Boston and Rory Ardmore was part of her past, she would recall this moment, when his arm was around her waist as she gazed upon his domain.

It seemed that he was no less affected by the view. "I never tire of this place," he said, maneuvering his horse down the heather-clad slopes toward the woods.

"I can well understand how you feel."

"Would that my wife had felt like that, Miss Maitland, but I fear she came here with the full intention of despising it. I was used quite cynically."

Lauren said nothing, but she couldn't help thinking that the cynicism with which he credited his late wife, could equally be credited to the way he and his brother were engaged upon the securing of the Ashworth fortune. She was regarded as a way of acquiring funds, which was precisely how Fleur had regarded her marriage.

He was conscious of having once again brought up the subject of his marriage. "It seems that once more I must crave your pardon, Miss Maitland."

"Why?"

"Because I am continually harping on about my disastrous venture into holy wedlock. I'm afraid the whole business still rankles a great deal. Maybe that is the lot of the deceived husband. He is the last to know, and the last to recover."

"Yes," she murmured, thinking about Jamie's affair with Emma. Rory disapproved of any marital infidelity, and had made that clear, but how much greater would his fury be if he knew that his brother's mistress was Fitz's wife? No doubt he would be outraged. Perhaps as outraged as she herself felt about his willingness to assist Jamie in his despicable pursuit of her fortune. Rory Ardmore, Earl of Glenvane, was guilty of double standards.

He glanced at her. "Is something wrong, Miss Maitland?"

"Wrong?"

"You seem suddenly preoccupied."

"I was thinking about what you said."

"Which thing in particular?"

"About your wife marrying you as a means to acquire funds. I think I know how you felt. The Ashworth fortune has proved a magnet for adventurers and the more disreputable gentlemen in society." She glanced briefly at him, and then away again.

He didn't respond and so she looked at him again. "I am not sought after for myself, but for my inheritance. It's a quite shameful fact, is it not?"

"Yes, Miss Maitland, quite shameful," he replied, meeting her gaze.

She marveled at his coolness. He was actively assisting his brother to do the very thing she was condemning, but he didn't flinch, or even seem vaguely uncomfortable. Lord Glenvane's conscience was quite clearly capable of astonishing selectivity. He was hurt and resentful about what had been done to him, but he did not think twice about trying to foist his feckless, unpleasant brother upon her.

But a moment later she was proved wrong about his apparent lack of discomfort. The horse stumbled a little, and his arm tightened around her waist as the animal regained its balance. "Are you all right?" he asked quickly, reining in.

"Yes." Thank you."

He hesitated. "Miss Maitland, I have the oddest feeling that an atmosphere has suddenly sprung up between us," he said.

"Oh?"

"Yes." He gave a slightly embarrassed laugh. "I trust you do not imagine that I am intent upon your fortune?"

"You, sir? Why would I think that?"

"I don't know, but after pointing out that you understood how I felt about Fleur's actions, your manner seemed to change a little."

"Lord Glenvane, I do not for a moment imagine you are interested in either me or my fortune, so please put such a thought from your mind," she replied. No, she thought, you're interested in using me to settle your brother's debts, and I should loathe you for it, but here I am, still beguiled by your smiles. I must be moonstruck.

He moved the horse on again, and they left the open mountainside to enter the woods, where the air was cool, and the smell of oak leaves and ferns filled the air. They had proceeded some way into the trees when they heard the sound of voices ahead, and gradually made out two riders, a lady and a gentleman. It was Mary and Fitz, and their laughter was easy and natural as they raced each other up the hillside. On suddenly seeing Lauren and Rory, they reined in in surprise.

Rory smiled at them both. "Good morning."

"Good morning," they replied in unison, exchanging brief glances between returning their curious gaze to the two mounted on the single horse.

Lauren could imagine their thoughts, and she endeavored to sound natural as she greeted them as well. "Good morning, oh, and happy birthday, Lady Mary."

"Thank you, Miss Maitland."

Rory looked at Fitz and raised an eyebrow. "Such energy and high spirits before midday? At your advanced age? I'm overcome with admiration."

Fitz grinned broadly. "The birthday child is fair wearing me out. You're right about the advanced age. I'm an old married man now and well past all this youthful exuberance, especially after one of your gargantuan Glenvane breakfasts!"

Mary could no longer contain her curiosity about finding her brother riding double with Lauren. She looked enquiringly at him. "I trust there hasn't been an accident? I mean, Miss Maitland's horse—?"

"It cast a shoe up on the ridge, and as luck would have it I was close at hand to rescue her," Rory replied. "We've left the horse at Rab Macdonald's until someone can attend to it." He smiled at his sister. "By the way, happy birthday, sweet eighteen."

"Thank you. I vow I expected to wake up this morning and feel entirely different, but I don't. Being eighteen is no more exciting than being seventeen."

"Don't complain, for when you are a Methuselah like me, you'll yearn to be eighteen again," he replied.

"You're not that old!"

"Old enough. I can give your antediluvian riding companion a year, anyway." Rory glanced at Fitz. "I trust you've left some breakfast for us weary travelers?"

"I believe there was a finnan haddie you might be able to salvage. No, I lie, we were actually the first to gorge; no one else was even up when we set off."

"What of Emma?"

"She's the original lazybones, I fear, especially when faced with the prospect of a ball which will go on until dawn. When I tried to interest her in getting up to accompany Mary and me, her response was to turn over and pull the bedclothes over her head, which action I took for a polite but firm no."

Rory gathered the reins. "Well, we'll leave you to your exercise, *mes enfants*. Don't wear my horses out, will you?"

"We won't." Kicking their heels, they rode on up through the woods.

Lauren turned to watch them. "They get on very well, don't they?" she observed, wondering if Rory had perceived his sister's feelings for Fitz.

"Yes, I suppose they do, but then they've known each other for a very long time—in fact, I think Fitz and I were here on vacation from Eton when Mary was born, so he's known her all her life. They are the best of friends."

Lauren said nothing more, for mere friendship was the last thing Lady Mary Ardmore desired from Lord Fitzsimmons. She continued to gaze after the now-vanished riders, and something occurred to her. "Lord Glenvane, what is a 'finnan haddie'?" she asked.

He threw his head back and laughed. "A Scottish delicacy of rare tastiness, Miss Maitland."

"Is it like haggis?"

"No, not at all like haggis." He smiled at her. "Finnan haddie is smoked haddock from the village of Findon, near Aberdeen, and it is the finest smoked haddock in the world, as I think you'll find if you trouble to sample it. I urge you to do so, for I am sure you will enjoy it."

"You wouldn't fib to me, would you, sir?"

"Me? Miss Maitland, I am the most truthful and trustworthy soul in the whole of Scotland."

Which didn't say much for the rest of his nation, she thought as he moved the horse on once more.

Soon they emerged at the foot of the valley and rode around the shore of the loch toward the castle. Lauren gazed at the castle windows, wondering if anyone was observing their return. Lord Glenvane and the Ashworth fortune riding double after setting off separately before breakfast! She hoped both Jamie and Isabel happened to glance out and see.

They rode across the neck of land to the castle, and then around the outer wall to the stableyard, where a groom hastened to take the reins, and Rory dismounted. "See that someone is sent up to the Macdonald croft to attend to Miss Maitland's horse. It's lame and has cast a shoe."

"Your lordship."

Rory turned to reach up to Lauren, and she slid down from the saddle into his arms. For the briefest and most breathless of moments she was in his embrace, and in the space of that heartbeat she was sure that he was as conscious of her as she was of him, but then slowly he released her. "Shall we go in, Miss Maitland?" he asked.

"Yes, of course."

They went through the little door into the courtyard. A cart had been sent out earlier to the icehouse deep in the woods on the far side of the loch, and now its load of ice blocks was being carefully lowered through a trapdoor into the cellars, where they would remain in the coldest place possible until required to chill the air at the ball that night. Summer balls were usually hot and uncomfortable, this was especially so in one of the hottest summers in memory. The ice placed strategically around the floor brought a much needed coolness to the proceedings.

Lauren paused for a moment in the courtyard, glancing through the archway into the gardens. One of the tree-covered islands on the loch had suddenly caught her eye, for it seemed particularly beautiful in the mid-morning sunshine. Its oak trees were luxuriant, overhanging the water as if they wished to conceal something hidden among them, and then she noticed what appeared to be a crumbling tower, its ivy-clad stones barely visible above the surrounding foliage. Framed as it was by the courtyard arch, the scene seemed like a work of art.

Rory followed her gaze. "Have you just noticed Holy Island's ruins?"

"Holy Island?"

"There was a monastery there—a small one, of course, since the island is hardly two hundred yards from end to end. It was razed by one of my less religious ancestors, who took exception to the constant wagging of disapproving monkish fingers. He was of a rather—er—orgiastic disposition, and the riotous goings-on here at the castle were just too much for the pious brothers to endure. They condemned him once too often, and so he put the torch to the monastery and banished them from the island."

"I'd love to go there."

"Then you shall. I will attend to it for you."

They left the courtyard and entered the great hall, where they were immediately greeted by the confusion of floral preparations as well as the noise of the breakfasting guests in the dining room. It seemed that nearly everyone had now risen from their beds, and were all around the breakfast table at the same time.

But as Lauren and Rory crossed toward the staircase to go to their rooms to change, Isabel called from the entrance of the dining room, having to raise her voice to be heard above the general noise all around. A bank of delphiniums and ferns hid Lauren temporarily from her view as she addressed Rory.

"Ah, there you are at last—" she began, but then she saw that he wasn't alone. "Good morning, Miss Maitland," she said coolly.

Lauren smiled. "Good morning, Lady Maxby," she replied.

Isabel came toward them, her bluebell eyes guarded and cool. She wore a white lawn gown that was scattered with embroidered pink roses, and her rich red hair was pinned up on top of her head. A white shawl trailed along the floor behind her, and Lauren knew that if there hadn't been so much clatter in the hall, the shawl would have been heard slithering like a snake.

Isabel halted before them, her gaze moving appraisingly from one to the other. "You've been out for a ride together?"

Rory shook his head. "Not exactly." He explained what had happened.

The bluebell gaze was icy as it rested on Lauren. A chance meeting? She doubted that very much, and was determined to wrest him from her unexpectedly persistent rival. She linked his arm. "Rory, I have something to speak to you about."

"But I was just about to change out of these things. Can't it wait a while?"

"It's important," she insisted.

Lauren gave a quick smile. "Er—if you'll forgive me, I'll go on up to my room," she murmured, and gathered her skirts to hurry up the staircase. She was well pleased about the encounter with Isabel and didn't need to glance back to know Rory was about to be quizzed about the ride. Oh, to be a fly on the wall for the next few minutes! He was only intent upon pairing the Ashworth fortune with his brother, but Isabel suspected him of entirely different motives.

She hurried past the room where she'd overheard that very telling conversation the evening before, and then made her way toward the tower where her own room lay. Passing a large window set back in a deep embrasure that was flanked by dark green velvet draperies, she noticed that it looked down over the terraced gardens, and she halted for a moment to look toward Holy Island.

She'd only been there for a moment or so when she heard a door open a little further along the passage. It was a stealthy sound, and she turned to peep around the draperies. She saw Jamie looking out of the doorway. He glanced cautiously along the passage in both directions, and then turned to nod at someone else in the room behind him. It was Emma. She wore a cherry-and-white seersucker gown, and her face was a little flushed as she paused to link her arms around his neck and kiss him briefly on the lips. Her body pressed voluptuously against his, and then she left him. As she passed Lauren's hiding place, she reached up to push back a loose pin in her honey-colored hair.

Lauren kept well back out of sight. So that was why Fitz's wife had declined to join him on his ride with Mary—she preferred to steal the chance to go to her lover!

Hearing the door along the passage close again, Lauren peeped out once more. There was no sign of Jamie, and Emma had gone. Taking the skirts of her riding habit, Lauren fled on toward her own room.

11

A little later, Lauren went down to the dining room. She did not feel at all tired after the ride; on the contrary, she felt quite refreshed and ready to enjoy one of the gargantuan Glenvane breakfasts to which Fitz had referred.

He had not exaggerated about the lavishness and variety of the table provided by the castle, as she saw the moment she entered the crowded dining room. The sideboards were laden with an astonishing array of silver-domed platters and the room was heavy with the smell of food, from bacon, sausages, warm bread, and coffee, to the more exotic aromas of kedgeree, deviled kidneys, and the much-praised finnan haddies. The chatter of conversation had not diminished in the time she had been changing, and it seemed that those guests who had finished were content to linger with their companions just to talk.

In the few seconds that Lauren stood in the doorway, she noticed that Emma was with Jamie, and that Isabel was seated beside Rory. Rory looked displeased about something, indeed it seemed to Lauren that he was decidedly irritated, although he strove to conceal the fact. Hester and Alex were at the other end of the table, deep in conversation with some old London friends, and they didn't notice her. Rory did, however, and to her surprise he immediately left his place to come to her. It was a courtesy which angered Isabel.

Rory smiled at Lauren. "Have you recovered from your exertions?"

"Most definitely, sir."

"I'm filled with admiration."

"Whereas I intend to be filled with finnan haddie," she replied promptly.

He laughed. "The thought of our best smoked haddock appeals to you?"

"A great deal more than the prospect of haggis, I must admit."

"Then filled with finnan haddie you shall be, Miss Maitland."

His good humor and apparent delight on seeing her again seemed quite natural, and, again, if it hadn't been for what she'd overheard the night before, she would have thought him sincere in his attentiveness. If only he were. If only he felt as much for her as she did for him . . .

He was about to escort her to the sideboard when suddenly Jamie appeared beside them. "Good morning, Miss Maitland."

"Sir." She glanced surreptitiously at Rory. His expression was mixed, although what that mixture was she couldn't quite tell.

Jamie smiled into her eyes. It was a practiced smile, smooth and confident. In his vanity it simply did not occur to him that his prey might not wish to be caught. "Miss Maitland, I was wondering if you would care to join me for a drive after breakfast? I have my cabriolet and thought you might like a tour around the loch?"

Rory replied before she could say anything. "You're too late, brother mine, for Miss Maitland is already spoken for. I'm rowing her across to Holy Island."

Lauren stared at him and then smiled a little apologetically at Jamie. "Another time, perhaps, sir."

He gave his brother a dark look, but then dissembled as he returned his attention to her. "Then at least allow me to assist you in the more mundane matter of selecting your breakfast," he said, offering her his arm in such a way that Rory would have had to make a thing of it to exclude him again.

Rory stepped aside. "Until a little later, Miss Maitland."

She smiled at him and then reluctantly accepted Jamie's arm. From the corner of her eye she saw that Rory did not return to his seat next to Isabel but left the room instead. She didn't know what to make of him, except to wonder how he could possibly still be assisting Jamie when he had quite deliberately put a stop to any thought of a cabriolet drive around the loch. Unless, of course, when they'd been in the courtyard earlier, he'd meant that he would personally take her to the island as soon as possible. But even as she considered this possibility, she discarded it, for if that had been the case, then surely he would have made certain that she understood.

Jamie had been lifting the domes off several platters for her, but she was so lost in thought about Rory that she wasn't paying any attention. He paused. "Perhaps you aren't hungry, Miss Maitland?"

She came back to the present. "Forgive me, I was thinking about something else."

"So I noticed." He smiled into her eyes again. "Would that I were the subject of those thoughts," he murmured, with just the merest hint of gallant flattery.

She feigned not to have heard. "To the matter in hand, sir. What's that?" She pointed to the platter he'd just displayed for her.

"Herring and potato cakes," he said flatly, a little disgruntled that his expert flirting wasn't earning the desired response.

"Oh. Well, I don't think I have a fancy for them," she said quickly, moving on to the next dome and lifting it herself. "And this?"

"Pigeon pie."

"For breakfast?"

"There are many who like it, but usually they are of

the older generation, who also like roast beef and ale at this time of day."

"Indeed?" She gave him an innocuous smile. "I fear there is only one thing I wish to sample this morning, sir, and that is finnan haddie."

He blinked. "You are acquainted with the dish, Miss Maitland?"

"I was told about it earlier, when Lord Glenvane and I were returning to the castle."

He became still. "You and Rory?"

"We were coming back from our ride," she said, being deliberately ambiguous.

She was rewarded by the slight darkening of his eyes. "It seems one cannot trust one's own brother," he murmured to himself, not realizing that he'd spoken loud enough for her to hear.

"Not trust one's own brother? What do you mean, sir?" she enquired innocently, determined to cause him as much subtle discomfort as she could.

He managed a light laugh. "I meant that Rory has stolen a march on me, Miss Maitland. Here I am, striving to ingratiate myself in your favor, but it seems he has beaten me to it."

She replied with a tinkle of false laughter, but did not confirm or deny any of his suppositions. Then she looked him in the eyes. "The finnan haddie, sir?" she prompted.

"Er—yes, of course." Trying to hide his annoyance with the way things were going, he ushered her further along the sideboard to another dome, which he raised with a flourish to display the succulent contents.

She gazed approvingly at the plump, straw-colored haddock. Smoked fish had always been one of her favorites, and this appeared to be particularly appetizing.

Jamie looked enquiringly at her. "Does it meet with your approval, Miss Maitland?"

"It does indeed, sir."

"Then please allow me . . ." Taking a warmed plate

and the fish slice, he deftly scooped a generous helping, then led her to the table, where he drew out her chair for her. She couldn't help noticing that there was a vacant place next to the one he'd selected, so it came as no great surprise when he sat down as well.

For the next half an hour he put himself out to be as attentive as possible. He obtained the perfect bread to go with the finnan haddie, and retrieved the silver cruet set from the other side of the table. He even poured Lauren's coffee, and then purloined the blackcurrant preserve so that she could finish her breakfast with something sweet. No one could have been more flatteringly considerate, but by the end of the meal she knew he was frustrated in the extreme, because each of his careful advances had either met with bland indifference, or had apparently not been noticed at all. She enjoyed her secret advantage over him. The Ashworth fortune was remaining tantalizingly out of his reach, and he was far too arrogant and conceited to guess why! She had wondered what Emma's reaction would be to his attentiveness to another, but Jamie's mistress appeared unconcerned. The likely explanation for this was that he must have confided his urgent need for a wealthy wife. Unlike Isabel, Emma certainly did not look as if she feared she was losing her lover to the impertinent upstart from Boston.

The dining room was gradually beginning to empty now, and as Lauren murmured that she had something to attend to in her room, Jamie detained her for a moment by getting up to pull her chair back, at the same time bending down to speak close to her ear.

"I crave two favors, Miss Maitland," he said softly.

"Sir?" She didn't look at him.

"Promise that you will honor me with a drive tomorrow and a waltz tonight."

"I'm flattered, sir."

"Do I have your promise?" he pressed, still standing with his hands upon the back of her chair.

"Unless I wish to remain pinned in my chair indefinitely, you leave me no choice, sir."

"Then I consider your word binding," he murmured, straightening to draw the chair away and allow her to get up.

She quickly withdrew from the room. Drive with him? Waltz with him? She would as soon walk barefoot over hot coals! She would have to dream up adequate excuses for reneging on both undertakings, for the last thing she intended to do was oblige him in any way.

The hall was still a scene of confusion and bustle as the ball preparations proceeded. The floral decorations were becoming more and more beautiful, with garlands twining around banisters, newel posts, suits of armor, and everything else that Tam's ingenuity happened upon. Bolts of the Ardmore tartan had been brought in to swathe around the walls, and there were silk ribbons of the same tartan pinned among the flowers. By the evening, the hall promised to be a veritable Scottish arbor of blooms and foliage.

Rory was waiting at the foot of the staircase. He'd plucked a carnation from a huge vase standing on the floor beside him, and was twirling it between his finger and thumb, raising it to his nose now and then to savor the scent.

He discarded the flower and turned as he realized she was approaching. "I trust you have no objection to my taking the liberty of asking your maid for these so that we can leave for the island straightaway?" He held out her shawl and parasol.

She looked at them, then raised her eyes to his. "I don't mind, Lord Glenvane, but I confess to a little surprise."

"Surprise?"

"When I mentioned going to Holy Island earlier, I didn't really know we had a firm arrangement to go there together now."

"We didn't." He held her gaze. "Do you mind?"

"I don't mind at all, Lord Glenvane," she replied honestly.

"Good," he murmured, placing the shawl gently around her shoulders. She took the parasol and accepted the arm he offered, and they went out into the courtyard. As they emerged into the gardens, they heard hoofbeats approaching the castle near the bridge over the River Vane, and they turned to see Fitz and Mary returning pell-mell from their ride. Mary's laughter rang out as she tried to outpace him, but as they vanished toward the stableyard it was Fitz who was in the lead.

Rory watched them until they vanished from view, but he didn't say anything to Lauren. Whether or not he was mulling over her comments of earlier, she couldn't tell, but surely it must be clear to him that his sister didn't regard Fitz simply as a friend. Lauren's eyes were thoughtful as she and Rory proceeded down through the gardens, for although Mary's feelings were occasionally written rather too large, Fitz's were far more difficult to gauge. If he were aware of how Mary felt, then he had no business at all spending so much time with her. He was older and supposedly wiser, and certainly should know better. On the other hand, if he secretly returned Mary's affections . . .

At last Rory led Lauren on to the jetty, where the rowing boats rocked on the crystal water. He stepped down into one of them, and then held his hand out to her. She descended gingerly, her breath catching slightly as the boat swayed.

"It's all right, I have you," he said, his fingers tightening over hers as he assisted her to the cushioned seat at the stern. A minute later he had cast off the mooring rope and the boat slid out on to the loch as he rowed strongly toward Holy Island.

Lauren lay back on the cushions at the stern, her face shaded by her parasol. The sunlight shone brightly upon her locket as she dipped her hand into the loch, savoring the current of the water as it swept through her fingers.

She could not help but be conscious of Rory, of the litheness of his muscular body as he rowed and the way the sun shone with almost blue lights upon his dark hair. This Scottish lord was the personification of temptation, kindling sensuous desires which warmed her very soul. To save herself from the perdition of unrequited love, she should leave Glenvane as soon as possible. But she knew she wouldn't. She'd stay, simply to be near him . . .

After about twenty minutes, they reached Holy Island, and the prow of the boat grated on the shingle of the small beach where they landed. Behind them the castle rose above its mirror image in the loch, and all around there were the splendid heights of the mountains. A light breeze rustled through the oak trees on the island, and the first thing that Lauren saw as she stepped ashore was an ancient stone cross, its weatherbeaten surface almost completely concealed beneath a cloak of shining dark green ivy. It faced toward the castle, and she felt that the monks must have placed it there as a deliberate admonishment when they found the then Lord Glenvane's activities too much for their pious sensitivities.

Rory dragged the boat a little further on to the beach and then indicated a barely discernible path leading between leafy banks. "This way," he said. It was so cool and shady on the island that she left her parasol in the boat and then followed him. Soon the loch was lost from view behind them as the thick greenery of the island closed around. There were wild roses and honeysuckle, and the moss beneath their feet was like a carpet, smooth and untrodden. The path led down a slight dip, and he turned to assist her up the other side, where the ground promised to be a little slippery. As he drew her safely toward him, she was again conscious of the electric sensation that passed between them. It was as if her whole body were alive, tingling the moment he touched her. Did he feel it too? How could he not, when it was so real it could almost be heard?

Because the island was so small, it wasn't long before they reached the center, where the ruined monastery stood in a dell. It was a quiet, impressive place, the ruined walls crumbling and yet still strong, as if they had done with aging and would now remain forever as they were. The crowding trees stole much of the sunshine, but there was a sunny bank nearby, and Rory led her there.

"Your green velvet sofa awaits, Miss Maitland," he said, referring to the thick moss.

She smiled as she sat down. "A sofa worthy of a palace, sir," she answered.

"In the early spring this place is white with snowdrops," he murmured, glancing around for a moment and then sitting down next to her.

She glanced around as well, and then thought about its rather disappointing history. "I wish the island had a more romantic story than a mere quarrel between stuffy monks and licentious lords," she said, pushing a stray wisp of hair back from her face as the breeze blew it loose from its pins.

"Then your wish is granted, for there is a legend that Mary, Queen of Scots, used to come here to meet her lover, the Earl of Bothwell."

"Really?"

"Oh, yes. Her affair with Bothwell was frowned upon, and so she kept it secret as much as she could by meeting him at night. It was autumn, a season of heavy mists hereabouts, and she was rowed over without anyone knowing. She was warned when it was time to return because she had arranged with the piper at the castle that he would play half an hour earlier than he should, thus giving her time to be rowed back."

"Bagpipes played at the castle can be heard here on this island?"

"Miss Maitland, there are those who declare with considerable feeling that the pipes can be heard from *any* distance," he replied.

"I will have to take your word for that, sir."

"Tonight you will have the evidence of your own ears by which to gauge."

"I will?"

He nodded. "There will be pipes in plenty at the ball, and all manner of other things Scottish and traditional, including my good self and all north-of-the-border gentlemen in full highland toggery."

"Do you cut a fine figure in a kilt, Lord Glenvane?"

"I will permit you to be the judge of that, but I'm told I have a pretty enough ankle." He smiled.

"I will be sure to let you know my opinion, sir."

"Just be gentle with my pride, for it is a fragile thing."

"I find that hard to believe."

"How cruel you are."

"There is safety in attack, Lord Glenvane."

He looked enquiringly at her. It was an expressive look, conveying so much more than the mere words he said. "Meaning by definition that there is danger in acceptance?" he asked quietly.

"Acceptance at face value, yes." They were fencing, and she knew it. Her heartbeats had quickened, and her mouth was suddenly dry. There was much, much more to this than idle banter, for behind it all they were both very serious indeed.

"Why should you not accept at face value," Miss Maitland?" he asked.

"Because things are not always what they appear to be, sir."

"I am what I appear to be."

"Are you?"

"Yes."

"I wish I could believe that, Lord Glenvane."

Suddenly he put his hand to her cheek. "Then believe it," he said softly.

The air was motionless around her, and all sound died away except for the pounding of her heart. A bewildering weakness spread through her, and her whole body ached with desire as he pulled her gently down on to the bank and then leaned over her. The sunlight was behind him, dazzling and distracting, and she felt a warm sense of inevitability stealing treacherously over her. Luxurious shackles bound her, and she was a willing prisoner as he kissed her on the lips.

12

LAUREN was overtaken by a sensuousness she never dreamed she possessed. Her lips softened and parted, and her body moved to meet his, molding to him as if it had been fashioned for just this moment. Kissing him was the most natural thing in the world, and the most exciting. Innocence slipped away from her fingertips and an instinctive knowledge took its place. The world spun, lifting her out of her hitherto chaste existence and carrying her toward a luxurious fulfillment. Consummation beckoned, promising all manner of sensual delights, but a cool voice whispered a warning. "Fool if you trust him, fool if you trust him . . ."

"No!" With a gasp she drew sharply away, and got up hastily from the bank. Her skirts brushed the ferns, and a slender branch from the oak tree overhead caught briefly in her hair, dislodging it from its pins so that it tumbled in confusion about her shoulders.

"Lauren—"

"I don't trust you, Lord Glenvane. I have no reason to, you see, because I know what fate you and your brother have plotted for me." Her voice shook as she struggled to gather her scattered senses.

He stared at her. "You what?"

"I overheard you last night, when you agreed to help him settle his gaming debts."

For a moment he was too thunderstruck to say anything, but then he ran his fingers slowly through his hair. "How much did you hear?"

"Enough to see through you now."

"Oh? And what exactly do you think you see now?"

"I see . . . " She faltered, for what *did* she see? How could it further his brother's cause if he himself made love to her?

His gray eyes were bright and intense. "It seems you cannot explain, for to follow your reasoning leads to a puzzle. What logic can there possibly be in my actions now?" he said softly.

Still she tried to fight the compelling sensuality which he had stirred within her. "I don't begin to know what passes for logic where you are concerned, Lord Glenvane."

"No, but *I* begin to understand *you* a little better. Suddenly I see the reason for your trickery before dinner, why you managed to prevent Jamie from escorting you, and then contrived to be seated next to me."

"A dextrous turning of the tables, you will agree," she replied defiantly.

"Oh, poetic justice, no less."

"I trust you also understand more what I meant when we rode back to the castle this morning?"

"About being pursued for your fortune? Yes, I understand."

"I also trust that you will convey my displeasure to your brother?"

"I will see to it that he desists forthwith; you have my word upon it."

"And your word is to be trusted, sir?"

"Yes. Lauren, you will never know how much I regret my equivocation where Jamie's plan was concerned. I didn't want to have any part in it, but at the same time I was trying to convince myself I didn't want you. It was impossible, for I want you too much."

Her breath caught, and she whirled about to face him properly. Was he trying to gull her with his practiced words? Or was there some truth in what he said? "Please

don't say that if you don't mean it," she begged, her wits
in such confusion that she could hardly bear it.

"I mean every word, Lauren," he replied quietly.

She was afraid of the consequences of believing him,
and that fear made her uncompromising. "If that is how
you feel, I find it inexplicable that you should agree to
your brother's suggestion. To say that you were trying to
resist me yourself just isn't good enough."

"It's the truth. Lauren, you have no idea how bitter an
experience my marriage was. It has curdled my whole
existence—at least, it has until now. Besides, I never for
a moment really believed Jamie would succeed with
you. In fact, in my heart of hearts I rather hoped you
would deal him the snub he deserves, for his gambling
debts have long since gone beyond anything reasonable.
I was shirking my own responsibilities, if you like, secretly wanting you to curb his excesses for me. He's a
grown man and should be displaying at least a modicum
of responsibility, but instead he frequents every gaming
hell he can find, and he pursues other men's wives. He's
hardly a jewel in the Ardmore family crown. But then
neither am I at the moment, I suppose." He added this
last on a scathing note of self-recrimination.

She glanced at him but said nothing. She felt dazed,
wanting him to be telling the truth, wanting him to really
mean the regret he expressed.

He went on. "Oh, I know that none of this excuses
me, and that to blame Jamie is a little base, but I'm trying to explain my actions. Lauren, I wanted to turn from
you, but every time you were there I wanted you more."
He looked at her locket as a shaft of sunlight flashed
upon it. "In the boat yesterday, when I learned about
your fiancé, I felt suddenly closer to you than ever. We
had something in common, you see, something that
erased the obstacles. You had as much reason to spurn
any thought of entanglement with me as I had with you.
Your fiancé died at British hands, and my marriage died

at American hands—the one was canceled out by the other. Do you understand what I mean?"

Her heart was thundering in her breast, but she clung to common sense as she nodded slowly. "Yes, I understand that, sir, but I do not understand why you have omitted all mention of Lady Maxby. What place does she have in all this?"

He looked away and drew a heavy breath. "When you arrived here and saw me with her in the garden, I had just told her that our—er—liaison was at an end. That was all it had ever been—a liaison. I have never offered her marriage or anything permanent and she was fully aware that that was how it was. Oh, I'd been trying to break it gently for days, but somehow the time never seemed quite right. I knew that I couldn't possibly allow things to continue between us while I was so preoccupied with you."

Recalling Isabel's manner during those first moments, Lauren could well believe that he was telling the truth. But Isabel's conduct since hadn't been that of a woman who meekly submitted to the ending of the liaison. "Do you believe Lady Maxby accepts the changed situation?"

"I'd be a liar if I said I did, but in the end she will have to accept it, because I no longer feel the same way about her. I will always regard her as a friend—we go back too far for that not to be so—but as a lover . . . " He shook his head. "What there was between us commenced when she'd been a widow for a year and did not endure on my side for longer than a few months. It was over for me before I went to London, and certainly long before I met you. I don't want to part from her on bitter terms, but I fear that in the end it may be the only way, for she insists upon trying to win me back."

"No woman finds it easy to be rejected, or supplanted by another."

"Women do not have the franchise on that, for I know only too well what it is like to be rejected and supplanted. Deceit and unfaithfulness are the two things I cannot endure, and that is why I am doubly ashamed of having briefly gone alone with my brother's stratagem. Forgive me, Lauren, forgive me for having let you down. You have invaded my life, and it is the sweetest invasion imaginable."

His words touched something deep inside her, and suddenly she knew that she believed everything he'd told her. "Oh, Rory," she whispered, stretching her hand out hesitantly toward him.

He seized it gladly and drew her down on to the bank once more. She went willingly, lying back in his arms. His lips were only inches from hers, and she could feel his heartbeats. His voice was soft.

"My confessions are almost complete, Lauren, but what I haven't confessed is the depth of my feeling toward you. It's more than mere attraction, and far more than desire. Lauren, I love you almost beyond all endurance."

Her heart almost stopped within her, and her green eyes were filled with tears of joy and disbelief. "You . . . love me?" she whispered.

"More than I have ever loved before."

"Oh, Rory . . . " His name was a sigh on her lips as she linked her arms around his neck to draw his mouth down to hers, and she pressed achingly against him. Her lips parted, and the tip of his tongue curled luxuriously against hers.

Passion stirred through her, a keen passion that was eager to cast restraint to the four winds. She craved him with an urgency that threatened to rob her of consciousness itself. She wanted to surrender right here on this mossy bank, to lie naked in his arms with the warm August sun on her skin, to feel his lips upon her breasts, to possess and be possessed . . . It was an almost irresistible temptation. They were alone, the moment was theirs, and so great was the tumult of desire that the remnants of her defenses crumbled away into nothing. If he wanted her now, then she was his.

But he drew back from the brink, cupping her flushing face tenderly in his hands and kissing her once more upon the lips. "To go further now would be to risk destroying what we have, and that is something I will not do. You must always be able to trust me, and you will not if I take you now, for in your heart of hearts you will wonder if my intention was only to seduce you. You are too precious to me for that." He stopped her protest with another kiss, and then smoothed the hair back from her forehead before gazing lovingly into her wide green eyes. "I feel as if you've been part of my life forever," he whispered.

"I know, for I feel the same."

"Oh, Lauren, my sweet, sweet Lauren," he breathed, pulling her into his arms and kissing her once more. His passion was more controlled now, but no less fierce for all that. Here on the island, for these few precious minutes, they were free to indulge their newly declared love, free to hold each other and say anything they chose. The moment they returned to the castle, propriety would bind them to correct behavior.

How long they lay together on the bank she didn't know, but it seemed all too short a time. Again it was Rory who brought the moment to a close, bending over to kiss her forehead before sitting up. "I think we will cause undue comment if we stay here much longer. There is nothing indecorous about a gentleman conducting a lady to see ruins upon an island, but that lady's character might be called into question if she lingers too long about what can only be a fairly short guided tour." He indicated the few scattered ruins in the dell before them.

She sat up as well, leaning her head on his shoulder for a moment. "I want to stay here forever. I love you, Rory," she whispered.

"And I love you. You've conquered my heart, Miss Maitland from Massachusetts."

Her lips parted to reply, but then another heavy curl of

her hair fell loose from its pins, and with a slight laugh at how disheveled she must look, she reached up to try to rectify matters.

"Allow me," he said, getting up and moving behind her to take out every last pin before shaking the heavy tresses until they spilled freely over her shoulders. Then he twisted the hair up into a smooth coil on top of her head, and replaced the pins. He stood back to admire his work. "You will do handsomely, now Miss Maitland."

"I'm alarmed at how expert you are with such things, sir. Just how many times have you had cause to attend to ladies' hair, Lord Glenvane?"

"Often enough to know what I'm doing," he confessed, smiling.

"Yes, I can imagine that is very true."

"You flatter me."

She met his eyes. "No, I merely see what other women see when they look at you."

"Well, Miss Maitland, knowing the effect you have upon those of my sex, I trust that you are not similarly well versed in the many ways of tying gentlemen's neckcloths?"

She smiled. "No, sir, I am not. Apart from you, there has only ever been Jonathan, and I confess to never having come so close to complete surrender with him."

"I would be inordinately jealous if you thought you had," he said softly, drawing her to her feet. "Oh, I don't know how I am going to manage when we return. I will want to kiss you all the time, but that wouldn't do at all, for it is not how one is expected to go on in polite society."

"Indeed it is not, sir."

"Propriety must be observed, and we must conduct ourselves with suitable decorum for the time being. There must not be any raised eyebrows concerning haste." He put his hand tenderly to her cheek. "One step at a time, Miss Maitland from Massachusetts, one step at a time . . ." He kissed her and then held her close, his cheek against her hair for a moment before he began to lead her from the clearing.

But she held back. "What will you say to Jamie?"

"The truth—that you overheard our conversation. He won't persist after that, I promise you." He smiled into her eyes. "Then, when the time is right, we will allow our love to be known."

She returned the smile.

His thumb caressed her palm. "I'll never fail you again, I promise," he said softly, and gave a rather incongruous laugh.

"What is it?" she asked.

"I was thinking of the entertainment I have planned for this afternoon. Madame Santini is to give her recital in the music room, and I shudder at the prospect. She arrived not long before we returned from Rab's, and she has a formidable repertoire at the ready. In my present mood I shall require earmuffs if I am to endure."

They laughed together as they walked hand-in-hand from the glade.

Lauren felt as if she were in a dream as he rowed her away from the island. The past hour had been the most wonderful of her life, and she was afraid that in a moment she would awaken. But as he smiled at her, while she leaned back upon the cushions with her parasol, once more trailing her fingers in the cool water, she knew that it wasn't a dream. She knew too that when she returned to her room at the castle she would remove Jonathan's locket and never wear it again.

If she had but known it, however, the locket was soon to be lost forever, and under circumstances which were by no means the accident they appeared to be.

13

AS the boat glided over the loch toward the castle, Lauren still found it hard to believe that she was suddenly so very happy. She gazed up at the flawless arc of the sky. "This is the most wonderful summer ever," she breathed.

Rory smiled. "True, but as far as the weather is concerned, you must shortly be prepared for a change for the worse."

She sat up slightly. "But the sun's shining, there isn't a cloud to be seen, and it's been like this for months!"

"I know, but a change is on the way, believe me."

"How do you know?"

He shipped the oars. "There is just something different in the air, a whiff of the sea."

She stared. "The *sea*? But it's miles away on the other side of Ben Vane!"

"Precisely. Believe me, over the years I've learned to read the weather in these parts, and when one can smell the Firth of Clyde, there's rain in the offing. Thunderstorms usually."

She suspected him of pulling her leg. "I don't believe you, sir," she declared.

"You will when the deluge begins and there's enough lightning to turn night into day." He grinned. "It's true, I swear it. If my father were still alive, he'd be vowing upon his gouty toe!"

She laughed then. "Oh, very well, I believe you. The weather is soon going to change."

He rowed on and as the boat neared the castle Lauren observed the gardens, where the guests strolling and sitting in the sunshine appeared to be only ladies. "Where are all the gentlemen?" she wondered aloud.

"In the billiard room where Fitz has taken on Sir Guthrie Dundee, an Edinburgh physician who is said to be the finest billiard player in Scotland. Needless to say, vast sums rest upon the outcome."

"I hope Fitz wins."

"Against Sir Guthrie? I doubt it. The man is a magician with ball and cue. Still, Fitz will be released from his misery in an hour's time, when Madame Santini's recital begins. I've left strict instructions that the billiard room is to be promptly vacated five minutes before her first song."

Looking at the crowded gardens again, Lauren was suddenly daunted by the prospect of encountering so many. She needed a little time to prepare herself after all that had happened on the island. She looked quickly at Rory. "Please don't return to the jetty. Can't we go ashore over there, closer to the bridge and the road into the courtyard? I don't want to see anyone else just yet."

Rory smiled. "Nor do I particularly. Very well, we'll avoid the jetty." He turned the bow of the boat slightly and then continued to row.

Jamie was no longer among the gentlemen in the billiard room, having lost interest in the play, and he'd been observing the boat for some time. As soon as he saw it wouldn't moor at the jetty, he followed it along the shore and was waiting as the prow grated slightly upon the shingle at the edge of the lake. He was suspicious that his brother wasn't serving his best interests, and that the Ashworth fortune wasn't being guided in his deserving direction.

Lauren's heart had sunk as she realized he was there, but there was nothing she could do but accept the hand he offered to assist her out of the boat. "Thank you, sir," she said reluctantly.

"Lemonade is being served in the garden, Miss Maitland. Perhaps you would care to accompany me there?"

Rory stepped ashore and spared her the need to reply. "I wish to speak to you in private, Jamie, and it can't wait," he said.

Lauren seized her opportunity. "I'll—er—go on, then," she said, and then walked quickly away. She didn't look back, not even when she heard Jamie's dismayed exclamation.

"She overheard?"

Her steps quickened still more as she made her way around the castle wall to go into the courtyard by the main gateway, and thus avoid the gardens and the ladies for the time being. Only when she reached the coolness of the courtyard did her pace slow a little, but almost immediately Hester came from the gardens on her way back into the castle. She wore a plum silk gown with a wide gray sash and a gray gypsy bonnet tied on with plum gauze, and there was a glass of chilled lemonade in her hand. She was rather pale, Lauren thought with concern. Hester saw her and halted.

"Ah, there you are, Lauren, I've been looking everywhere for you," she said, coming over to her. "Wherever have you been? We haven't had a chance to talk much since we arrived here, and I feel I've been neglecting you."

"You haven't been neglecting me any more than I have you," Lauren replied, looking at her a little anxiously. "Are you feeling well, Hester? You seem decidedly pale."

Hester gave a rather self-conscious smile. "I've felt better."

"What's wrong?"

"I don't know. It started last night after dinner. I was perfectly well, and then suddenly I felt decidedly queasy, but it passed off again and I dismissed it. But then the queasiness returned briefly this morning, and now it's come over me again. I was just about to go and lie down for a while. And before you say it, no, I do *not* think it is anything to do with that wretched red grouse!"

"I didn't say a word."

"No, but you thought it."

"Well, Hester, you have to admit that it is rather a coincidence," Lauren pointed out.

"It's two days since I ate at the Crown & Thistle."

"Sir Sydney Dodd wasn't taken ill straightaway."

Hester sighed. "I still don't think there is a connection. I've simply contracted a bad humor, and it will soon pass."

"I hope you're right."

Hester eyed her. "Enough of my indisposition. Let's talk about you instead, Coz. I've been hearing all manner of intriguing things about your activities. I'm told, for instance, that you and Rory went for a ride this morning."

"Well, it wasn't quite like that, but we *did* come back together from our respective excursions."

Hester was disappointed. "So he didn't invite you to join him?"

"Not then, no."

"But he has since?" Hester's eyes widened hopefully.

"Yes, he's just brought me back from seeing the ruins on Holy Island."

Hester's lips parted. "You went alone with him?" she breathed.

"Yes."

"There! I knew it! He's smitten with you, isn't he, and if I'm not mistaken, you're smitten with him as well. I can see it in your eyes, and in that telltale blush on your cheeks! What have you been up to, Lauren Maitland?"

"Hush," Lauren said quickly, for it seemed that Hester's voice echoed rather alarmingly around the courtyard.

Hester spoke in a whisper. "I trust you mean to tell me, for I shall burst if you don't!"

"Very well, I'll tell you, but not here."

"Come into the garden and we'll take some lemonade together."

"I thought you were feeling unwell."

"There is no better remedy than the prospect of a titillating gossip."

"It isn't *that* titillating," Lauren replied as Hester linked her arm and virtually propelled her into the garden, where the other ladies were like butterflies among the flowers. Their summer gowns ranged across the colors of the rainbow, from the most daring of reds to the softest of violets, and the light chatter of their conversation drifted on the warm air. Lauren looked quickly along the lake shore, and was just in time to see Jamie striding angrily away from Rory, who lingered for a moment by the boat and then followed. It was clear that Jamie wasn't the least pleased to discover that the Ashworth fortune was wise to him and that he was therefore bound to stay out of reach. He'd have to find another means to settle his debts.

Mary was in the gardens, wearing a particularly becoming shade of apricot. She was seated in an arbor with Isabel and Emma, and was doing her best to appear lighthearted and carefree. They were all laughing at something Emma was reading aloud from a rather lurid gothic novel she'd brought with her from London. Isabel glanced across as Lauren and Hester made their way down toward the well, which offered the only reasonably secluded part of the gardens. Her blue eyes became veiled and anticipatory, and a sleek smile played momentarily upon her lips before she returned her attention to Emma's reading.

Reaching the well, Hester made herself comfortable on the seat, and then beckoned to one of the maids serving the lemonade. She waited impatiently until Lauren had been supplied with a glass, and then urged her to begin.

"Oh, *do* tell, before I burst!"

Lauren hesitated before commencing. "You must

promise me you won't breathe a word of this, not yet, anyway."

"Of course."

"I mean it, Hester. Not even to Alex."

"If that is your wish."

"It is." Lauren drew a long breath, and her eyes began to shine with irrepressible happiness. "Hester, Rory and I love each other."

Hester's jaw dropped, and she nearly spilled her lemonade. "I . . . I beg your pardon?" she said weakly.

"We declared our love on Holy Island, and sealed it with many more than just one kiss."

Hester's green eyes threatened to pop out of her head, then she gave Lauren a rather cross look. "This is a jest, is it not? Wagers are the order of the day, and you have something resting upon whether or not I will swallow such a tall tale!"

"It isn't a jest, and there isn't a wager. I'm telling you the truth, Hester. Indeed, it is so much the truth that I confess I would have surrendered all had he wished it. My proper upbringing did not count for anything in the way I felt, I promise you."

Hester stared at her, and then drained her glass of lemonade before fixing her cousin with a determined gaze. "I want every detail, and if you leave anything out I will beat you with your parasol!"

"I don't know about *every* detail, but I will tell you most of it." Lauren related what had happened, commencing with what she'd overheard before dinner the night before, and ending with the return to the jetty, when Rory had immediately taken Jamie aside. "And there you have it," she finished. "I'd just come up from the lake when you saw me in the courtyard, and as we were coming to sit here, I saw Rory and Jamie leave. Jamie appeared to be somewhat—er—dismayed."

"I'll warrant he was!" Hester then gave an incredulous laugh. "So I was right all along about Rory's feelings for you. Oh, what a stir there will be when this gets out!

Lord Glenvane, who was cruelly treated by his wife, now takes another of her countrywomen to his heart. And my American cousin, who lost her first love six years ago in the war with Britain, now falls head over heels for a British aristocrat. It will rattle the teacups for weeks!"

"You make it sound like a scandal," Lauren said, a little put out.

Hester put a quick hand on her arm. "Oh, please don't think that, for it wasn't my intention. I was only pointing out that it is a very intriguing situation, as I think even you must admit."

"Yes, I suppose it is," Lauren conceded.

Hester gave another laugh. "I can't believe all this has been going on. To think that I was conscience-stricken about neglecting you, but all the time you've been so busy that you haven't had time to even think about me!"

"There is an element of truth in that," Lauren admitted ruefully, for Hester hadn't crossed her mind very much over the past few hours. Suddenly her attention was drawn once more to Mary, Isabel, and Emma, on the terrace above. Seeing Mary striving to appear happy on her eighteenth birthday was really quite sad. Rory's sister was sweet and charming, and Fitz was gallant and good-humored. They belonged together, not kept apart by his hollow marriage to a faithless wife.

Lauren looked at Hester. "Actually, if you want a proper scandal, then I think you need look no further than Lady Fitzsimmons," she said, deciding that the time was right to confer about Mary's secret situation.

"What do you mean?" Hester asked curiously.

"I wasn't going to say anything, and in a moment I'll tell you why I've changed my mind, but first I must explain about certain things I've discovered." She informed a deeply shocked Hester all about the goings-on at the Crown & Thistle, and the bedroom tryst before breakfast that very morning.

Hester gaped. "There . . . there isn't any mistake?" she asked then.

"None at all. You and Alex were right about her that day in Bond Street. She isn't to be trusted at all, and as for Jamie—"

"They are both monstrous! How *could* they do it to poor Fitz?"

"Keep your voice down," Lauren urged, glancing around for fear that her cousin's indignation would attract attention.

"I don't know how I'm going to be civil to either of them."

"You'll manage somehow, I'm sure."

"But my loyalty is to Fitz," Hester protested.

"Exactly."

Hester looked enquiringly. "What do you mean?"

Lauren took another deep breath. "There is still more to all this."

"More?" Hester squeaked. "Good heavens, I shall soon require the *sal volatile*."

"This is the last thing, I promise. It concerns Fitz and Lady Mary."

Hester blinked. "You aren't going to tell me that they are also engaged upon an affair?"

Lauren smiled, and looked up toward the trio seated in the arbor on the next terrace. "Not exactly, but I believe Lady Mary *is* in love with him, and I am beginning to suspect that in spite of himself, Fitz returns the feeling."

"You seem very certain," Hester replied, watching Mary.

"I am, I suppose." Lauren explained her observations since first seeing Mary and Fitz in the music room. "And earlier today, when Rory and I were setting off for Holy Island, they returned to the castle in truly high spirits. I can't believe that Fitz, who is a man of the world, isn't aware of the effect he has upon Mary, and since he is obviously honorable, I can only believe that he is unable to help himself from spending so much time with her."

"And therefore he returns her love?"

"It seems probable. Don't you agree?"

Hester thought for a moment and then nodded. "Yes, knowing Fitz as I do, I think I have to."

"Hester, now that I'm so happy myself, I want them to be happy too."

"Noble sentiments, Coz, but hard to put into practice. There is the small matter of Emma. She *is* Fitz's wife, and even though you and I may think he is in love with Mary, we might be wrong."

"Possibly, but I don't think so, and that's why I decided to tell you. I think Fitz returns Mary's love, and if that is so, then they deserve to be together. Emma certainly doesn't deserve any consideration."

"I agree with you there."

Lauren sighed. "I don't know what we can do about anything, but at least if we put our minds to the problem . . . "

"We'll both keep a sharp eye open. At the moment, that's all we *can* do."

"Yes."

Hester raised a wry eyebrow at her. "Now, are you quite sure that you've told me everything? You haven't any more salacious tidbits to lay before me?"

"None at all."

"I'm relieved to hear it. You're a very dark horse, Cousin Lauren, a very dark horse indeed."

"It's just that I've happened to be in the right place at the right time, or the wrong place at the wrong time, depending upon your point of view." Lauren looked anxiously at her. "Please don't say anything to Alex about Lady Mary and Fitz, for as you've pointed out, I might be entirely wrong about the whole thing."

"My lips are sealed about this entire conversation."

"Thank you."

Hester suddenly put a warning hand on her wrist. "I fear we are about to receive a visitation—two cats and a kitten from the next terrace."

Lauren's heart sank but she managed a bright enough smile as Isabel, Mary, and Emma descended the garden steps and then came toward them.

Isabel was almost effusively friendly, her skirts rustling prettily as she sat next to Lauren. "My dear Miss Maitland, I have a great favor to ask of you."

"A favor?"

"Yes. It concerns your locket. You see, I've been telling Mary how much like her mother's it is, and I was wondering if you would be so kind as to show it to her now?"

Lauren didn't want to do any such thing, but reluctantly she held the locket up while it was still around her neck, but that didn't suit Isabel. "Oh, no, she can't see it properly like that. May I?" Without really waiting for permission, she reached around Lauren's neck to unfasten the chain and take the locket to show the others. But as she turned with the locket in her hand, suddenly it slipped through her fingers, and fell between the wide squares of the grille over the well. It vanished from view, and after a second or so they all distinctly heard the distant splash as it fell into the water far below.

Isabel was instantly distraught. "Oh, no! How clumsy of me!" she cried, leaping to her feet and staring at the well. Tears filled her magnificent eyes and her lips quivered before she hid her face in her hands. Emma rushed to comfort her, as did Mary, who was torn equally between reassuring her and telling Lauren how dreadfully sorry she was about the loss of the locket. Hester put a gentle arm around Lauren's shoulder and said nothing.

Isabel's distraction was a thing to see. No one could have been more upset and remorseful, and no one could have drawn more attention to the mishap. She sobbed and begged Lauren's forgiveness, and made a great deal of unnecessary noise about the loss of the locket, which inevitably brought many other ladies to the scene to see what had happened.

Lauren did her best to make little of the incident, but

it wasn't an easy task when the guilty party was at such pains to keep the matter on the boil. It was several minutes before Mary and Emma were able to persuade a still-weeping Isabel to come into the castle to lie down for a while.

As the other ladies drifted away again, Hester glanced down into the darkness of the well. "Oh, Lauren, your lovely locket."

"As it happens, I wouldn't have worn it again anyway. Not now."

Hester smiled at her. "No, I suppose it wouldn't be entirely suitable, would it? All the same . . . "

"It wasn't an accident."

"No, she did it quite deliberately. Odious creature. She's obviously beside herself with jealousy over Rory."

Lauren watched as Isabel was ushered, still weeping, into the castle. "I have a horrid feeling that she has more than this in store for me."

"What do you mean?"

"I don't know yet, but she's made her animosity plain enough to me in private."

Hester shivered suddenly. "The breeze has picked up a little, and I haven't got my shawl," she said.

Lauren glanced up at the sky. "Rory said the weather was going to change."

"Actually, it may not be the weather at all, for I've begun to feel a little unwell again."

Lauren was anxious for her. "Perhaps a doctor should be sent for?"

"No, I don't want to make a fuss. I'll just lie down for a while, and forgo the delights of Madam Santini's concert. Did you know about that, by the way?"

"Yes, Rory told me."

"I'm sure I won't be missed from the proceedings, and if I have a good rest, I'll be all right again in time for the ball."

"Yes, but—"

"No, Lauren, I really don't want to see a doctor." Hester got up and glanced down into the well again. "I hope you're wrong, and that Isabel isn't plotting something."

"I hope so too, but I fear I'm only too right," Lauren murmured as she got up and began to make her way with Hester up toward the castle.

14

TRUE to her word, Hester took to her bed on returning to her room, and Lauren immediately sent for someone to bring Alex from the billiard room, where Fitz had eventually been defeated by Sir Guthrie, although as it turned out the match had been much closer than expected.

Hester's indisposition put all thoughts of billiards and wagers from Alex's mind, for he was greatly concerned that the Crown & Thistle's red grouse was at last doing its worst. The unfortunate Sir Sydney Dodd was still confined to his bed feeling very unwell indeed, and Alex had visions of the same unpleasant fate befalling Hester. Sir Sydney had a fixed loathing of doctors and all things medical, and simply would not be budged on the matter of sending for the doctor from Dumbarton. Hester, on the other hand, was simply convinced that such a course was totally unnecessary, as she insisted she was only a little under the weather. Faced with such intransigence, Alex allied himself with Lauren in an attempt to persuade his wife to see the doctor, but nothing would move her. In the end Hester became a little cross with both of them, and so they left her alone and made their reluctant way to the music room and Madame Santini's recital.

In spite of his anxiety over Hester, Alex was keen to hear the famous soprano, but Lauren wasn't interested in the least. Too much had happened today for her to find such a recital to her taste. The likes of Madame Santini were never soothing, and the thought of all those high notes was really quite wearing. Her lack of interest in the entertainment became even more pronounced when on arriving in the music room she heard Tam making Rory's excuses to the imposing Italian *diva.*

"His lordship craves your indulgence, madam, but something very urgent has required his attention, and—"

She waved him away impatiently. A very large, florid lady, she was clad in clinging pink satin, and when she drew in a huge breath and nodded to the waiting pianist, she rather resembled a plump rosebud bursting into full bloom. "I sing now," she announced imperiously, as if the presence of the Earl of Glenvane was of no consequence whatsoever—which it probably wasn't.

Tam withdrew prudently, just as the first trilling notes of a *lied* by the Austrian composer Herr Schubert rang out over the assembled audience. Lauren also decided upon retreat, and Alex hardly noticed as she followed the steward discreetly from the room. It soon turned out that she and Rory were not alone in crying off the musical interlude, for Mary hadn't attended either, as Lauren discovered when she reached the top of the staircase and paused to watch the continuing preparations in the hall below.

The decorations were now virtually complete, and everything looked very lovely indeed. Tam had resumed the task of supervising the servants putting the final touches to the special stands where the blocks of ice would be placed shortly before the ball began. These stands were placed at regular intervals between the sofas, and had been elegantly adorned with luxuriant ferns, to enhance the impression of coolness. Flowers had been decked everywhere, even around the hammer-beams, and the floor had been carefully sanded, with the stencilled shapes of moons and stars scattered all over it. Lengths of the green-and-blue Ardmore tartan were festooned over the walls, and there were bows of the same tartan fixed among the flowers. It was very traditional and Scottish, Lauren thought approvingly as she gazed at the scene, and it would make Lady Mary Ardmore's eighteenth birthday ball an occasion to remember forever. But then, this was a day for others to remember, not just Mary . . .

Lauren's thoughts drifted back to the island, and the minutes she'd spent in Rory's arms. Yes, this was indeed a day to remember. She was dragged back to the present by the sound of the main door opening and closing. Mary came in and made her way around the edge of the sanded floor toward the staircase. She still wore the apricot gown she had had on earlier, and she was carrying a little posy of flowers from the garden. There was a blush on her cheeks and a shine in her eyes as she held the flowers to her nose and breathed deeply of their scent. It was then that Lauren recalled not having seen Fitz at the recital either. Had he and Mary been together in the gardens?

Mary hurried up the staircase and halted on seeing Lauren. "Oh, hello, Miss Maitland. Don't you care for Madame Santini's singing?"

"Don't you?" Lauren countered with a smile.

Mary smiled as well. *"Touché.* To be honest, I am reminded of caterwauling, and so I'm going to my room to paint for a while."

"Paint?"

"With watercolors. I love to do it, and spend hours at my easel."

"What do you paint?"

Mary hesitated. "Flowers mostly," she said then, and raised the posy to her nose again.

"I trust you have an enjoyable few hours," Lauren replied.

"I will. I will see you later, Miss Maitland. Oh, by the way—"

"Lady Mary?"

"I'm truly sorry about your locket. If it were not for me, it wouldn't have been lost."

"It was hardly your fault, Lady Mary." No, it was Insufferable Isabel's!

"Not in the true sense of the word, no, but I still feel to blame. I trust you will be able to forgive me."

"There is nothing to forgive, but if it will make you feel better, then of course, you have my forgiveness." Lauren smiled at her.

"Thank you, Miss Maitland. Now, I really must get on with my painting." Gathering her apricot skirts, Rory's sister hurried away.

Lauren returned to her room, and hadn't been there long when she remembered the birthday present she had brought for Mary. It was a fan she had brought with her from home, and of which she was particularly fond, but because it was exquisitely painted with scenes of Boston it seemed an appropriate gift. Maybe there wouldn't be a suitable moment to give it to Mary at the ball, so perhaps the sensible thing would be to take it to her now, while she was in her room.

Madame Santini's singing still echoed through the castle as Lauren left her room with the fan, to go down the hall to ask Tam for directions to Mary's room. Her route necessarily took her past the room where the night before she had eavesdropped upon Rory and Jamie. Now, as then, the door stood open; now, as then, her curiosity got the better of her. But as she started to go inside she had the oddest feeling that someone was watching her from the staircase end of the passage. She glanced swiftly around, but there was no one. The feeling lingered for a moment and then faded, and so she went into the room.

It was a library, with arched gothic bookcases of such height that a wheeled stepladder was required to reach the upper shelves. Those walls which were not covered by the bookcases were paneled with dark, richly carved oak, and there were several ancient portraits above the elaborate wooden fireplace. The windows faced toward Ben Vane, and the afternoon sunlight streamed brightly into the room, falling right across the huge leather-topped desk where, unseen at first, Rory stood examining the contents of a large jewel box that was beautifully inlaid with ebony and mother-of-pearl.

He smiled and spoke softly. "To what do I owe this unexpected honor?"

She gave a start, and whirled guiltily around. "Rory! I didn't know you were there."

"So I noticed," he said, still smiling as he came around the desk toward her. He pushed the door to, and then took her in his arms, pressing his lips to her throat.

She went eagerly into the embrace, and closed her eyes with a soft moan as he kissed the pulse in her neck. Shivers of delight passed over her as she was awakened to the same exquisite desires she had experienced on the island. The flare of passion was instant and compelling, an aching need which seared through her as he raised his head to press his lips over hers. Her body felt as if it were melting against his, and she was conscious of his arousal. She could hear the blood pounding in her ears, and feel discretion slipping inexorably away. Take me, take me now . . .

With a slow sigh he drew back, leaning his forehead tenderly against hers. "You tempt me almost beyond endurance, my darling," he whispered.

She closed her eyes, savoring the delicious sensations which quivered through her as he stroked her hair. "I love you so much, Rory."

"As I love you, dear God as I love you . . . "

There was a soft sound at the door. They both heard it and leapt guiltily apart. Lauren remembered having felt as if someone had been watching her as she came into the room and she held her breath as Rory went quietly to the door. His fingers closed over the handle, and then he opened it suddenly and stepped outside, but the passage was empty. He stood there for a moment and then came back in, closing the door behind him again.

"We must have imagined it," he said.

"Both of us."

"I have to confess that Glenvane abounds in quite determined mice, too determined for the few castle cats to triumph over." He smiled and took her hand to draw her close once more, but she had found the incident disturbing and shook her head.

He understood, and touched her cheek with his fingertips. "I don't know how I will endure the ball, seeing you, dancing with you, and not being able to embrace you in front of them all."

She closed her eyes again, putting her hand briefly over his, and then she moved away a little. Common sense had to prevail, and all her other senses must be denied that which they craved. She cast around for something distracting, and her glance fell upon the fan in her hand. "I . . . I was on my way to see Mary when I came in here. I have her birthday gift and wanted to ask someone the way to her room."

He took the fan, and opened it over his palm to examine the little painted scenes. "It's very beautiful."

"Yes."

"Are you sure you wish to part with it?"

"Well, I admit to being very fond of it, but somehow it seems the perfect thing to give your sister."

"I know she will like it immensely."

"You really think so?"

"Of course." He smiled, tilting her face toward his and brushing his lips briefly over hers. "And as to find someone to take you to her room—well, you have found him."

"I don't want to take you away from whatever it was you were doing before I interrupted," she said, glancing at the open jewel box on the desk.

"Actually, I was also engaged upon a birthday gift for Mary," he said, returning to the desk. "It was my mother's wish that Mary have a certain ring on her eighteenth birthday, and I simply can't find it."

Lauren joined him by the desk, and gazed at the treasure trove of jewels in the box. Her breath caught with admiration. "A veritable pirate's hoard," she murmured, touching a strand of pearls which had tumbled over the side.

He smiled. "My mother was very fond of jewelry."

"She had exquisite taste," Lauren said, picking up a golden bracelet set with opals.

Rory nodded. "Yes, she did. Ah, here is the ring." He held up a richly ornamented band of gold which flashed with diamonds. "It was her betrothal ring, and it mattered to her that it went to Mary."

"I can understand that."

He put the ring into the pocket of his waistcoat and then took out a locket. "This is the locket which so resembles yours."

Lauren took it for a moment. The two pieces of jewelry were indeed very alike, but there was no doubt that Lauren's had been more ornately decorated.

"Lauren, I'm so very sorry about what happened to yours. Isabel is quite devastated."

"Is she?"

"But of course." He searched her eyes. "You evidently don't think so."

"Rory, she loathes the very sight of me, and I promise you there wasn't anything accidental about the way my locket was lost. It was all carefully contrived." She handed back the locket.

"I will question her—"

"No." Lauren put her hand gently over his. "The locket was no longer of great consequence to me, for I would never have worn it again. As a memento of the past it had some significance, but it wasn't precious any more."

"Are you absolutely certain?"

In response she moved closer to him, linking her arms around his neck and stretching up to kiss him lingeringly on the lips. "I'm quite, quite certain," she whispered.

He held her for a long moment, and then went to replace the locket in the jewel box, which he locked and took to one of the bookcases. To her surprise, she saw that it wasn't a bookcase at all, but a carefully concealed hiding place. He put the box inside and then turned the key on the cupboard door, before putting it in his waistcoat pocket alongside the ring for Mary.

He looked at Lauren again. "By the way, as you know, I spoke to Jamie earlier. I think that in spite of himself he now views you with grudging respect for the way you manipulated everything last night. I do not know that he will be able to look you in the eye when next you meet, but he has bowed to the inevitable and now accepts that the Ashworth fortune is not for him."

"What of his debts now?"

"I'll bail him out just once more. After that, he really is on his own." He looked away for a moment. "It's a terrible thing to say, Lauren, but although he is my brother, and I love him, I no longer like him particularly. He has changed for the worse since meeting his married inamorata."

Lauren lowered her eyes. Should she tell him what she knew? Or would such a revelation cause more trouble than it was worth? She didn't want to be responsible for driving an even greater wedge between the brothers.

As she deliberated, Rory gave her a quick smile. "I digress, do I not? Come, I'll take you to Mary now." He went to the door and opened it stealthily, peeping out once more to make absolutely sure there wasn't anyone there to see them leave the library after being closeted alone together. She was forcibly reminded of seeing his brother do exactly the same thing earlier that very morning, when Emma had left his room . . .

"All's clear," he said, stepping outside.

She followed him out into the passage and they walked away from the library.

Mary's room proved to be almost directly above the library, with windows looking across the loch toward Ben Vane. It was a pretty room, with curtains and bed hangings of rose velvet and all manner of feminine clutter, from an untidy dressing table lavishly hung with frilled muslin to a selection of shawls scattered on the bed, as if their owner had given up attempting to select the right one.

The tall window was open and Mary was standing by her easel in the embrasure. She wore a blue linen smock over her gown, and there was a smudge of paint on her nose. Whatever she'd been painting had been hastily hidden from view beneath a cloth, and she looked a little flustered as her maid announced Rory and Lauren. Putting her brushes into the jar of water beside her paints, she quickly wiped her hands on a towel and came to greet them.

"Two visitors? How very agreeable," she said, glancing back at the easel as the breeze from the window threatened to dislodge the cloth she'd put over it.

Rory took the diamond ring from his pocket, and pressed it into her palm. "Mother wanted you to have this today, and I'm honoring her wish."

Mary gazed down at the ring. "Oh, Rory," she murmured, slipping it on to her finger and then admiring it.

"It seems the perfect fit."

"It is." She hugged him. "Thank you."

"It's Mother's gift, not mine," he said, returning the hug before releasing her. "Now, if you will both forgive me, I really do have much to do, and am not simply crying craven where Madame Santini is concerned. A sheaf of legal documents awaits my immediate attention, and I've put it off for long enough."

Inclining his head to them both, he withdrew from the room, but at the opening and closing of the door, a draft swept through the room and the cloth over Mary's easel fluttered to the floor, exposing the painting beneath.

Mary gave a cry of dismay and hastened to replace the cloth, but it was too late, for Lauren had already seen the portrait of Fitz. It was an excellent likeness, and very lovingly painted. To Mary he was a hero—strong, romantic, and chivalrous, a veritable Sir Lancelot—and that was the Fitz who gazed from the easel. Bronzed and golden, all he lacked was the suit of shining armor.

Hot color flooded into Mary's cheeks as she replaced the cloth, but she knew her secret could not help but be out now. "I . . . I suppose you think me very foolish," she said, not looking at Lauren.

"No, of course I don't."

"I didn't want anyone to know."

"I'd already guessed," Lauren replied frankly.

Mary's eyes flew toward her. "Guessed? How?"

"I saw it in your eyes."

"Oh, and I thought I was being so circumspect." Mary went to sit on the bed, leaning against one of the posts. "May I confide in you, Miss Maitland?"

"Of course you may."

"It's so hopeless, but I can't help it. I cry myself to sleep most nights."

Lauren went to sit next to her, and put a comforting arm around her shoulder. "Does Lord Fitzsimmons know how you feel?"

Tears suddenly brimmed in Mary's eyes, and she nodded. "Yes, and he feels the same for me."

"He does?"

"Yes. Oh, *please* don't tell anyone, not even your cousin, for I really shouldn't divulge such secrets to anyone at all, but I do so need to talk to someone."

"Your secret is safe with me, although I should tell you that Hester already knows I suspect you to be in love with Lord Fitzsimmons. Oh, don't look so anxious, for she has already given me her word she won't relay anything to anyone else."

A little reassured, Mary searched for a handkerchief to mop her eyes. "I didn't ever imagine that I would fall in love with Fitz. Not Fitz. I've known him all my life, you see, right from the day I was born. I didn't realize how I felt until the day I heard he was married. It broke my heart, and I cried for days. Then he came here on his own to see Rory, only Rory had just left for America.

Jamie wasn't here, either." A dreamy look entered Mary's dark eyes. "We were thrown together, if you like, and it was the most wonderful time of my whole life. He told me that he was unhappy in his marriage, that he and Emma are oil and water, chalk and cheese . . . I found myself telling him that *I* loved him, that *I* yearned to be with him always. At first he was startled, for I really don't think it had entered his head, but then he thought about it and began to see, as I had done, that true love had been there in front of him all the time. He won't take it any further, though—he's too worthy for that. He wouldn't do anything to put my reputation at risk, and he knows that the merest whisper about us would do just that. Lady Mary Ardmore and Lord Fitzsimmons—such a scandal."

Lauren's heart went out to her. "You mustn't give up hope, Lady Mary."

"I have to, for he is married to Emma, and that is the end of it. Oh, what is it about us Ardmores that we love so foolishly? First there was poor Rory and his entanglement with Fleur, and now me. As for Jamie, well, he has never loved wisely and sometimes I think he never will."

Lauren didn't know what to say.

Mary wiped her eyes again and then gave a sheepish smile. "This won't do, or I'll have horrid red eyes at the ball tonight."

Lauren remembered the fan. "I almost forgot the reason I came here. This is for you."

The diamonds on Mary's finger flashed as she took the fan and opened it, and her breath caught with delight as she saw the scenes painted on it. "Oh, how lovely! And such magnificent painting! Whoever made this is an artist indeed."

"I'm glad you like it."

"I can't possibly accept, for you must love it dearly."

"I can always get another, and I really do want you to have it."

"Thank you, Miss Maitland. For everything."

"I haven't done anything."

Mary smiled. "You have. You've listened to me. It's a relief to have unburdened myself."

"If I can help at all . . ."

"Thank you."

Lauren left her then, and returned to her own room. She was now more determined than ever to do what she could to help Lady Mary Ardmore find true happiness. Something had to be done!

15

THE sun was beginning to set as the ball commenced. Music echoed over the loch—sometimes the refined notes of the orchestra and sometimes the stirring skirl of bagpipes—and added to both was the laughter and witty conversation of the guests as they applied themselves to the business of enjoying such an elegant occasion in surroundings that were both romantic and steeped in history.

No setting could have been more perfect for the eighteenth-birthday celebrations of a young Scottish lady from so ancient and revered a family, and no one present could honestly have found anything to complain about regarding the sumptuousness of the decorations or the lavishness of the hospitality. Glenvale Castle was at its magnificent best, and few grand houses south of the border could have rivaled it tonight.

Lauren's preparations were almost complete. She wore an ice-green taffeta gown that swept low over her breasts, and there were pearls in her ears and around her throat. Her hair was twisted up into a knot at the back of her head, with a wreath of leaves encircling the knot. Her arms were sheathed in long white gloves and she carried a white silk fan embroidered in gold.

She would already have left to go down to the ball had not Peggy noticed that a pin had come loose in her hair, and she was therefore still seated before the dressing table when Hester tapped at the door and came in, having pronounced herself much better after her rest. She wore sapphires and a silver lace gown. A jeweled comb sparkled in her dark hair and she brought with her the fresh flowery fragrance of lilies of the valley. There was no doubt that she looked better than she had earlier, but she couldn't fully disguise the fact that she was unwell. However, it wasn't the pallor beneath the rouge which caught Lauren's immediate attention, but rather her urgent excitement.

"Lauren, I must speak to you! In private," she added, glancing at Peggy.

The maid swiftly put the finishing touches to Lauren's hair and then withdrew. As the door closed behind her, Lauren turned at the dressing table to face her cousin. "Whatever is it?" she asked curiously.

"Alex believes he's remembered where he saw Emma and it's so astonishing that I simply had to come to tell you straightaway." Hester sat on the edge of the bed. "Lauren, when he was in the billiard room earlier with all the other gentlemen, he happened to read something in a newspaper he found lying on a chair. It was a recent paper and there was an item tucked away in a corner inside which he managed to read before Jamie called him away. When he returned the newspaper was gone, and he now thinks Jamie took it."

"Took it deliberately, you mean?"

"Alex believes so, on reflection. Anyway, the article was about Robert du Maurier having died in prison, and—"

"Who's he?" Lauren interrupted.

"Oh, of course, you won't have heard of him. It was quite a *cause célèbre* about four years ago. Du Maurier and his wife ran a rigged gaming hell in Brighton—at least, it turned out that it was rigged—but at the time it was simply very popular among gentlemen who liked to wager on whatever they could. Du Maurier, who was an Irishman from Dublin in spite of his French name, was always seen on the premises, but his wife seldom was; indeed, very few people knew what she looked like.

Anyway, before he knew me, Alex went there with some acquaintances and on that occasion Mrs. du Maurier *did* appear, albeit fleetingly. He is convinced that she and Emma are one and the same, and Fitz *did* meet Emma in Dublin, if you recall."

Lauren stared at her.

Hester leaned forward, her eyes bright with excitement. "The whole point of this is that when du Maurier was arrested, his wife escaped. Lauren, if Alex is right, and Emma is really Mrs. du Maurier, it means that Fitz cannot possibly be legally married to her. You see, the newspaper specifically stated that the late Mr. du Maurier's *wife* is still being sought for her part in running the club. If there had been a divorce, then she would have been referred to as his *former* wife. Now, I don't for a moment imagine that any of this is known to Fitz, which means that she deceived him and committed bigamy, and if Jamie did deliberately remove the newspaper, then maybe he is aware of her true identity. It's all guesswork of course . . . "

Lauren rose slowly to her feet. "Yes, and based upon whether or not Alex has remembered correctly. After all, he only saw this Mrs. du Maurier once."

Hester sighed. "I know, but he's convinced about it. If only we could prove it."

"Proof is essential," Lauren agreed, going to the window and staring out at the dazzling sunset on the loch. "Hester, there is something I must tell you. It concerns Lady Mary."

"Oh?"

"You know I said earlier that I believed she was in love with Fitz?"

"Yes."

"Well, she is; she has admitted it to me."

"Does he love her?"

Lauren faced her. "It seems so, but he is doing the noble thing. Hester, this really mustn't go any further, for if it does—"

Hester interrupted a little reproachfully. "Lauren, I haven't breathed a word, not even to Alex when he told me his suspicions about Emma being Mrs. du Maurier. You asked for my discretion, and you have it completely."

"Forgive me, I didn't mean . . . " Lauren's voice died away a little awkwardly. "It's just that I did promise her she could confide in me."

"And so she can. In fact, she can confide in both of us, if she wishes, for we can both be trusted to show every discretion." Hester smiled and got up from the bed. "Oh, if *only* we could prove Emma's guilt, then maybe Mary and Fitz would have a chance of happiness, for he would be free to pay open attention to her."

Lauren turned from the window. "We decided earlier that we'd have to think of something, and now we must apply ourselves even more."

"Inspiration hasn't descended upon me yet," Hester said ruefully.

"Nor upon me." Lauren looked at her. "How is the queasiness now, by the way?"

"Still there a little. I feel wishy-washy and lackluster."

"Are you sure you're up to this ball?"

"Miss a ball? Me? Lauren Maitland, the day has yet to dawn." Hester smiled.

"Neither Alex nor I want to have you swooning away."

"I won't."

"You must promise me one thing," Lauren fixed her with a determined look.

"Yes?"

"The moment you feel even vaguely odd, you must say so, and either he or I will accompany you to your room and stay with you."

"Lauren—"

"Your word, Cousin."

Hester sighed crossly. "Oh, very well." She glanced at

the clock on the mantelshelf. "Come on, we should go down."

When they reached the staircase, they had to pause halfway down to gaze in delight at the dazzling scene that greeted them. The pipers on the gallery were playing the first part of a reel, a strathspey, and there was much merriment as a sea of dancers whirled to the music. The ladies were beautiful in jewels, silks, and plumes, and some of them also sported tartan silk scarves which were pinned over their shoulders with glittering brooches. The gentlemen were either in formal black evening coats and white silk trousers, or in dashing highland dress, with kilts, sporrans, black velvet jackets, and spills of lace at their throats and cuffs. The ice blocks were already lending coolness to the air, and champagne was flowing freely, as was refreshing lime cup for those who preferred a less alcoholic drink. But above all there was whisky, some of it in punch, some neat from the decanter. Nothing could have been more breathtaking than the flowers which had taken so long to arrange, and no ballroom could have set off such a very Scottish occasion more fittingly.

Lauren's attention was drawn to one of the sets, where she noticed Emma and Fitz dancing together. Emma looked very lovely in midnight blue satin and diamonds. She laughed as she moved, but her glances were for Jamie, not her husband. Rory's brother stood at the side of the floor, a glass of whisky in his hand as he watched his mistress. He wore highland dress and it suited him well. Lauren paid him scant attention, except to hope he'd forgotten requesting her to honor him with a dance, for it was Emma she was really interested in. Was it really possible that Emma was the infamous Mrs. du Maurier? And was it also possible that Jamie knew? Maybe he'd taken the newspaper innocently, or maybe it had been very intentional indeed, a precaution against Alex's memory being jogged about what he'd once seen in Brighton.

Mary stood with Rory at the foot of the staircase, receiving the guests. She was enchanting in rose silk, and she wore a blue-and-green Ardmore tartan silk scarf which was fixed to her waist and then over her shoulder with a gold brooch. Lauren couldn't help noticing with some pleasure that she carried the fan from Boston.

Like Jamie, Rory wore highland dress, but Lauren thought it suited him far more. He had the looks, build, and presence to carry off such a flamboyant costume, and of all the gentlemen present who wore similar clothes, he was by far the most dashing.

Hester nudged her suddenly. "Don't look now, but the she-cat of Maxby is coming down the stairs behind us," she hissed.

With that Isabel spoke. "Why, if it isn't Mrs. Kingston and Miss Maitland, and both of you looking so very charming."

They turned reluctantly. She was wearing crimson silk, sheer and low cut, and her beauty was very predatory as she halted. Her russet hair was piled up on top of her head and threaded with diamonds, and more diamonds flashed at her throat. She smiled a little, snapping her fan open and shut as she ignored Hester and gave Lauren her full attention. There was no trace now of the false remorse she'd shown that afternoon after managing to drop the locket into the well; on the contrary, she was flagrantly hostile.

"I have a warning for you, Miss Maitland," she said softly, her voice only just audible above the sound of the bagpipes.

"A warning?"

"For your own good, of course."

"Oh, of course," Lauren replied, reminding herself that this woman had lost Rory and therefore held no trumps.

"You would be advised to pay heed, Miss Maitland, or it will be the worst for you."

Hester was incensed. "Isabel, is it your habit to issue threats?"

Isabel took no notice. "My advice is that you make arrangements to leave Glenvane without delay. Indeed it would be sensible if you left first thing in the morning."

Hester was aghast. "Isabel!"

Lauren met the malevolent bluebell gaze. "And why should I do that, Lady Maxby?" she asked coolly.

"Because, as I've already said, it will be the worst for you if you don't," Isabel replied.

Hester gave her a contemptuous look. "This does you no credit, Isabel."

Isabel's eyes flickered briefly toward her. "This has nothing to do with you, Hester; it is solely between your cousin and me. Suffice it that if Miss Maitland insists upon remaining here where she isn't wanted, then she will suffer the consequences. She has been warned." Flicking her fan open again, she swept on past them and down the staircase, where she made much of greeting Rory. She presented her cheek to be kissed, she smiled, and she dazzled, but still she suffered the humiliation of seeing how his gaze was easily drawn away toward Lauren.

He left his former mistress and came lightly up to where Lauren stood with Hester, and after greeting the latter with every courtesy, his eyes became very warm and dark as he bowed over Lauren's hand.

"You look exquisite," he murmured, then he gave them both an arm to descend to the hall just as the reel ended and the pipers were replaced by the orchestra for a waltz.

Lauren barely had time to speak to Mary before Rory invited her to dance. He whirled her away on to the crowded floor, his arm around her waist as they waltzed. She was floating. The orchestra's playing faded away into the background, and it was as if they were alone, dancing on an empty floor. An electricity passed between them, tingling to their very fingertips, and she was sure that there was an aura surrounding them, glowing and setting them apart. Surely everyone could see, everyone could tell how much in love they were. But as the sounds of the ball returned, and reality swept over her, she saw that no one was looking. No one else had seen that shimmering halo.

Knowing the waltz would have to end and they would have to part again, Rory tightened his arm around her waist. "I love you, Miss Maitland from Massachusetts," he murmured.

She smiled up into his eyes. "I love you, too," she whispered.

"It would be reprehensible if I were to ask you to dance again straightaway, and so I must contain myself, but I *will* ask you again. You have my word upon it."

"I trust it will be another waltz?"

He smiled. "What else can it be when I need to hold you?"

Her fingers curled in his, and they danced a little more before he spoke again. "What say you to my highland togs?"

"You are very splendid, sir."

"I trust you mean the compliment."

"Oh, I do, my lord," she breathed, gazing up at him. "I have found you irresistible each time we've met, but tonight, in your kilt and lace, I find you even more attractive. I desire you, Lord Glenvane, and I am not ashamed to say it."

"Oh, Lauren, would you have me make love to you right here and now?" he whispered, unable to help pulling her even closer.

She wanted to laugh her happiness aloud, to fling her head back and exult in the sheer rapture of knowing he loved her. This was joy of a kind she'd thought lost to her forever on the day Jonathan had died, and it was hers again now, here at Glenvane Castle on this most wonderful of nights. She had crossed the Atlantic with such reluctance, not wanting to set foot in Britain, but, oh, how glad she was that she'd come!

All too soon the waltz was over and they had to part. It was hard to turn away from each other, but they knew they must, for tonight was Mary's night and they didn't want to draw any attention away from her.

For the next hour or more Lauren danced with a succession of partners, although not Jamie, who did indeed appear to have forgotten her. She was even enticed into a set for a rather too lively highland fling. She wasn't alone in not knowing the steps, and the resultant shambles caused a great deal of hilarity. It was after the fling, when she'd retreated a little breathlessly from the floor, that she was at last reunited with Rory.

She didn't know he was there until suddenly he caught her hand and without anyone knowing drew her into the adjacent dining room, where supper would soon be served. They hurried across to the door on to the garden terrace, and then out into the warm night air. Lanterns twinkled everywhere, even on rowing boats out on the loch, and the gardens were like fairyland itself as Rory led her away from the castle and down to the water's edge. There were other guests enjoying the night, but no one paid any attention to anyone else, and no one saw Lord Glenvane taking Miss Maitland in his arms to kiss her on the lips with a passion which consumed them both.

16

IT was a long kiss, savored to the full, and neither of them was conscious of anything else in the word except the ecstasy flooding their veins. Their hearts beat swiftly, pounding together as breathless desires swept them along.

Lauren's very soul longed to capitulate, and she didn't know how long she could endure without the slaking of the unbearable thirst he'd aroused. She wanted him, and the feeling knew no bounds of chastity or propriety. Her true sensuality had been awakened at last, and she knew herself as never before. She wasn't meant to be prim and correct, always mindful of etiquette and manners; she was meant to share voluptuous passions with this one man. This one man . . .

He tore his lips away and crushed her close, whispering against her hair. "Dear God, I cannot go on like this. I need you, Lauren, and now that I know you feel the same way, there is only one course to be taken."

"Course?" she breathed, still lost in the beguiling sensations which swirled through her mind and body.

"Mere seduction will not suffice, for I must have you completely. You must be properly mine, and I yours." He cupped her face in his hands, his eyes bright in the lanternlit darkness. "You must be my bride, Lauren; you must be mistress of both the castle and its lord."

"Marry you?" she breathed, caught off guard.

He smiled, his thumb moving softly over her cheek. "Does such a prospect hold no attraction for you?"

"It's not that . . . "

"What then?"

"I know how determined you were never to take another bride."

He searched her eyes. "Lauren, I know that you aren't another Fleur, for you are all that is honest and true. I also know that after all that has passed between us today, we must never allow anything to part us. We were made to be together, my darling, and I want to cherish you as you should be cherished. I want you to share my love, my title, my fortune, and my future, and so I ask you to be my bride."

"Oh, Rory—"

He brushed his lips softly over hers. "Be my countess, Lauren," he whispered.

"But there is so much to think of . . . " His lips were distracting, denying her the will to reason.

"What is there to think of, except that we love each other and are free to marry?"

Her wits seemed to have been scattered into the night. "But my home is thousands of miles away, and I belong there, not here."

"Look into my eyes and say that, Lauren. Glenvane has been waiting for you, and you should be its mistress."

She met his gaze and then turned to look at the brilliantly illuminated castle.

He stood behind her, his arms lovingly around her waist as he whispered a line of a poem in her ear. "If thou woud'st view fair Glenvane aright, go visit it by the pale moonlight." He gave a low laugh. "I know the poet was actually writing about Melrose Abbey, and that the ring around tonight's moon quite clearly heralds a dire change in the weather, but the sentiments are appropriate to Glenvane, don't you agree?"

Glenvane in the pale moonlight? With Rory Ardmore's arms around her? She leaned her head back against his shoulder. "Yes, I agree," she murmured.

"Can you leave this place and its master, my darling?" he asked softly.

She closed her eyes. Leave? She was bound to Glenvane forever. "No, I can't," she replied softly.

"Will you marry me?" he asked again.

"Yes. Oh, yes . . ." She turned back into his arms, and a searing joy seized her as he crushed his lips to hers.

How long they remained there by the water's edge she didn't know, for the minutes passed in a succession of tender words and loving kisses, but at last they knew they must return, and as they made their way back up through the illuminated gardens, Lauren knew that she had made the right decision. Nothing and no one mattered to her more than Rory Ardmore, and to leave him would be like leaving her very heart.

As they reached the terrace by the dining room, he drew her into the shadows for a last kiss, and then he gazed tenderly into her eyes. "Tonight is Mary's night, but tomorrow is ours, and I will tell the world that I have won your hand. The niceties of taking our time have no place in the way I feel, and I cannot bear the thought of having to conduct myself formally whenever I am with you. I need to touch you, hold you, tell you how much I love you, and I cannot do that if we observe all the usual tedious rules of waiting for a suitable length of time, *et cetera, et cetera*."

"I feel the same, but are you quite, quite sure you want to marry me?" she whispered.

"Without any shadow of doubt. Are you quite certain as well?"

"Yes."

"Then it is sealed."

A group of guests emerged on to the terrace and they drew apart. Shortly after they rejoined the rest of the ball, and he was obliged to resume his duties as host. The last thing Lauren felt like was dancing with anyone but him, and so she politely declined a gentleman who invited her for a polonaise. Instead she sought Hester.

She found her with a group of other ladies on a sofa near the staircase, and Hester was glad of the excuse to leave them.

"Oh, I'm so glad you've come, for I'm bored beyond belief by all that chatter about fripperies. I swear that if I hear one more suggestion as to how one can wear lace, I will suggest wearing lace stays and nothing else!"

"Mrs. Kingston, I'm shocked."

"Oh, perhaps I'm just finding them tiresome because I'm not feeling quite the tippy."

"Have you had enough of the ball?" Lauren asked with swift concern.

"No, not exactly, for I've been giving a certain matter my full consideration," Hester replied mysteriously, nodding toward Mary, who stood nearby with a large group of companions. "I've been watching her, Lauren, and although she's putting on a brave face, I can tell she's utterly wretched. She tries not to look at Fitz, and he tries not to look at her, but they can't help themselves. It's so unfair, especially as Emma is what stands between them, and not only is she horridly unfaithful but she may not even be legally his wife anyway!"

"Don't say it too loudly," Lauren said, glancing around a little uneasily, for it seemed that Hester had spoken rather vehemently.

"Oh, I'm sorry, it's just that I feel so angry about it."

"I know; I feel the same."

"It would be good if we could find some proof that Emma is really Mrs. du Maurier," Hester mused.

"Proof? Such as?"

"I don't know. Anything." Hester drew a long breath. "There won't be anyone in her room now," she said slowly.

Lauren drew back. "Go there and search it? Is that what you're suggesting?"

"Why not?"

"What if we're caught?"

"Who will catch us? Everyone is down here, and if

Emma's maid is still there, we won't go in anyway. Isn't it worth a try? Isn't poor Mary worth helping?"

Lauren followed her gaze toward Mary again, and she remembered how touchingly sad Rory's sister had been that very afternoon. "Yes, she's worth helping."

"Then shall we sally forth on our stratagem?"

"Now?"

"When better?" Hester tapped her fan against Lauren's arm. "Come, Coz, it's positively our duty to help true love upon its proper course."

"Very well, let's to it," Lauren replied with sudden resolve, and the cousins linked arms to walk to the staircase.

"By the way," Hester murmured as they ascended, "I have to say that you were quite obviously telling the truth about you and Rory. I vow I thought he would eat your hand when you arrived at the ball, and then, when you danced at waltz together, I feared he would devour the rest of you as well! You've snapped him up, Coz, and right from under the noses of half of London's eligible ladies. If I were of a wagering nature, I would lay odds that you won't return to Boston to live. No, indeed."

Lauren smiled but said nothing. Time enough later to relate what had happened by the loch a short while ago.

They hurried away from the staircase, and the sounds of the ball became more muffled behind them. There was hardly anyone to be seen in the passages, for everyone was either at the ball or enjoying the lesser festivities in the servants' hall; at least, that was what the two conspirators hoped as they made their way to the room Emma shared with Fitz. At the door they paused. Was Emma's maid inside? After a moment Lauren decided to make certain by knocking. There was no response, and so she knocked again, louder this time, but still there was no response. At that she took her courage in both hands and turned the handle. The room beyond was almost in darkness.

Hester peered in as well. "It's too dark to see properly," she whispered. "I'll go to our room and light a candle with Alex's lucifers. I won't be a moment." She hurried away.

Lauren lingered in the doorway, fearing that at any moment one of the guests would return for something forgotten and see her. At last Hester hastened back again, shielding a lighted candle with her hand. As she reached Emma's room, her steps faltered and she thrust the candle into Lauren's hand and then leaned back against the door jamb. Her face had suddenly gone very pale, and an anxious Lauren could see that she was trembling.

"Hester?"

"I'll be all right in a moment. I tried to hurry too much, and got myself all of a pother." Hester smiled a little ruefully. "I felt so much better that I quite forgot how unwell I was earlier today," she explained.

"Perhaps we should abandon this exercise—" Lauren began. But Hester shook her head.

"No, now that we've thought of it, we must carry it through. I loathe Emma for what she's doing to Fitz. Even if she isn't Mrs. du Maurier, and is legally married to him after all, she's still breaking her marriage vows by taking Jamie as her lover."

"I could not agree more," Lauren replied with feeling. She glanced back along the passage before going into the room.

Hester followed, and they closed the door behind them.

Lauren turned to face her. "You stay by the door."

"But—"

"No buts, Mrs. Kingston. You're not feeling well, and so you must stay quietly by the door and listen for anyone coming."

"Keep watch?"

"Yes."

Hester sighed. "Oh, very well."

Lauren glanced around the shadowy room. It was a large chamber, larger than hers, and even in the dim light she could see that it was richly gilded. There was gilding on the ceiling plaster work, on the painted paneling on the walls, and on the heavily carved bed, but apart from this the predominant color was silver-gray. The curtains hadn't been drawn across the window, which stood open to the summer night, and she could hear the ball more clearly now. When she went to the window to look out, she saw that the castle wall dropped directly into the loch close to the dining room terrace and to the gardens where she and Rory had been together a short while before.

There were still guests strolling beneath the lanterns, and she knew that if anyone glanced up at the window they might notice the flickering candlelight within. Swiftly she drew the curtains and then glanced around the room once more before going to the dressing table. She put the candle down to open the first drawer, not really knowing what she was looking for, and certainly not expecting to find anything incriminating, for if Emma really were Mrs. du Maurier, it was hardly likely she'd leave proof where it might be happened upon.

She went through all the drawers and found only the things one would expect. Then, just as she was about to start on the wardrobe, Hester gave a startled hiss from the door.

"Someone's coming!"

Lauren snatched up the candle, and as one she and Hester dashed behind the curtains at the window. Hester immediately made to blow the candle out, but Lauren swiftly tossed it outside into the loch, for an extinguished candle had too distinctive and noticeable a smell, and if anyone entered the room, they would know immediately that someone else was there.

Hearts beating anxiously, they waited in the darkness, praying that whoever it was would walk straight past the room. But their prayers were not answered, for to their dismay the door opened and someone came in.

Hearts pounding in their breasts, Lauren and Hester peeped secretly through a provident crack in the curtains. They saw not one but two figures briefly outlined against the brightly lit passage as they entered the room. Then the door closed once more, but not before the cousins had recognized Jamie and Emma.

For a moment the room remained in darkness, but then a lucifer flared into light as Jamie lit a candle on the mantelpiece. Emma went to him then, slipping her arms around his waist and reaching up to kiss him on the lips. For a moment or so he returned the kiss, but then he pulled sharply away.

"No, not here . . . "

"Scruples, my darling?" Emma gave him a seductive laugh.

"Possibly. Look, Emma, why come here, to this room? If we must be alone as you wish, then surely my room would be more wise? Fitz might miss you and come looking." He glanced uneasily toward the door, obviously exceedingly ill at ease.

"Fitz?" Emma was greatly amused. "My darling, he is too busy feasting his eyes upon your little sister. Oh, don't look so shocked, for he is far too noble to do anything but look. Why, he's even too noble to tell me he regrets marrying me. He's guessed that I'm being unfaithful."

Jamie was appalled. "Fitz knows about me?"

"You may rest easy, for he has no idea. So, you see, we can be quite private here." Emma moved closer to him again.

"I'd still feel safer in my room."

"With old Dodd suffering from a surfeit of rich food in the adjacent chamber? Come now, Jamie, moaning and groaning he may be, but his hearing is still as sharp as ever, and you know he has a reputation second to none when it comes to scandalmongering. There never was a nosier old tabby than he—I vow he'd put any gathering of dowagers to shame."

Jamie nodded. "You're right, I suppose."

"Of course I am." She put her arms around his neck. "So why waste time in chattering, when we could be . . ."

Her voice died away on a suggestive note, and Lauren and Hester looked at each other in dismay, but to their relief Jamie was still far too uneasy.

He unlinked Emma's arms and moved away. "No, I can't . . ."

"What's wrong?"

"You know what's wrong."

Emma leaned back against one of the carved bedposts, her eyes shining in the candlelight as she surveyed him. "Yes, you are put out that the American creature was apparently wise to you all along."

"I don't deny it, but there is more. I'm referring to our liaison. I hate deceiving Fitz, for he is my friend, and when I think of it I'm deeply ashamed."

"You think I revel in it?"

He looked at her. "Yes, I do."

"Is your opinion of me so low?"

"I know what you are capable of."

"Given the chance, this particular leopard can change her spots," she said softly. "I want that chance, Jamie, and time is running out. You see, I fear you may be right after all, and my past may be about to catch up with me. Oh, don't look so alarmed, for no one has said anything, or even hinted. It's just that since you told me about that business with the wretched newspaper, I've noticed that Alex Kingston looks at me a little oddly. If he hasn't remembered, then he soon will, just as that American creature might suddenly recall seeing me at the Crown & Thistle."

"No one saw either of us at the inn—I've already told you that. And as for Alex remembering Brighton—"

"I know that it's an outside chance, but it's still a risk.

I remembered him because of his golden hair, so there might easily be something about me that will make him recall. Oh, Jamie, I'm so afraid of what might happen if that happens." Emma's voice caught.

Behind the curtains, Lauren and Hester exchanged glances again in the darkness. There was now no doubt in their minds that Emma was Mrs. du Maurier and that Jamie was fully acquainted with her shadowy past.

17

AROUSED to a need to reassure and protect his mistress, Jamie went to her and pulled her swiftly into her arms. "You won't be caught, my darling, for no one will ever find out about Brighton. Your secret is safe with me."

"I know you can be trusted, but I feel suddenly more vulnerable than you will ever know," Emma whispered pathetically, clinging to him as if he were her savior. "I couldn't bear to go to prison, Jamie, or maybe even be transported . . . "

"That will never happen," he breathed, his lips moving against her hair.

"But it might." Her voice dropped to a pleading whisper. "Please change your mind again, my darling. Let us carry out Isabel's suggestion, and—"

"I can't." Abruptly he released her.

"Is your brother more important to you than me?" Emma challenged, a wounded note entering her voice.

"No, you know that isn't so."

"I don't know any such thing, Jamie. All I know is that you are putting his feelings before my chance of happiness."

"We could be happy together without resorting to theft."

Behind the curtains, Lauren's eyes widened with surprise. Theft? What were they talking about?

Emma's tone was crisp. "There is no happiness in

penury, my darling, as you must concede, given your recent scramble to stay out of jail."

"But to do as we first planned would be to . . . to . . . "

"Bring back dear Rory's most painful memories? I hardly think that his temporary discomfort is worth putting before our well-being, my love. Oh, he will be sunk in gloom for a short while, but that is all, and after that he will hardly notice what has been done."

"Hardly notice? Emma, he will be devastated, believe me. Haven't you observed him this past day or so? If he were led to believe that history was repeating itself—"

"It will pass," she insisted, seizing his hands and making him look into her urgent eyes. "Jamie, we must do it while we have the chance, for if we don't, then it may be too late, and I will pay a very high price indeed. Besides, why should Rory be considered? Simply because he has belatedly deigned to hand out his largesse? For that you are prepared to put *me* in jeopardy?"

"That's hardly fair, Emma."

"Isn't it? Rory could afford to bail you out a thousand times over, and yet he cut up rough this time. Now, because it suits him for some reason, he has decided to be benevolent again, and you are so pathetically grateful that—"

"You may view it as pathetic gratitude, Emma, but I prefer to regard it as a timely rescue. I don't want to continue as I have been; I want to change."

Emma breathed out with a slow smile. "Ah, so you and I are the same, are we not?" she murmured. "I want the chance to change, and so do you. If we carry out Isabel's plan, then we will both achieve what we wish for so much. Please, Jamie, do it for me."

"Emma . . . "

"If you love me, truly love me, you will put me first," she begged, moving toward him again and coiling her arms around him. She was spellbindingly beautiful in the gently swaying candlelight. Jamie would have had to be made of ice to resist, but he wasn't made of ice; he was in Emma's seductive thrall. As she raised her lips toward his, he gave a groan of capitulation and swept her roughly into his arms, kissing her as if he would consume her completely.

Lauren watched and saw how weak he was. Of the two, it was Emma who was strong. She held sway over him, and even though he clearly wished to break free, he was trapped by his desires. He wanted to turn his back on everything, but she was temptation beyond endurance and she wasn't slave to her senses as he was to his. Emma was cool and calculating, determined to have her own way at all costs. His conscience subsided, and he was at her bidding once more.

Emma's body curved richly against his as she whispered to him. "It's agreed, then? We do as Isabel wants?"

"Yes." The single word of consent was dragged from him.

She was exultant. "My darling . . . "

"Emma, when we start anew, it must be different."

"Oh, it will be, my dearest, I promise." Emma was prepared to concede anything—for the time being, at least.

He kissed her, lingering over the moment as if he wished it would never end, but now that she had won him over, she knew only too well how to keep his desires at fever pitch. She drew back. "We must make our plans."

"We already have. We will proceed as we decided before."

She smiled. "Exactly as then?"

He hesitated but then nodded. "Yes."

"To the last glittering detail?"

"I've said so."

"I just have to be absolutely sure, Jamie, for if your conscience is likely to reassert itself—"

"It won't. I've given my word, and that is the end of it."

"Good, for with so much going on tonight, we won't be noticed."

"Tonight?"

She looked at him. "That is what we decided before, and I think it is the best plan."

"I know, but the weather is changing, and there'll be a storm before the night is out."

"The weather is excellent," she replied, echoing Lauren's own words on the loch that morning.

"If you'd lived here all your life, Emma, you'd know the signs as I do. The sea is in the air."

"You sound like a country wisewoman," Emma said scornfully. "Oh, come on, Jamie, forget your weather divining and agree to do it tonight."

"Emma, it may be really hazardous," he warned.

"Please, Jamie," she interrupted softly, pressing against him once more.

He couldn't deny her anything; reluctantly he nodded. "Very well, if you are absolutely set on it."

Pleased to have achieved her way yet again, Emma smiled, but then seemed to remember something. "We mustn't forget our side of the bargain."

"Bargain?"

"Isabel thought of it all, and did not do so purely out of the goodness of her heart. She must benefit too."

"Emma—"

"She's my friend, and in difficulty because of the Maitland *chienne*."

Lauren stiffened in the darkness.

Jamie gave a brief laugh. "Emma, the advent of Miss Maitland isn't of any consequence where Rory's feelings for Isabel are concerned. His affections had been on the wane for some time before he'd even heard of Lauren Maitland!"

"She is convinced he can be won back, and I believe she is right."

"Emma—"

"Please, Jamie. It's all very simple, and may even give

us more time. If the one item is found where it shouldn't be, then the inference will be that everything else will be discovered nearby, and while the Maitland creature is blamed for everything, we will be able to cover the miles."

Jamie didn't reply, and once again it was plain he was reluctant to do as she wished. Emma decided not to give him the opportunity to back away, and quickly she went to extinguish the candle. "There is no time like the present," she said. "Everyone is at the ball, and the coast will be clear."

"If there were any other way—" he began.

"There isn't," she interrupted bluntly, then she softened. "Oh, Jamie, it will be all done in a few minutes, and then we can return to the ball. For the moment anyway."

"It all feels so very wrong."

She laughed a little in the darkness. "My poor darling. But never mind, for soon it will all be behind us, and we'll be free to do as we please."

They went out, and as the door closed behind them, Lauren and Hester stepped cautiously from behind the curtains. The air was heavy with the smell of candlesmoke as they looked at each other.

"What do you suppose they're up to?" Lauren asked.

"I don't know, but it sounds a little sinister. They mean to steal something, that's clear enough." Hester sighed. "Do you know, I almost feel sorry for Jamie, for he quite clearly has reservations."

"Not enough to haul him back from the brink. He's being led by the nose, and my opinion of him has now sunk even lower. He certainly doesn't have my sympathy," Lauren replied.

Hester glanced around again. "Well, we aren't going to find anything here, so perhaps it would be more sensible to go back to the ball and keep an eye on them there."

Lauren nodded reluctantly. "Yes, I suppose so. Somehow I feel we should tell Rory, but I don't know what to say."

"You can hardly tell him you *think* his brother is about to steal something," Hester pointed out. "I'm afraid that we'll just have to hold our tongues for the moment, until something becomes a little more clear. Then we can tell Rory."

"They mean to implicate me in whatever it is. Hester, I'm a little afraid—"

Hester squeezed her arm. "We'll be on our guard. Come on, let's go."

They slipped out and closed the door behind them, before hurrying back to the ball, where, if they had but known it, disaster awaited for Hester. She felt the queasiness return as she and Lauren were descending the staircase, but this time it was far worse than before, and was accompanied by dizziness. Her steps faltered and she gave a gasp as she tried to hold on to the bannister to steady herself, but consciousness was deserting her. Her legs lost their strength and the lights and noise of the ball began to recede into darkness. Lauren screamed as her cousin pitched down the staircase, tumbling down like a puppet to lie motionless at the bottom.

The ball came to a shocked standstill. The pipers had been playing, but now their music faltered on discordant notes, and everyone turned. Gasps rippled around the suddenly silent room as all eyes flew to Hester's still figure.

Lauren hurried down the staircase, her skirts rustling as she reached the bottom and knelt anxiously beside her cousin. "Hester? Can you hear me?" she cried, her voice catching with alarm.

But still Hester just lay there, her eyes closed and her face deathly pale. Alex hastened distractedly over and tried to gather his unconscious wife into his arms to carry her up to her room, but Rory halted him.

"Have a care, Alex, for she may have broken bones," he said gently, and then knelt down next to Hester to see if he could tell.

The guests pressed anxiously around, and there was very little sound as Rory looked at Alex again. "I think it's all right to move her. Take her to your room, and I will send someone for the doctor in Dumbarton. I fear it may take some time, as there is no guarantee that he will be immediately available—"

"Just see that he comes as soon as humanly possible," Alex interrupted, scooping Hester up from the floor and beginning to carry her up the staircase. Lauren immediately hurried with him, and Rory straightened, turning to Fitz, who stood nearby.

"Mary's ball mustn't end like this."

"I'll see that it doesn't," Fitz replied, reaching out to take Mary's hand and then leading her through the gathering to the center of the floor. He nodded at the pipers, and immediately they struck up once more. As the jaunty notes of another reel rang out over the hall, everyone moved away to form sets and commence to dance. But although the ball had been resumed, the atmosphere had changed and few really felt like going on.

Rory beckoned to a footman. "See that a rider is dispatched for Dumbarton on the fastest horse in the stables."

"Your lordship." The footman bowed, and hurried away.

Rory then made to follow Alex and Lauren up the staircase, but Isabel appeared at his side. "I will come too, Rory, for I may be of some help," she murmured.

He smiled, but shook his head. "You will be of more use to me lending your invaluable assistance down here."

Her lovely blue eyes were wide and understanding. "Possibly, but it wasn't you I was thinking of. Poor Miss Maitland looked very upset, and may need a little comfort. Oh, don't look like that, for I know that she and I haven't exactly hit it off, but maybe now is the time to put that right. I know I've lost you, and I do accept the situation, truly I do, but if we are still old friends, as I believe we are, then you must allow me the chance to make amends."

He smiled again. "As you wish," he said, offering her his arm.

But as they proceeded up the staircase, there was a glimmer of anticipation in Isabel's eyes. She wasn't a reformed character, nor was she in the least contrite; on the contrary, she was as determined as ever to win Rory back, and a moment before she had perceived Emma on the gallery. Emma had nodded, signifying that all had been accomplished, so now it was simply a matter of waiting until the time was right, at which moment the Maitland creature would rue the very day she first set eyes upon Rory Ardmore.

Lauren was still oblivious to the trap yawning so close, for Hester's accident had driven all else from her mind. Alex was distraught as he laid his wife on the bed and then took her hand to try to arouse her. Rubbing her cold fingers, he gazed anxiously at her ashen face.

"Hester? My darling, please open your eyes," he begged, his voice catching with emotion.

Lauren stood beside him and put her hand on his shoulder. "I . . . I'm sure she'll be all right, Alex," she murmured, but the words sounded lame. Hester looked so deathly, and her eyelids didn't flicker at all. If it were not for the fact that she was still breathing . . .

Rory and Isabel came quietly into the candlelit room, and Lauren's heart sank as she saw the latter. Oh, no, not now . . .

Rory came to the bedside, slipping his hand into Lauren's for a moment. "How is she?"

"There's no change at all."

"I've sent someone for the doctor, but I can't promise when he'll arrive. "It's a good two-hour ride to Dumbarton, and then he may have been called out elsewhere. We can only wait."

She nodded. "I understand. Oh, I feel so guilty."

"You? Why?"

"Yes, she hasn't been feeling well all day today, and I allowed her to talk me out of sending for the doctor earlier on. If only I'd been a little stronger."

"It's hardly your fault, and from what I know of Hester, you'd find it impossible to make her do anything she didn't want to."

Isabel reached out to touch Lauren's arm. "Is there anything I can do, Miss Maitland?" she asked, her gaze full of concern and sympathy.

"No, thank you," Lauren replied, trying not to sound as stiff and frosty as she felt.

Isabel lowered her lovely eyes for a moment. "Please accept my olive branch, Miss Maitland, for I readily admit to having been at fault in the past. But with poor Hester lying so ill, it seems unthinkable that we two should remain at odds. I have conceded defeat, and now wish to sign a peace treaty, if you will agree." She smiled.

The last thing Lauren felt like was forgiving and forgetting, for this odious creature had issued threatening ultimatums that very evening! Isabel was a chameleon, changing her color to suit the situation, and for some reason it suited her now to talk of olive branches and peace treaties. But Lauren knew that her own private reservations had no place in the proceedings at a time like this. For both Hester's and Alex's sake she would be a chameleon too.

She smiled at Isabel. "A peace treaty it is, Lady Maxby."

"Please allow me to at least secure us both a refreshing glass of lime cup, for it's very close." Isabel looked at Rory. "Do you think we're due for some thunder?"

It was a subtle way of reminding him that she, Isabel, had also lived in this part of Scotland all her life, and therefore knew as well as he how to read the changes in the weather. Lauren glanced away.

Rory went to the window and looked out at the summer night. "Yes, I'm sure so. It's been on the cards since about midday."

Isabel gave a light laugh. "I know, for I could smell the Firth of Clyde."

He glanced back at her and smiled.

Lauren felt excluded, just as Isabel intended she should. She looked toward the window and the shadowy outlines of the mountains. A bank of cloud had now concealed the moon, and she knew that all the predictions were right. Soon there would indeed be a storm, but she prayed with all her heart that it held off until the doctor arrived.

18

HESTER regained consciousness about an hour after daybreak, but was very poorly indeed, complaining of feeling very sick and aching all over. She was also very shaken by the severity of her fall, and after taking a soothing draft of orange-flower water had drifted into what appeared to be a comfortable sleep. Alex was a little reassured but was still anxious for the arrival of the doctor from Dumbarton, of whom there would not be any sign for several hours yet.

Lauren had changed out of her ballgown into a yellow-and-white gingham day dress. She was in no mood to bother with complicated coiffures, and so Peggy had simply brushed her hair loose, and tied it back with a yellow ribbon. The retreat of the sun behind a lowering sky meant that there was a noticeable coolness in the air, and so she carried a warm white woolen shawl. There was as yet no real sign of the promised storm, although thunder could be heard in the far distance and Ben Vane was from time to time enveloped in mist.

With so many other guests to consider, Rory was obliged to proceed with the entertainment and diversions already arranged, and so after breakfast he and a number of the gentlemen rode up to the moors for some grouse shooting, and the ladies adjourned to the croquet lawn, which had been laid out near the bridge. Mary did not accompany them but chose to sit in Hester's room with Lauren and Alex, which pleased Lauren considerably.

But Isabel also chose to sit in the room, which didn't please her at all.

Isabel seemed set upon being the personification of kind concern, and made so much of their new so-called friendship that Lauren found it difficult to move without finding Isabel at her elbow, or speak without Isabel being the one to respond. It was quite infuriating, but Lauren bit back the irritation, for Hester's sickroom was hardly the place to say what she really thought of dear Lady Maxby, who had apparently been plotting with Emma and Jamie to do something which would incriminate the visitor from Boston. With Isabel now behaving in such an unnerving way, Lauren wondered again if she should say anything to Rory. But Hester's advice still held good, for what could he be told? And now, with Hester herself unable to confirm or deny anything that the plotters said . . .

The doctor arrived at noon, and to everyone's relief pronounced Hester to be in no danger. There were no broken bones or any sign of internal injuries after the fall. And after examining the unfortunate Sir Sydney Dodd as well, the doctor declared that both invalids were suffering the consequences of the dubious fare served by the Crown & Thistle. In his opinion the grouse had probably been hung for far too long, and the ill humors present in them had been transferred to the unfortunates who had dined upon them. There was nothing for it but to wait for the ill humors to be finally expelled, and in the meantime both patients must rest as much as possible. They were not to be subjected to any anxiety or noise, and frequent drafts of orange-flower water were recommended. Only if stomach pains were complained of was laudanum to be administered, and then sparingly. Hester knew very little of his diagnosis, for she slept throughout most of his examination.

After issuing his sterling medical advice, the doctor immediately started back for Dumbarton. As he urged the refreshed horse out of the courtyard, he passed a traveling carriage that was just arriving. It was a splendid vehicle, with a coat of arms on its gleaming gray-lacquered doors, and it was conveying a very late guest, a gentleman whose presence was to have a devastating effect upon Lauren's happiness. He was shown up to his room, and after changing adjourned to the dining room to partake of some excellent cold pigeon pie and Bordeaux wine.

As Hester continued to sleep, Mary decided that it would be most agreeable if those around the bedside went to the solar to enjoy a dish of hot chocolate. Alex could not be persuaded to leave his wife, but although Lauren didn't want to go anywhere with Isabel, she knew that to refuse would be churlish, and so the three ladies left the bedroom together. Lauren was soon to wish she had never left Hester's side; indeed she was to wish many things before the next dreadful hour was over.

Before entering the solar, Isabel suddenly remembered something she wanted from her room and hurried away, promising to rejoin the others in a moment or so. This she did, although before sitting down she went to the window behind Lauren's sofa to look out over the loch for a moment. It was as she did this that, unseen, she placed Lauren's reticule upon the arm of the sofa. Lauren's attention was on Mary, and she didn't notice anything amiss.

Everything commenced reasonably enough, with the three sitting down with their chocolate and debating whether or not the thunderstorm would eventually descend upon Glenvane. This led to the observation that the grouse shooting and croquet playing would come to grief if it did, and to Isabel remarking that Jamie and Emma would also get a drenching.

Lauren looked swiftly at her. "A drenching?"

"Why, yes. They've gone out for a drive in his cabriolet, and I do not believe the hood is very efficient."

Mary sipped her chocolate. "I didn't know they'd gone out on their own. Have they been gone long?"

"Oh, I don't really know," Isabel replied vaguely, but her glance slid briefly toward Lauren's reticule. It was a glance which Lauren failed to intercept.

Isabel put her chocolate aside and got up. "Maybe they're on their way back to the castle now," she murmured, crossing toward the window behind Lauren again. As she did so, she contrived to knock the reticule to the floor. It fell, spilling its contents over the carpet.

"Oh, dear, I'm so sorry!" Isabel cried.

Lauren looked blankly at the reticule. How on earth had it come from her room? She hadn't brought it. Puzzled and a little uneasy, she bent to gather the spilled contents, but Isabel did so first.

"Oh, Miss Maitland, you must think me the most clumsy creature on earth. I—" Isabel's voice broke off on a startled gasp, and slowly she straightened.

Mary looked swiftly at her. "What is it? What's wrong?"

Isabel seemed at a loss for words, and could only point to the items that had fallen out of the reticule. There, gleaming gold among them, was the locket from the Glenvane jewel box.

Shaken, Lauren stared at it, as did Mary, and then Isabel gave a light laugh as she retrieved it. "Has Rory made a declaration and sealed it with a gift, Miss Maitland?"

"I—" Lauren broke off before really replying. What could she say? Yes, that a declaration had been made, but no, the locket had nothing to do with it?

Isabel spoke again. "Have you nothing to say, Miss Maitland?"

"Er—no, Lady Maxby, Lord Glenvane did not give me the locket; indeed I have no idea how it came to be in my reticule. As it happens, I don't even know how my reticule came to be here in this room, for I didn't bring it." No, dear Isabel brought it! Too late she saw how the sleight of hand had been achieved, and too late she began to understand what Emma and Jamie had been talking about the night before. Find one item in Lauren Maitland's possession, and believe that the rest would be nearby? Had the entire jewel box been stolen? Was that how the two lovers intended to gain funds? Her mind raced as thought succeeded thought . . .

Mary looked most confused. "You—er—didn't bring it, Miss Maitland?"

"No."

"But, surely you must have done so."

"I assure you I didn't, Lady Mary. I really do not know anything about the locket, or how it came to be in my reticule. I swear that it has nothing to do with me." Lauren's cool green eyes swung accusingly toward Isabel.

Rory's former mistress was equal to the moment. Without a word she placed the locket on the table, where it lay shining almost defiantly. Lauren felt wretched as she looked at it. Oh, if only Hester were well enough to be at her side now, to confirm what they'd both overheard.

Isabel looked at Mary. "Maybe this is someone's notion of a practical joke, but it could be more serious than that. Perhaps it would be wise to see if the rest of the jewels are safe," she suggested.

Mary got up swiftly. "Yes, indeed," she replied, and hurried out.

The moment she'd gone, Lauren turned to face Isabel. "Don't think I don't know what's going on," she said quietly.

"I beg your pardon?"

"Don't play the innocent, Lady Maxby. Lady Fitzsimmons put the locket in my reticule last night, didn't she? And you have just brought the reticule here, with the sole purpose of 'finding' the locket inside it."

Isabel was taken a little by surprise, for she hadn't realized that once again Lauren was aware of too much, but she was sufficiently composed not to be ruffled. "I have no idea what you're talking about, Miss Maitland, but if Lady Fitzsimmons knows anything about the locket, I am sure she will be able to confirm as much when she and Jamie return."

"If they return," Lauren replied.

"If? Good heavens, Miss Maitland, what are you suggesting?"

"Simply that I will be very surprised indeed if Lady Mary finds the jewel box, because it has been stolen by Lady Fitzsimmons and—"

Lauren broke off, for at that moment they heard Mary's hasty footsteps returning, and then she came into the solar in a very agitated state. "The bookcase door has been forced and the jewel box has gone!" she cried.

Isabel turned swiftly toward Lauren. "You were right, Miss Maitland. How very intuitive you are, to be sure."

Mary looked at them in bewilderment. "Intuitive. I don't understand."

"Miss Maitland has just told me that she didn't think you'd find the jewel box, although her suggestion as to the thief, or thieves, is rather bizarre. It seems she has a theory that Emma and Jamie are the real culprits, although why she should think such a preposterous thing is beyond me."

Mary stared at Lauren. "Emma and Jamie?" she repeated faintly. "Why on earth do you think that, Miss Maitland?"

"I . . . I'd rather not say, not at this point," Lauren replied lamely, wishing again that Hester were at her side right now, for it was quite impossible to make any real charge without her cousin's testimony. Isabel's choice of words was particularly appropriate, for such an accusation would indeed sound preposterous in the extreme, especially as everyone in the castle was under the impression that Jamie and Emma had only gone for a drive.

Isabel affected to be a little incensed at her reticence.

"Come now, Miss Maitland, you cannot say outrageous things and then decline to expand. Unless, of course, you know full well that they are innocent, and you yourself are the guilty party."

Mary gave a gasp, and her hand crept anxiously to her throat. "Oh, Isabel, how can you suggest such a thing?" she whispered.

"As easily as Miss Maitland finds it to accuse your brother and my best friend," Isabel replied promptly.

Lauren was icily furious, as well as alarmed at the way things were going. "I am not the guilty party in this, Lady Maxby."

"No? It seems to me that you've been caught red-handed, as the saying goes. You have stolen the jewel box and have kept the locket close because it reminds you of the one that was lost down the well. No doubt the rest of the jewels are somewhere in your room."

"I refute every word you say, Lady Maxby!" Lauren cried. It was all falling horridly into place now, and she had been trapped. Who would believe she hadn't stolen the locket, perhaps even the whole jewel box? And while she stood accused, and fruitless searches were made for the rest of the Glenvane jewels, the real culprits put more and more miles between themselves and the scene of their crime. How useful an implement she was for the two unprincipled lovers and how clearly had jealous Isabel used the situation to try to turn Rory from his new love. Lauren could have wept with frustration and wretchedness, for now she also understood what painful memories he would relive as a result of all this. He would be forced to recall Fleur and how she'd stolen the same jewels for her lover. He would also have cause to wonder if Lauren Maitland, Fleur's countrywoman, had failed him by also attempting to purloin the jewels. Yes, history would indeed seem to be repeating itself, and Isabel would be there at his side, offering comfort and understanding . . .

Mary was upset and close to tears. "Did you do it, Miss Maitland?" she asked unhappily.

"Lady Mary, I swear I am innocent." Lauren looked urgently at her. This couldn't be happening. Let it be a dream . . . But it wasn't a dream, for she could see doubt in Mary's dark brown eyes.

Isabel was contemptuous. "Why should we believe you, Miss Maitland? You knew about the second locket, indeed you were with Rory in the library only yesterday, and he showed it to you."

Lauren's eyes flew toward her. "So it was you listening at the door, was it, Lady Maxby?" she fired back.

A dull flush suffused Isabel's cheeks, but she held her ground. "You knew about the locket, and you saw where the jewel box was kept."

"I didn't steal it, nor did I take the locket. Why would I?"

"To replace the one you lost," Isabel replied. "Who knows why a magpie is a thief, all one knows is that he *is* a thief."

"I am not the thief on this occasion, Lady Maxby."

"Ah, yes, I was forgetting. Emma and Jamie are the villains, are they not?" Isabel gave a cold laugh.

There were footsteps and male voices in the passage as Rory and his friends returned from their grouse shooting. Lauren's heart sank. Oh, Rory, you have to have faith in me. I didn't do it, truly I didn't.

He was laughing at something as he came in. His hair was tousled from the ride, and there was color in his cheeks as he spoke to one of his companions. "That will teach you to arrive late in the proceedings and then boast about being fresh as a daisy, Dickon," he said, and then realized there was an atmosphere in the room. His smile faded as he surveyed the faces before him.

"What is it? What's happened?"

Mary ran to him and flung himself tearfully into his arms. "Mother's jewel box has been stolen!"

"What?" He was startled as he held her close.

Isabel stepped forward. "It's true, Rory, and I rather fear that your Miss Maitland knows much more about it than she's prepared to admit."

He looked at Lauren. "What is this, Lauren?"

"I'm innocent, Rory. I swear that I am."

Isabel gave a scornful laugh. "Innocent? And yet you have some of the booty in your reticule? Oh, come now, Miss Maitland, we aren't fools." She pointed at the locket on the table.

Rory released Mary and looked at Lauren again. "Was the locket in your reticule?"

"Yes, but I deny all knowledge of it. I didn't put it there, Rory, nor did I take it or the jewel box from the library."

Seeing him hesitate, Isabel moved closer. "She wanted to replace the lost locket, Rory, and decided to take the whole jewel box. It's plain enough."

Lauren rounded upon her. "Nothing could *replace* the locket I lost, Lady Maxby, and I resent the suggestion that it could. That locket was the only tangible memory I had of someone I once loved very much, someone who has been dead for six years, and because of your deliberate clumsiness, it is gone forever!" As she spoke, she wished she'd chosen her words more carefully, for she'd made it sound perilously close to anguish over losing her last link with Jonathan. She glanced at Rory's face and saw in his eyes that that was indeed what he thought. "Rory, I—"

But Isabel had no intention of allowing her to plead her case with him. "Because of my *deliberate* clumsiness? Miss Maitland, I accidentally dropped the horrid thing into the well, that was all."

"We beg to differ on that point," Lauren replied coldly. She could sense Rory's growing disquiet. He already knew her suspicions regarding the loss of Jonathan's locket, but Isabel was so very convincing, and the evidence was overwhelming.

Isabel's bluebell eyes flickered. "Attempt to differ if

you wish, Miss Maitland, but you cannot shift the blame on to me, or upon poor Emma and Jamie, as you have already endeavored to do."

Rory turned swiftly toward her. "Emma and Jamie? What have they to do with this?"

Isabel gave Lauren a scornful look. "She claims that *they* have taken the jewel box. Have you ever heard anything so ridiculous? And even if they had, why on earth would they leave the locket in her reticule? I vow the creature isn't even a convincing liar."

"That's enough, Isabel." Rory looked at Lauren again. "Why have you accused my brother and Lady Fitzsimmons, Lauren?"

"Hester and I overheard . . . " Lauren fell silent, and then looked regretfully at him. "Hester is still too indisposed to deny or confirm anything I say at this point."

Isabel sighed. "How very convenient," she murmured.

Lauren turned urgently to Rory. "I haven't done any of the things of which I stand accused. I swear it upon my honor."

The assembled gentlemen had listened with some amazement to all that was being said, and now one of them spoke. It was the gentleman who'd arrived as the doctor had departed, and who Rory had referred to as "Dickon."

"Er—Miss Maitland, with all due respect, may I ask if the lost locket was the one you showed me in London early last month?"

A cold finger passed down Lauren's spine as she recognized the voice. It belonged to Sir Richard Finchley, the man she'd fobbed off in London with a tale of a fiancé and an imminent wedding.

"Is it the same one, Miss Maitland?" he enquired again. He was a handsome man, with blond curls and knowing eyes, but although he was much sought after by the ladies of London, she liked him as little now as she had then.

There was nothing for it but to reply truthfully. "Yes, Sir Richard, it was the same locket."

"Forgive me, but I seem to recall you telling me that the

gentleman whose likeness appeared inside it is your fiancé, a Captain Hyde, who, far from being dead, is expecting you back in Boston in the new year to be married."

Isabel could not believe her ears. If she'd planned it, this intriguing development could not have come at a more opportune moment!

Lauren stared wretchedly at Sir Richard. Why had she decided to spare his feelings by resorting to a white lie? He had been importuning her, and should have been dealt a monumental snub! If she'd told him the truth—that she loathed the sight of him—this would not be happening now.

Sir Richard gave a faint smile. "Did I perhaps misunderstand what you told me, Miss Maitland?"

"No, sir, you didn't misunderstand, indeed you have recalled everything quite accurately." Lauren's unhappy gaze moved to Rory.

Sir Richard cleared his throat. "Quite so," he murmured, taking out a snuff box and flicking it open to take a pinch.

Isabel was exultant, although she strove mightily to conceal the fact. Oh, what sweet fortune! The creature was condemned out of her own lips! Deceit and infidelity were the two things Rory abhorred above all else, and his Miss Maitland was apparently guilty of both. Another Fleur, to be sure.

Rory glanced around the room. "I would be grateful if you would all leave, for I think it is time Miss Maitland and I discussed certain matters," he said stiffly.

Everyone did as he requested, although Isabel paused reluctantly in the doorway. She wanted to be there, to hear every word, but she knew that would be impossible, and so unwillingly she went out as well.

As the door closed softly behind her, Rory faced Lauren. "Well? What have you to say to me, Miss Maitland?"

The use of her surname delivered full warning that he already believed her to be guilty.

19

HE was so cold that Lauren couldn't respond. She was conscious of a very distant roll of thunder somewhere beyond the surrounding mountains, and she was equally conscious of the frantic thundering of her own heart. There was a veil over his eyes, a shadow which shut her out and prevented her from reading his thoughts.

"Have you nothing to say, Miss Maitland?" he inquired coolly as he went to the window and looked out over the darkening waters of the loch.

"Miss Maitland? So formal, Rory?" she replied, finding her tongue at last.

"It must be thus, for I have learned the hardest way of all that only a fool entrusts his faith to his heart."

"I love you, Rory," she said simply, pleading with her eyes.

"So did Fleur, or so she would have had me believe."

"I'm not Fleur, Rory."

"I wish I could take your word on that, but I cannot. You have been found with my mother's locket in your possession, and—"

"Yes, but—"

But he ignored her attempted interruption. "And you have apparently accused my brother and Lady Fitzsimmons in connection with this. Now it also seems that you've also lied either to me or to Sir Richard about the existence of a fiancé. Deceit of one sort or another appears to be your trademark, Miss Maitland, and although

I thought I knew you, it's now quite clear that I do not. You are a stranger to me, madam."

"I haven't changed; I'm the same now as—"

His eyes swung coolly toward her. "No, you probably haven't changed, it's just that the scales have gone from my eyes and I begin to see you in your true light."

"So I'm condemned before I've uttered a word in my own defense?" she breathed. "I had hoped for better from you, Lord Glenvane." His title was stilted upon her lips. Oh, Rory, Rory, please don't let us sink to this! Her eyes were bright with unshed tears as she faced him, willing him to soften a little, to give her the benefit of the doubt. Didn't she deserve at least that small concession?

"And I had hoped for better from you, madam. You complain of being condemned unheard. Very well, I await your explanation. First of all, I wish to know how my mother's locket came into your possession, where the rest of the jewels are to be found, and why you so improbably point the finger at my brother and Lady Fitzsimmons?"

The tears still shimmered in her eyes. "The truth frequently sounds improbable, sir," she replied. "If I intended to lie to hide my own guilt, I would invent a more plausible tale."

"I'm still waiting, Miss Maitland," he pointed out tersely.

She drew a long breath. "As you wish, Lord Glenvane, but I don't think that you will like what you hear; indeed, I know you won't. To explain how I believe the locket came to be in my reticule, I must first inform you that Lady Fitzsimmons is the married woman with whom your brother is conducting a liaison."

His lips parted. "That can't be so!"

"I saw them together at the Crown & Thistle before I knew who either of them was."

"Do you really expect me to believe that? I know Jamie is many things, Miss Maitland, but I cannot accept that even he would put horns on a friend as close as Fitz."

"It is the truth. I noticed Lady Fitzsimmons at the inn because she was so obviously waiting for someone and had removed her wedding ring. I could see the white line it left on her finger. Then when Hester and Alex came downstairs, she took one look at them and fled. From that I gleaned that she knew them and didn't want to be seen, especially as the removed wedding ring suggested she was waiting for a lover. That night I was awoken by the sound of a vehicle arriving at the inn, and when I looked out I saw Jamie getting out of his cabriolet. He went up to Lady Fitzsimmons's room on the other side of the gallery from where I was, and when she admitted him they embraced. He left at about dawn and she remained in her room. I think her intention was to stay well and truly out of sight until Hester and Alex had gone."

He had returned his attention to the scene beyond the window, and when she finished he remained silent for a moment. "And Hester can corroborate this?" he asked then.

She lowered her eyes. "No."

"So it would simply be your word against theirs?"

"Yes."

"And if they really were these lovers, they will claim it is a case of mistaken identity, just as they would claim the same if they were *not* the people you saw at the inn. *Impasse*, I think," he said dryly.

"Lord Glenvane, I am telling you the truth. The man and woman I saw meeting at the inn were definitely your brother and Lady Fitzsimmons. I've also seen them in compromising circumstances here in the castle." She explained how she'd seen Emma leaving Jamie's room.

His gray eyes flickered briefly toward her. "How unfortunate that you were again alone, Miss Maitland, for once more it will come down to your word against theirs."

"That does not make my story untrue, sir," she pointed out.

"No. To return to the inn. If it was clear to you that the lady you saw knew Hester, did you draw your cousin's attention to the fact?"

"No."

"May I ask why?"

Lauren felt wretched as she met his eyes, for she knew that her reason would not please him at all, but if he demanded the full truth, then that was what he would get. "I didn't say anything because I foolishly imagined that the lady was locked in a disastrous marriage, and that maybe her assignations were her only happiness."

"And therefore her infidelities were excusable? How telling such reasoning may be of your own philosophy, Miss Maitland," he murmured.

Her eyes flashed at that. "And your response, sir, is very telling of your bitter nature, that you needs must see your wife's image in me as well!"

"Perhaps I see what is there to see, madam!" he snapped. "You have just admitted to me that your reason for holding your tongue about what happened at the inn was because you sympathized with an adulterous wife! Am I right in my analysis of your statement?"

There was nothing she could say, for when he put it like that, yes, she had so sympathized.

"You offer no alternative explanation, Miss Maitland?"

"Nothing that would make any difference."

He surveyed her for a long moment, his eyes dark with anger, then he drew a long breath. "Very well, your story is that Jamie and Emma are lovers. What bearing can that possibly have upon the theft of the jewel box?"

Lauren didn't quite know where to start.

"I'm waiting, Miss Maitland," he said with exaggerated patience.

"I will put it as succinctly as I can, sir. Your brother is not only in financial straits at the moment, he is also very much under Lady Fitzsimmons's influence, and she isn't at all what she appears to be. Far from being your friend's legal wife, it appears she is bigamously married to him."

Rory gave an incredulous laugh. "Your inventiveness goes from strength to strength," he murmured.

"As does your capacity for determined resistance to the truth, sirrah," she countered swiftly.

"The truth, Miss Maitland, this convoluted yarn is a work of complete fiction! Now, if you have more to add to your so-called explanation, I wish you would do so," he snapped.

"I was endeavoring to do so. As I was saying, Lady Fitzsimmons isn't Lady Fitzsimmons at all, but a certain Mrs. du Maurier, who is being sought by the authorities because she and her recently deceased husband ran a crooked gaming hall in Brighton. But when he was arrested, she escaped. It seems that your brother is perfectly well aware of all this."

His eyes were very cold and bright. "I will not believe it," he breathed.

"Lady Fitzsimmons has had cause to fear that her past is about to be exposed, and so she wishes to run away and start a new life. Your brother wishes to do the same in order to be free of his debts. They decided to go together, and to use your mother's jewels for funds, a suggestion which was apparently first put to them by Lady Maxby."

"Isabel? Oh, come now—"

"Lord Glenvane, I am trying to tell you everything you need to know, so please allow me to do so. As I was saying, the plan was originally Lady Maxby's, her motive being that she wishes to compromise me beyond all hope of redemption, a purpose in which she has apparently succeeded beyond her wildest hopes. But it seems that your brother was suffering pricks of conscience, both over his liaison with Lady Fitzsimmons and over his betrayal of your trust. But she dominates him, and last night persuaded him to proceed with the plan because she is afraid that Alex will remember having seen her once at the gaming hell in Brighton. She is right to so fear, because he *has* remembered, and that is why Hester and I went to Lord and Lady Fitzsimmons's room last night during the ball to search for any evidence about Mrs. du Maurier."

"Why didn't Alex see fit to say anything to anyone else? To Fitz, or maybe even to me?"

"He wasn't sure enough for that. He read in a newspaper that Mr. du Maurier had died in prison, and his memory was jogged."

"In other words, he thought he saw a resemblance between Lady Fitzsimmons and this du Maurier woman, but that is all?"

"He was sure the two were one and the same, but he couldn't swear upon a Bible, if that is what you mean." Lauren raised her chin slightly. "I'm not inventing any of this, Lord Glenvane. You may ask Alex if you wish."

"Oh, I will, believe me, for he is so far your only apparent proof of anything. Until now you've only offered Hester, who isn't in any state to say or do anything. Very well, we've got as far as searching the room. What happened then?"

"While we were there, Lady Fitzsimmons and your brother came in, and Hester and I had to hide. We overheard everything they said, and that is how I am able to relate it all now. It came as no real surprise to me that the jewel box is missing, for the business with my reticule had forewarned me. The locket found its way into my possession by nefarious means, Lord Glenvane, but mine was not the hand behind it. Your brother and Lady Fitzsimmons stole the jewel box and removed the locket for Lady Maxby. *She* then put the locket in my reticule to blacken me in your eyes. She believes she can win you back, and maybe she can, for in truth I now realize that I know you as little as you say you know me. As to the rest of the jewels, you may count upon it that they are in the cabriolet with your brother and Lady Fitzsimmons, who are most certainly not merely out for a pleasant drive. They have run away, sir, as you will very soon discover."

Rory stared at her and then gave a dry laugh. "Miss Maitland, I saw them leave, and they certainly didn't have sufficient baggage with them to commence a new life."

"They aren't fools, sirrah. They need all the time they can win, and that is why they have gone along with the part of the plan which incriminates me. While the finger of suspicion is directed toward me, they are in the clear, are they not? And what need do they have for baggage? They have the jewels, and as soon as they reach Glasgow they can purchase whatever they require."

He faced her across the room. "May I ask why you were so intent upon exposing Lady Fitzsimmons?"

Lauren looked away. Should she tell him about Mary and Fitz?

"Well?" he prompted.

"Because if Lady Fitzsimmons's marriage is bigamous, Lord Fitzsimmons would be a free agent, and that would be of immense importance to him and to the person he really loves."

"Who?" he demanded.

She shook her head. "I'm not going to tell you that, sirrah, for the confidence isn't mine to tell, but if you think about it, perhaps the identity of that person will dawn upon you, although I doubt it, since you are apparently blinkered even when the truth stares you in the face!"

"I have certainly been blinkered where you are concerned, madam!" he replied acidly.

"And I where you are, sirrah!" she fired back. Anger surged through her now. He was quite determined not to believe anything she said, and no matter how convincing an explanation she offered, he would continue to accuse her of lying!

"How have I deceived you, madam? Have I forgotten to mention a betrothed? Maybe there is someone in Edinburgh who has conveniently slipped my mind for the time being?"

"How frequently you resort to sarcasm, sir. I haven't forgotten anyone, for there is no one to forget."

"No? Then Sir Richard was mistaken after all? He misunderstood completely when you told him about your fiancé in Boston, and the forthcoming marriage in the New Year?"

"No, he wasn't mistaken, for that is indeed what I said to him, but it was said with a view to getting rid of him. He was pestering me; indeed, I feared he was about to ask for my hand, and so I forestalled him by inventing both a fiancé and a wedding."

He was contemptuous. "Oh, I can almost believe *that*, Miss Maitland, for invention is most certainly your forte! I vow you exult in it!"

"As you wallow in the role of the injured husband, sirrah! You hug it to you like a hair shirt, to remind yourself all the time of how badly you were treated. Poor Lord Glenvane, deceived by his monstrously unfaithful wife and left to lick his wounds ever after. It's set to be your eternal excuse for everything, a revered relic to be dragged out when things don't go quite as you wish, and will serve as a timely reminder that everyone must tread carefully for fear of wounding your sensitivities. Ah yes, dear star-crossed Rory, we must always bear his sad past in mind, for he suffered so very much. Let him be rude, arrogant, overbearing, unapproachable, impossibly stubborn, and bigoted in the extreme, for his failings are understandable after what was so foully done to him!"

The angry recriminations spilled from her lips, and when she'd finished she was so aghast that she closed her eyes. She shouldn't have said all that.

There was a deafening silence, and then he turned and walked to the door. "I don't believe there is anything more to be said, do you? While your cousin is still so ill,

I have no objection to your remaining here, but I'd be obliged if you'd leave Glenvane as soon as possible after her recovery."

"Nothing would induce me to remain here, sir," she whispered, turning away so that he couldn't see her tears.

The door closed behind him and Lauren hid her face in her hands, her shoulders shaking as she wept silently. Six years ago her life had been left in fragments by losing Jonathan. Now it had happened again, only this was far, far worse. Rory was lost to her as sure as Jonathan had been, but she would suffer the pain of knowing that she had lost him because of the lies and machinations of others. And because of her own unguarded tongue.

Suddenly she knew she couldn't stay at Glenvane a moment longer, not even for Hester, who would soon be well again anyway. No, it would be best if this place and its master were put into the past without delay. Lauren looked out of the window toward Ben Vane. There was still cloud swirling around the summit, but the storm had held off for so long now that she was sure it wouldn't come at all. If she took a portmanteau and a good horse, she could reach the Crown & Thistle before the afternoon was out. It was hazardous, but not beyond her riding capabilities, and it would spare her the pain of Isabel's gloating triumph and Rory's cold contempt. Hester would understand.

Gathering her skirts, she hurried from the room. Her mind was made up. She'd spent her last night at Glenvane Castle. Tonight she would sleep at the Crown & Thistle, and tomorrow she'd hire one of the inn's chaises to commence the return journey to London, where she would arrange passage for Boston on the earliest available ship.

20

HER decision irrevocably made, Lauren remained in the solar only long enough to have recovered her aplomb sufficiently to put on a brave face, and then she hurried back to her room, where she found Peggy engaged upon repairing the torn hem of a muslin morning gown.

The startled maid listened in dismay to her mistress's plan. "Leave?"

"Yes."

"But—"

"I don't intend to explain, Peggy, for it's too long a story. Nor do I intend to change my mind, so please do not attempt to persuade me. I'm leaving Glenvane right now, and that is the end of it." Lauren turned for the maid to begin undoing her gown.

Peggy hesitated, but then reluctantly reached up to the fastenings. "How long do I have to pack, Miss Lauren?"

"*We* won't be packing, Peggy, for I'm going on my own. All I'll need is the small portmanteau, for it can be hung over my saddle and won't be seen beneath my cloak. I want everyone to simply think I've gone out for a ride." Lauren looked away. If the ploy was good enough for Jamie and Emma, then it was good enough for her as well . . .

Peggy was now thoroughly alarmed. "You're *riding*, Miss Lauren?" she gasped.

"I'm perfectly capable, Peggy; I did it often enough at home."

"Yes, but you knew the countryside there." Peggy glanced out of the window at the lowering skies and cloud-enveloped mountains.

"I know this countryside sufficiently. I simply have to follow the route the carriages took to come here, and once I'm at the Crown & Thistle I shall hire a chaise. With luck I should be in Dumbarton, or maybe even Glasgow, by nightfall. As to the weather, it's been like this since first light without deteriorating, and I see no reason why it should suddenly do anything different now."

"Please take me with you, Miss Lauren."

"No, Peggy, for you can't ride."

"Then take Mr. Kingston's traveling carriage," the maid suggested desperately.

"And how will I accomplish that without everyone knowing? Mr. Kingston's coachman is hardly likely to obey my instructions without first checking with his master. Peggy, there is nothing to be gained by arguing further, for I will not be moved on this. I'm going to ride to the inn, and that is the end of it. And you aren't going to tell anyone until I'm well on my way. Is that clear?"

The maid colored a little, for she had decided privately that the moment her mistress had set off on this ill-advised ride, she would raise the alarm. "But . . . but what of me, Miss Lauren? What will happen to me?"

"Mr. and Mrs. Kingston will take care of you, and if you tell them that I wish you to follow with all my belongings, they will see that you do. As to your plans after that . . . "

"Plans, Miss Lauren?"

"Your London footman," Lauren reminded her.

Peggy lowered her eyes.

Lauren managed a smile. "Don't look so crestfallen, Peggy, for if you wish to remain in England, I have already said that I will understand. And if you decide to return to Boston, then that will be acceptable as well. For the moment, however, my own plans are that I am going to leave this place and its master, and nothing will change my mind. I want your word that you won't say anything until I am long gone."

"Miss Lauren—"

"Your word on it, Peggy," Lauren demanded.

"Yes, madam," the maid replied, but her fingers were crossed behind her back.

"Then let's get on with it, for I wish to be free of this place as quickly as possible."

Peggy's lips parted to protest again, but then she caught her mistress's savage eye and fell silent. Nothing more was said as Lauren's gown slithered to the floor, and the maid went to bring the riding habit from the wardrobe.

After the savage accusations and reproaches of his parting with Lauren, Rory had gone out into the gardens to try to cool his fury. He was still trembling with bitterness as he reached the well and sat down. Running his fingers through his hair, he drew a long breath and then gazed up at the clouds mushrooming so darkly overhead. What a fool he'd made of himself over Lauren Maitland. Against all the odds, he had made the same mistake twice.

But as he closed his eyes, he was with her again on Holy Island. She was so warm and pliable in his arms, and her kisses had been made in heaven itself. Surely she had meant every loving word and sweet caress? Surely not even Mrs. Siddons could have played such a convincing role? He didn't want to believe ill of Lauren—in fact, the very opposite was the case—but he'd paid a savage price in the past for trusting unwisely.

He opened his eyes again, his gaze drawn to the grille over the well. Her locket lay somewhere down there, but the question was, had it fallen by accident or had it been deliberately thrown? It had to be admitted that Isabel was quite capable of such an act. She would stoop to many a devious ploy in order to have her own way.

He leaned back thoughtfully. Isabel had accused Lauren of stealing the entire jewel box, and he, in his anger and hurt, had believed it too, but what possible reason did Lauren have for taking anything? She was a wealthy woman, she had no need for funds, and if replacing what had been lost was so important to her, then all she had to do was wait until she became Countess of Glenvane, and the second locket would have been hers anyway. No, Lauren didn't have any reason for such a theft. But maybe Jamie and Emma did. What if Lauren's story about Mrs. du Maurier were true? If so, Emma most definitely needed a small fortune in order to run away and live her new life in luxury. She was a woman with expensive tastes and nothing less would do. And what if Jamie were indeed under her spell? He was impressionable enough to succumb to a stronger will, and Emma certainly possessed that. And if, as Lauren claimed, the plan had been hatched when Jamie had still to learn that he would again be bailed out of debt, then he had also had a need for instant funds.

Getting up, Rory began to walk back to the castle. Lauren had said that Alex knew something, and so that was where the questioning would begin. If Lauren were telling the truth, then the sooner he got to the bottom of it all, the better.

He was to find he could question Hester as well as Alex, for she had just awoken and was propped up on a mound of pillows. The dreadful queasiness had subsided and it seemed that the revenge of the Crown & Thistle was at last in retreat. She was pale and wan, but felt much improved as she sipped a welcome dish of tea and spoke to Alex, who was seated on the edge of the bed holding her hand. They both looked up in surprise as Rory came swiftly in.

He paused as he came face to face with both of them, for he knew that their replies now would either confirm everything Lauren had said, or damn her forever. He wanted her to be vindicated—dear God, how he wanted that—but he was so afraid that she really had failed him in every way . . .

Seeing his hesitancy, Alex got up from the bed. "What is it, Rory? Is something wrong?"

"Yes, I fear it is, Alex."

Hester looked curiously at him. "Can we help, Rory?"

He paused, and then looked at Alex. "What can you tell me about Fitz's wife and an article you read in a newspaper?"

Alex cleared his throat, and then glanced uncomfortably at Hester.

Rory looked quizzically at him. "Well?"

"Look, Rory, it may be something, and it may be nothing. It's just that I'm pretty sure that Emma Fitzsimmons is the same woman I saw at a gaming hell in Brighton."

"Du Maurier's place?"

"Yes. You remember the furor?"

"It was a notorious enough scandal at the time. I gather you believe that du Maurier's missing wife and Fitz's wife are one and the same?"

Alex nodded. "Yes. Well, as you probably remember me saying at our dinner in London, from the moment I met her with Fitz, I've had the oddest feeling I'd seen her somewhere before, but I couldn't recall where. Then, when I came here, I read the newspaper article regarding Mr. Du Maurier's recent death in prison, and suddenly I remembered. Look, I can't swear upon oath, but I'm convinced that my suspicions are correct, and if they are, then she can't possibly be Fitz's legal wife." Alex drew a long breath. "You see my dilemma, do you not? If I say anything, then I am obliged to accuse her of bigamy and the Lord knows what else, and I don't want to jeopardize my friendship with Fitz."

Rory was silent for a moment and then went to the bedside. "Hester, I have been speaking to Lauren, and she has made a number of claims, not only about Emma but also about Jamie. She says that you can corroborate a great deal of it."

"Yes, I can. Rory, whatever Lauren has told you, it is the truth."

"Forgive me for saying this, Hester, but you and Lauren are cousins, and have become very close in a short time. I have to wonder if you would support her regardless."

Alex stepped indignantly forward. "I say—!"

Rory held up a hand to him. "Please bear with me, Alex, for this is very important." He looked at Hester again. "Can you tell me what you know?"

"To see if my story matches Lauren's?" Hester was taken aback.

"Something of the sort, yes."

"But why would you doubt her?"

"Please, Hester, just tell me what you know."

"Very well, but . . . " She broke off awkwardly, for to tell him anything meant to bring Jamie into it.

Rory understood. "I've already been told about my brother's apparent part in the scheme of things, Hester. I just need to hear your side of it all."

"I would prefer it if Lauren were here as well."

"Just tell me, Hester."

"As you wish," she agreed reluctantly. "I didn't know anything at first, but then Lauren told me what she'd seen at the Crown & Thistle, and about Emma leaving Jamie's room that morning, when she was supposed to be still sleeping in her own bed after her tiring journey the day before. Anyway, not long after Lauren told me all this, Alex read the article in the newspaper and remembered where he'd seen Emma. Lauren and I then got together at the ball to search Emma's things for any proof. We were thus engaged when she and Jamie actually came in and almost caught us red-handed. We managed to hide and therefore overheard everything they said. She and Jamie are most definitely lovers, and she is Mrs. du Maurier." Hester looked apologetically at Rory.

"Jamie knows all about her, Rory, but although he is reluctant to continue with some plan they have, he is very much under her influence."

Rory met her eyes for a long moment. "What was that plan, Hester?" he asked then.

"I don't exactly know, for it wasn't quite clear. One thing I do know, and that is that they intend to implicate poor Lauren in some way, but then it is all—" She broke off, not knowing whether she should mention Isabel's apparent part in it all.

"Tell me everything, Hester," Rory pressed gently.

She glanced at Alex, and then at Rory again. "From what Jamie and Emma said, the plan is Isabel's. She's very jealous indeed, Rory, and has made herself exceedingly unpleasant to Lauren since we arrived here. She even threatened her with all manner of ill unless she left Glenvane immediately. That business with the locket was no mishap; it was done deliberately, no matter how many crocodile tears Isabel shed at the time. I don't know whether she did it out of spite or whether there was more to it; I only know that it wasn't an accident."

Lauren had been telling the truth. Rory knew it now and wished he hadn't doubted her. He looked away for a moment. "I think we may now be sure that there was more to it. The plan was to take my mother's jewel box. Emma and Jamie intend to use the contents to start a new life together; indeed, it appears they've probably already left. The locket was removed from the box and hidden in Lauren's reticule in order to make it appear as if she'd taken not only it, but the entire box. And while I am busy accusing Lauren of everything, the real culprits make good their escape," he finished.

Hester stared at him. "How do you know all this?"

"Because a great deal has happened since you fell at the ball last night." He told them briefly about the finding of the locket, and the discovery that the jewel box had been taken as well.

Hester sat up, her face growing pale. "You must believe me when I say that Lauren is innocent, Rory! She simply wouldn't do any of those things. I know she wouldn't."

"I know that too. Now." He ran his fingers wearily through his hair.

"What will you do?" Hester asked gently.

"Well, first of all I will request Isabel to leave, for my friendship with her must necessarily be at a complete end. As for Emma and Jamie, I fear that if I wish to retrieve the jewels, I have no option but to inform the authorities about everything. It won't be easy to accuse my own brother and know that he will be imprisoned for what he's done, but this is one thing I cannot forgive."

"And what of Lauren? Now that you know she hasn't lied about anything—"

"Hasn't lied about anything? Maybe not where the jewels are concerned, but I fear she has about other matters," he replied unhappily.

"What are you saying, Rory?"

"What do you know of her life in Boston?"

Hester was startled. "Boston? In what particular way?"

"I refer to her betrothal to a Captain Hyde."

She stared at him, and then laughed incredulously. "But surely Lauren explained all about it?"

"I want you to explain."

Her smile faded. "Am I to understand you believe it to be true?"

"Is it?"

"No."

"Sir Richard Finchley believes to the contrary," he replied, relating the story that gentleman had told.

"Yes, he was meant to." Hester briefly described what had really happened. "So you see, Sir Richard was making a nuisance of himself, and Lauren invented the whole thing to get rid of him. There isn't any Captain Hyde, nor is there to be a wedding in the new year. In my opinion, she was unnecessarily lenient where Sir

Richard was concerned, for he was less than gentlemanly in his pursuit of her. He'd have had a flea in his ear from me, and no mistake." Hester looked anxiously at him. "Rory, have you and Lauren fallen out over what Sir Richard says?"

"That, and this other wretched business with the jewel box," he confessed.

Hester gave him a reproachful look. "How could you, Rory? How could you possibly think such ill of her? She is the most genuine person I know, and she loves you. If you let her go now, than I will know you to be a prize fool!"

Alex shifted uncomfortably. "I say, Hester, that's a bit strong."

"He deserves it," she replied angrily.

Rory cleared his throat. "Yes, I do deserve it."

"The real villains are Jamie, Emma, and dear Isabel, who is the most cat-clawed creature I ever met. So if you've accused my cousin of any wrongdoing, then I suggest you go and beg her forgiveness right now, sir, for everything she has told you has been the complete truth."

Before he could reply, Alex suddenly spoke up. "Aren't we forgetting something in all this? What of poor Fitz? We have to warn him what's afoot. He'll be devastated to find out about Emma."

Hester looked wryly at her husband. "Devastated? Alex, he'll be over the moon."

Alex was bewildered. "I trust you mean to explain?"

"I was right when I said that Fitz regretted marrying Emma. I vow that if he could turn the clocks back, then he would. His heart is given elsewhere. That's why Lauren and I wanted to find proof about Emma being Mrs. du Maurier, so that Fitz could be freed to follow his heart."

"Follow his heart where? Who is his real love?" Alex asked.

"Well . . . " Hester glanced uneasily at Rory, for it would hardly do to name his sister.

Rory searched her face and then his eyes cleared. "Mary? Is that what you're saying? Fitz and my sister?"

"Don't be angry, Rory, for it's true love. I know he's much older than she is, but—"

"I'm not angry, damn it, unless you count my fury with myself for not having observed it on my own. If Mary loves him, and he loves her, then I won't stand in their way. Better that one Ardmore finds happiness than none at all."

Hester's attention was upon Rory. "Two Ardmores can find happiness, provided the one I'm looking at right now has the honor and courage to do the right thing. I trust you mean to crave Lauren's pardon, sir?"

"You know I do."

"I don't know any such thing, sir. You've disappointed me, Rory Ardmore, for I thought more of you than this. It seems you are not the man I thought you were, and maybe you do not deserve my cousin."

Rory smiled a little wryly. "I *know* I don't deserve her, Hester, but I promise you this; I will never fail her again. The moment I've dispatched Isabel and made the necessary arrangements about informing the authorities what's happened here, I'll go to Lauren. And if I have to beg her on bended knee to overlook my failings, then that is what I'll do."

Suddenly the door flew open and a very distressed Peggy hurried in. "Mr. and Mrs. Kingston, oh, please, you must do something immediately!" she cried, coming to an abrupt standstill as she saw Rory.

Hester looked anxiously. "What is it, Peggy?"

"It's Miss Lauren, madam. She's gone."

"Gone? What do you mean?"

"Just that, madam. She's taken a horse to ride to the Crown & Thistle, where she means to hire a chaise to return to London." The maid looked accusingly at Rory.

He seized the maid by the arm. "How long has she been gone?" he demanded.

"About an hour, sir. She made me promise not to—"

"And she's definitely gone to the Crown & Thistle?"

"Oh, yes, sir."

Without another word Rory strode from the room.

Hester and Alex looked at each other in dismay, and then Hester's breath caught as a flash of lightning illuminated the dark skies outside. It was followed by a roll of thunder. The storm which had threatened all day was at last about to break.

21

THE same lightning and growl of thunder shuddered overhead as Lauren urged her horse up the narrow tree-choked glen toward Ben Vane. The portmanteau bounced against the pommel before her, and her cloak fluttered and flapped as the wind gusted down from the open slopes ahead. She felt an occasional raindrop touching her face, but she didn't falter in her resolve to leave Glenvane forever. Tears were damp on her cheeks and she had to swallow back sobs as she rode out of the trees on to the open moorland which stretched up toward the summit of the ridge.

The little River Vane splashed between the rocks beside the track, and she could hear curlews calling over the heather. More lightning scarred the heavens, followed by a roll of thunder which seemed to wander all around the mountains as she reined in to look back at the castle and loch in the valley far below. The loch was gray, and there weren't any reflections upon the water. She could see Holy Island and just make out the ruins hidden among the trees. More tears wended their way down her cheeks. She had thought herself in paradise the day she'd gone there, but it had been a fool's paradise . . . How little it had taken to shake Rory's faith in her. He had claimed to love her and had offered marriage, but at the first moment of doubt she had been dashed aside.

Another gust of wind lifted the hem of her cloak and tugged at her hood as she continued to gaze down at

Glenvane for the last time. She had dreamed of such happiness with Rory, she had really believed herself destined to become his countess, but it had all turned to dust. She had deluded herself and had paid a very painful price. Now her heart was broken and all she wanted to do was escape, not only from Glenvane but from Britain itself. She belonged at home in Boston and she would never return here.

Turning her horse, she urged it on once more. Please let the weather hold off a little longer. Let her be safely in the lee of the mountains before the storm unleashed its full fury. She could feel that fury approaching now, like an electricity in the air, tingling over her skin and making her want to shiver.

A low cloud drifted over the incline ahead, a thin mist which would soon obscure the view behind her. As she rode into it, she resisted the desire to look back again. Rory Ardmore and all that he entailed meant nothing in her life from now on. The mist closed over her, swirling as she passed. There was no wind now, only an eerie stillness where the sound of her horse seemed to be magnified ten times over. Each rattling stone, each breath, echoed on all sides, and she could hear the roar of the waterfall as if it were only a few yards away. Lightning flashed again, turning the pale vapor to a brilliant silver-blue, and almost immediately there was a shuddering clap of thunder which seemed to shake the very mountain.

Lauren's horse was frightened, tossing its head and capering around in panic. She managed to keep control, but in the split second of lightning, she saw something which made her gasp. Jamie's overturned cabriolet lay by the ford just ahead. Its wheel had evidently become stuck in a deep rut, and the shafts had broken as the little vehicle tipped over. There was no sign of the horse, nor was there any sign of either Jamie or Emma.

Alarmed, Lauren dismounted, keeping a tight hold on the reins as she led the nervous horse toward the capsized vehicle. It lay like a toy, looking so fragile and unsafe that it seemed impossible anyone would wish to drive it at the breakneck pace judged *de rigueur* by gentlemen such as Jamie. Where were they? Had they continued their journey on the horse?

As the thought occurred to her, she heard Emma's raised voice. "We *must* go on, Jamie!"

The sound came from the direction of the waterfall. Lauren tried to peer through the curling mist. "Lady Fitzsimmons?" she called.

There was silence.

"Lady Fitzsimmons?" Lauren called again, and this time she heard footsteps.

"Miss Maitland?" It was Jamie. His figure was at first indistinct in the veils of moisture in the air, but as he came closer she saw him more clearly. Emma's figure loomed out of the mist as well. She was clutching something—it was the jewel box.

Jamie was astonished to see Lauren. "What are you doing here, Miss Maitland?" he asked.

"I—"

But before the words of explanation had left her lips, there was another jagged flash of lightning—so close that the air ticked—and almost immediately there was a mighty clap of thunder. Lauren gave a cry of alarm, but her horse was absolutely terrified, rearing away and almost snatching the reins from her hands. Somehow she managed to keep hold of the distracted animal, but her ankle twisted painfully.

Jamie dashed forward to assist her, grabbing the reins and managing to soothe the horse before tethering it to a nearby thornbush. Then he turned anxiously to her as she bent to rub her ankle. "Are you all right, Miss Maitland?"

Lauren winced with pain. "My ankle, I've wrenched it."

Emma stood nearby, making no move to help in any

way. She glanced toward the horse. "Leave her, Jamie, for we can escape now."

"We can't," he replied shortly.

"Yes, we can. We have her horse, the jewels, and—"

"I said no," he replied, turning to face her.

"If her safety is so important to you, we can tell them at the inn that—"

"No," Jamie said again.

Emma's eyes hardened. "If you don't come with me, I'll go alone. I'm not about to give up now, not when it's almost accomplished. Have you any idea what awaits me if I'm caught?"

Jamie looked at her without emotion. "Emma, I no longer care, for I'm ashamed of everything I've done since meeting you." He turned back to Lauren. "Miss Maitland, if you can sit on this rock over here, I'll take a closer look at your ankle."

It was painful to put her foot down on the ground, but somehow Lauren managed it, hobbling to the rock and then sitting down thankfully as he knelt to gently begin to unhook the laces on her boot.

Emma's eyes hardened, and as soon as his attention was diverted, she moved quietly to the horse. She glanced back over her shoulder, but he was still intent upon Lauren's injured ankle. Slowly she opened the portmanteau and pushed the jewel box inside, but there wasn't much room, so it only rested precariously on the top. Then she untethered the reins and began to mount, which was not an easy task to accomplish in her flimsy rose muslin gown and tight-fitting pelisse.

It was Lauren who realized what was happening. "Look! Quick!" she cried.

Jamie leapt to his feet and whirled about, just as Emma gathered the reins to urge the horse away. He caught the bridle, and the frightened horse whinnied and reared. Emma tried to beat him with her fist and his grip slackened for a moment. It was all she needed. Digging her heel into the horse's flanks, she urged it away again, but as she did so the jewel box was dislodged from the portmanteau and fell to the ground.

Emma didn't wait to see if she could retrieve anything. It was all up with her, and she knew it. She flung the horse away into the mist, and soon the drumming of its hooves died away, leaving only the endless rushing of the waterfall.

Lauren looked at Jamie. "Why didn't you go with her? You could have escaped and left me."

"My integrity has returned, albeit a little belatedly, Miss Maitland," he replied, smiling a little ruefully at her. "I've hardly been a credit to the British aristocracy, have I?"

"No, I suppose not," she admitted.

"Maybe it's too late to redeem myself entirely, but at least I've done something toward salving my conscience." Suddenly it began to rain heavily, a torrential downpour which almost drowned the noise of the waterfall. Quickly he pushed the jewel box under a thornbush, and then helped Lauren to her feet. "We must get to the cave behind the waterfall; it's dry there," he said, putting his arm around her waist and supporting her as much as he could as they made their way around the pool.

As they reached the cave, there was another flash of lightning, and the accompanying thunder brought an even greater deluge of rain from the lowering heavens. Jamie set her gently down on the dry floor, where she could lean back against the wall of the cave. "Are you comfortable?" he asked.

"As comfortable as I can be. I don't think I've sprained it badly, just given it a sharp pull. It will be better soon."

"As soon as the weather clears a little, I'll begin the walk back to Glenvane to bring help."

"What happened to your horse?" she asked.

"When the cabriolet overturned, the shafts broke and I tried to unharness it, but it made off before I could see that it was secure. The cloud was so damp and cold that

Emma and I had no option but to take refuge in here and hope that the weather soon cleared, but it closed in more and more, and then the thunderstorm began. Emma wanted to go on after the storm, but I saw the accident as a sign. I've known for some time that everything connected with her was wrong, but somehow I couldn't break free. Then, quite suddenly, just before we heard you calling, I knew that I couldn't go on. The jewels had to be returned to Rory, and I had to sever all connection with Emma. We were arguing about it when you arrived." He went to the entrance and stood gazing out at the dismal scene. "What were you doing up here?" he asked without looking back at her.

"I was leaving Glenvane," she replied honestly.

He turned. "Leaving?"

"Your scheming with the locket achieved its purpose."

"Oh." He came back to sit next to her. "How did you know?"

"Hester and I were eavesdropping last night." She told him about searching the room and hiding behind the curtain.

He looked away, his eyes filled with remorse. "I don't know what to say, Miss Maitland, except that I will explain the truth as soon as I see Rory."

"And incriminate yourself?"

"I have no alternative if I'm ever to live with my conscience." He ran his fingers through his hair, a gesture which keenly reminded Lauren of his elder brother. "I rue the day I ever set eyes upon Emma, for it was a day I took leave of my senses. Oh, I don't claim that she was the sole cause of my fall from grace, for I know my faults. I enjoy a wild life, I gamble foolishly, I have regrettable morals where the fair sex is concerned, and I've found it only too easy to ignore my conscience in the past. But I wasn't exactly bad. I've been bad recently, however. Very bad indeed."

"I will speak up for you."

"You? Why on earth should you, of all people, wish to do that?" he asked in some surprise.

"Because you wouldn't leave me here, and because your resistance means that the jewels are safe after all." She smiled in the shadows of the cave. "I guess Rory will be angry with you at first, but I'm sure he'll forgive you."

"Possibly. Or maybe he's at last had enough of me. God knows, I deserve to be kicked out on my elegant rear."

"Everyone's allowed one dire error of judgment. Lady Fitzsimmons was yours, and I rather fancy that the first Countess of Glenvane was your brother's, although no doubt he believes he has suffered two such blows."

"Two?"

"As I said, your trickery with the locket worked admirably. I am accused of stealing both it and the whole jewel box, and I also stand accused of omitting to mention my fiancé back in Boston, as well as nuptials in the new year."

"Miss Maitland, I may have dabbled where the locket was concerned, but I don't know anything about fiancés in Boston, or about nuptials in the new year."

She smiled again. "I know you don't, for the latter items are my own silly fault." She explained about Sir Richard and her white lies.

"My brother is a fool," Jamie observed flatly.

"He was badly hurt in the past."

"Oh, there's no doubt about that. Because of Fleur he was even prepared to go so far as to let the title pass to any of my heirs, rather than risk marriage again to produce an heir himself. That is, until he met you." Jamie studied her. "I don't know how far things had gone between you, but I know he loves you very much. I guessed it when he went to such lengths to escort you during the boating party, and I suspected it again when he was so loath to have anything to do with my ungentlemanly plot to pursue you for your fortune. I knew it beyond all shadow of doubt when he tore a strip off me after bringing you back from Holy Island. I may not be his favorite person at the moment, but that doesn't prevent me from knowing him like the back of my hand."

"I wish that he did love me, but I fear his feelings cannot be very deep. If they were, he wouldn't have accused me so easily. No, he was too swiftly over his so-called love, but at least I discovered it sooner rather than later."

"I think you are wrong, Miss Maitland."

The downpour began to relent, dying gradually away until it was a mere scattering of raindrops, and as it did so, they both heard Rory's voice in the distance.

"Lauren? Can you hear me?"

Her breath caught, and Jamie rose swiftly to his feet to hurry out of the cave, where the rain had dispelled virtually all the low cloud.

"Rory? We're at the cave!" he shouted, cupping his hands to his mouth.

After a moment they heard hoofbeats, and suddenly Rory was there. He reined in, and dismounted, looking incredulously at his brother. "Jamie? What in God's name—?"

"Miss Maitland is safe, Rory. She's in here. I'm afraid she's hurt her ankle."

Jamie led him inside, and Rory immediately crouched down beside her, taking off his glove and putting his hand to her cold cheek. "Lauren?" His gray eyes were anxious. She could smell the rain on him, the wet of his clothes, and the wet leather of his gloves.

"I did not think we would ever meet again, sir," she replied levelly, longing to be in his arms, but still not sure of him.

He looked at Jamie. "How are you here with her?"

"Didn't you see what's left of my cabriolet? I suffered an ignominious overturn and my horse escaped," Jamie replied dryly.

"And Emma?"

Jamie explained all that had happened, and as he finished, Lauren spoke up swiftly.

"So, you see, not only are the jewels safe after all, but your brother put me before his escape. He could have left on my horse with Emma, but he refused because I was injured. He'd already changed his mind about leaving, you must believe me," she pleaded.

He searched her pale face. "You wish me to forgive him?"

"Yes."

He smiled a little. "Then I will," he said softly.

His smile turned her foolish heart over. He wasn't lost to her! There was still some warmth in his heart!

Jamie breathed out with relief. "I won't let you down again, Rory."

"You'd better not, for next time I'll personally hang, draw, and quarter you." Rory straightened. "I take it your former sweetheart is now well on her way to the Crown & Thistle?"

"Yes."

"Well, I may be prepared to give you another chance, but I'm not about to let her get away entirely, not after that du Maurier business, and certainly not after her bigamous dealings with poor Fitz. I shall report to the authorities that she's been at Glenvane, and they will take up the pursuit."

Jamie nodded but then looked guiltily at Rory. "I knew she was still Mrs. du Maurier," he confessed.

"I know you did. It doesn't become you."

Jamie lowered his eyes. "If I could undo it all, I would, believe me."

"I've no doubt." Rory's glance moved to Lauren. "We would all like to do that from time to time," he added quietly.

Jamie looked out of the cave. "Do you trust me sufficiently to let me ride back to the castle for help?"

Rory nodded. "Yes."

"I won't let you down."

"I know."

Jamie hesitated, and then went to hug his brother close for a moment. "I'm sorry for everything, Rory. Truly I am."

Rory returned the embrace, and then pushed him out of the cave. "Don't dawdle, and for pity's sake don't stop for any pretty face you may meet along the way. With your luck, it will be another delightful villainess looking for an accomplice!"

Jamie grinned at him, and then hurried out to the waiting horse. As Rory stood by the cave mouth watching him, Lauren managed to struggle to her feet and lean back against the wall.

"Am I forgiven too, Rory?" she asked quietly.

He turned swiftly and came to her. "You haven't done anything wrong. *I* am the one who should be forgiven. I know what a fool I've been; Alex and Hester have told me everything."

"Hester? How is she?"

"Much better. Well enough to wrap her tongue around me in no uncertain way." He smiled. "Not that I needed to be told how abominably I've behaved." He caught her fingers tightly, his thumb caressing her palm for a moment.

The caress brought tears to her eyes. "Do you still love me, Rory?" she whispered.

"With all my heart."

"I said such dreadful things to you . . ."

"I was hardly innocent on that score." He put his fingertips to her cheek. "Lauren, I cannot endure without you, and I still want you to be my wife."

Foolish tears shimmered in her eyes, and a soft sigh slipped from her as he kissed her. Her body began to stir with the rich desire she always felt when he was near, and shivers of joy passed through her as his lips moved to her throat. The time was right, so very right. She needed to be his completely, body and soul . . .

"I was thinking . . . " she whispered. "It will be a long time before Jamie returns with anyone."

"A very long time," he replied, raising his head to look into her green eyes.

"Must love wait for a wedding band?" she asked, her voice so soft and caressing that it was almost deafened by the sound of the waterfall.

"Cardinal rules should not be broken, Miss Maitland," he murmured, his lips brushing hers again.

"But they can be, can they not?"

"Yes, they can be."

"Then let us break this rule now, Lord Glenvane. Let us flout convention and anticipate our vows."

"Are you set upon seducing me, madam?" he breathed, his fingers curling luxuriously in her hair.

"Yes. Oh, yes."

"Then I shall not resist," he whispered, his lips and tongue teasing hers.

She gave in to the waves of tantalizing desire which had seized her. He was hers, won in sweet victory. Her highland conquest. Her handsome earl. Her beloved Rory. They belonged together now—heart, body, and soul.

SPECIAL REGENCIES TO CHERISH